The Golden Chain

The Golden Chain

Margaret James

Copyright © 2011 Margaret James

First published in hardback as *The Long Way Home* by Robert Hale
in 2006

Published 2011 by Choc Lit Limited
Penrose House, Crawley Drive, Camberley, Surrey GU15 2AB
www.choclitpublishing.co.uk

The right of Margaret James to be identified as the Author of this Work
has been asserted by her in accordance with the Copyright, Designs and
Patents Act 1988

A CIP catalogue record for this book is available
from the British Library

ISBN 978-1-906931-64-3

Mixed Sources
Product group from well-managed
forests and other controlled sources
www.fsc.org Cert no.TT-COC-002063
© 1996 Forest Stewardship Council

Printed in the UK by CPI Cox & Wyman, Reading, RG1 8EX

This story is for dear Min, ever the best of friends.

Acknowledgements

A big thank you to everyone at Choc Lit for all their hard work on this novel.

Prologue

March 1926

It wasn't so much a nightmare as a mystifying dream.

Whenever Daisy Denham had the dream, she woke up tangled in her bedclothes and soaked with perspiration. Of course, this wasn't unusual in India, especially when the summer was coming, the temperature on the plains was rising, and it was time to go up to the hills.

'What's the matter, sweetheart?' asked her mother, after Daisy had woken up at three o'clock one morning, shouting to somebody in her dream to stop, to wait, to come back – please! The ayah had gone running in a panic to rouse Mrs Major Denham.

'I had that dream again.' Daisy sipped slowly from a glass of juice. 'I saw the lady, the one I always see.'

'You saw her face?'

'No, Mum, it was blurred. It's always blurred. I know she's young, and has black hair like you. But she isn't you. I'm sure I've met her once in real life. But I don't know where.'

'What did she say to you?'

'Nothing, she never speaks. She just stands there, looking at me. Then she goes away. Mum, she worries me.'

'She's just a dream.' Rose stroked Daisy's long, fair hair back from her sticky forehead. 'I dream about all sorts of things,' she added. 'I see people I know I've never met and go to places I know I've never been.'

She picked up Daisy's empty glass and smoothed the linen sheets. 'Try to go back to sleep now, dear,' she said. 'You're going to have a busy day tomorrow. Or I should say today.'

'Did you finish my dress?'

'Yes, and it looks perfect. The style and colour are just right for you. Dad's bearer has polished up your shoes, and I've had all your ribbons starched and ironed. You're going to be the star of Mrs Colonel Norton's little show.'

'What about my dad, do you think he'll come?'

'He says he hopes to get away. But he's got a lot to do right now, as well as getting all the transport organised for when the mothers and children go up to the hills.'

'I wish he could come with us.'

'I do, too. But when he has some leave, I'm sure he'll join us for a couple of weeks. Come along, my darling, settle down. Ayah, stay with missy baba until she goes to sleep.'

So the ayah squatted by the bed, crooning softly in soothing Hindustani. The lady with black hair had vanished. As her ayah sang a lullaby, Daisy felt herself falling asleep.

Rose went back to her bedroom, where she found her husband was awake.

'So Daisy had that dream again,' said Alex.

'Yes, she did.'

'We ought to tell her, don't you think?'

'What would be the point? Alex, she's only ten years old. She's such a happy child. She has a good life here with us. Why should we rake up all that stuff again?'

Chapter One

The show had clearly been a huge success, for now the village audience rose as one. They clapped and whistled and stamped their feet. As Daisy took her final bow with all the other performers, she scanned the rows of faces. But she couldn't find the person she had hoped would come.

The clapping finally died away. The other singers and dancers skipped and scurried off the stage. Daisy followed them to the dressing rooms, where the happy buzz of conversation raised her spirits, just a little.

She came out of the makeshift green room to find Alex Denham waiting with her hat and coat and gloves. 'You were excellent, darling,' said her father. 'Your song and dance act was the best thing in the show.'

'Do you think so, Dad?' said Daisy, looking all around for someone else.

They pushed their way into the crowded lobby of Charton village hall, where Alex nodded to acquaintances and was told by everyone his daughter was a star. But Daisy couldn't see the person whose opinion mattered most. 'Where's Mum?' she asked.

'She couldn't make it, sweetheart.' Alex shrugged apologetically. 'She had one of her headaches, and had to go and lie down.'

Daisy's shoulders slumped. Why was her mother being like this? Why had she changed? When the Denham family had left India the previous year and come to live near Charton, a honey-coloured, stone-built village on the Dorset coast, the previously sociable, gregarious Rose Denham had made no effort to fit in.

A few months after they'd arrived, Daisy had been asked if she would like to be in a concert which the schoolmistress Miss Sefton was organising at the village hall. Rose had not forbidden it, but she hadn't shown any interest, either.

Since the family had come back to England, Rose had turned into a different person. While the Denhams lived in India, she had been involved in everything. The social life of the cantonment had revolved round Mrs Major Denham. She had organised all kinds of shows and fêtes and parties. She'd encouraged Daisy to join in amateur dramatics, let her perform in all the variety shows in the cantonment theatre, sent her to have dancing lessons, singing lessons, made her costumes. But not any more.

'Where are the brats?' asked Daisy.

'In the car,' said Alex. 'They enjoyed themselves. They were telling everybody you're their grown-up sister, and they clapped and cheered like anything. Do you want to stay for a while and chat, or have a glass of cordial and a bun?'

'No, Dad, let's go home.'

So Daisy and Alex said goodnight to a red-faced and happy Laura Sefton, who had masterminded the event, and looked relieved that it had gone so well. Now the cottage hospital would be that much closer to getting its new ward.

Alex and Daisy walked across the cinder patch to where he had parked the battered Riley he'd been left in Henry Denham's will. The brats were in the back, kicking and punching one other, but broke off when their father and sister got into the car.

'Look, it's Greta Garbo,' sniggered Stephen, grinning like a monkey.

'You were so embarrassing, Daze.' Robert, the bigger and stronger twin, grabbed her round the neck and made her choke. 'When you croaked that song about picking lilac, I was nearly sick.'

'Yeah, me too,' said Stephen, Robert's faithful echo. 'When you sat on that tree stump and sang about the moon in June, you looked like you were going to lay an egg.'

'Your eyes were bulging, like someone on the lav. A lady said you needed Beecham's Pills.'

'Hark the herald angels sing, Beecham's Pills are just the thing!' sang Stephen, in a high falsetto.

'You danced like Mr Hobson's donkey, and – '

'Daisy, take no notice,' interrupted Alex, turning round to glare at the two boys. 'Belt up, you little blighters, or I'll thrash the pair of you.'

Although their father had never laid a violent hand upon them, the twins heard the authority in his voice. They belted up at once.

'I know it's difficult, but we must give it time,' said Alex, as he drove home to Melbury House. They'd come back to England the previous October, after Alex had been injured in an anti-British riot, and obliged to leave the army. 'Dorset's so very different from Delhi, after all.'

'Damn right it is – no money, freezing cold, no servants, living in a ruin,' whispered Robert, confident he was on his father's deaf side, so Alex wouldn't hear him, even if Daisy did.

'We'll be fine, you'll see,' continued Alex. 'I know this winter's been a challenge. We've all had coughs and colds. But the spring and summer are wonderful in England. You chaps can learn to swim. We'll go for picnics on the beach.

I'll find some ponies for you, and then you can go riding.'

'It sounds lovely, Dad,' said Daisy loyally, even though she didn't much like riding, and though she hated England and everything about it.

The damp and dismal countryside was ugly and depressing. The glass-green sea looked freezing. She didn't want to dip a toe in it, much less learn to swim. The beach was covered with sharp shingle or big pebbles, not with golden sand. The constant cold poked freezing fingers through her clothes into her very bones, and she'd given up all hope of being warm again.

Every time she walked into the village on an errand for her mother, the locals said hello. But then they gawped and goggled so much you would have thought she had three eyes. Whenever she went into the village shop, the woman behind the counter was very friendly and polite. But the other customers stared and muttered. Then they grinned like idiots if she turned round suddenly and caught them gawking, like a lot of fools.

They parked in front of Melbury House, which Alex had inherited from his guardian Henry Denham along with the old Riley. In its dilapidated state, the house was probably worth about as much as the rusty motor. Or maybe even less.

'You two can get the coal in,' Alex told the twins, as he parked the Riley. 'Make the fire up in your mother's bedroom, wash your hands, then go and fetch the supper trays Mrs Hobson will have left for us, and bring them to the drawing room. There'll be a good blaze there. Off you go, then – at the double.'

'God, we're nothing but child slaves,' groaned Stephen, but he went with his brother to the stables where the coal was kept, leaving Alex and Daisy on the steps of the old house.

'You were very good, you know,' said Alex.

'You're just saying that.'

'I mean it,' Alex smiled encouragingly. 'You're very talented. Your mother and I have always thought so. You mustn't take any notice of the brats. They're only ten years old. They say the sort of beastly things that boys of their age do. I should know. I used to be like them, many years ago.'

'I can't believe you were as foul as those two,' muttered Daisy.

'Oh, I was much fouler!' Alex grinned and shook his head. 'I was a sullen, sulking horror. If you don't believe me, ask your mother.'

'Why didn't she come?' asked Daisy.

'I told you, love, she had a headache.'

'Yes, but Dad – '

'Come on, let's go in and see if she feels better.'

They found Rose lying on the threadbare sofa in the shabby drawing room. The fire had burned itself almost to ashes, and shadows from the oil lamps danced and flickered around the walls and ceiling, so all the cracks and stains weren't quite as noticeable as they were in daytime.

Alex drew the rotting velvet curtains, sending them rattling along the tarnished metal poles.

'Alex?' Rose opened her eyes 'Daisy, you're back already? How did it go?'

'She was wonderful. They clapped and cheered like maniacs. You would have been so proud.' Alex sat down on the sofa and took Rose's hands. 'Goodness, Rose, you're freezing! Why didn't you pull those blankets over you?'

'I fell asleep.' Rose smiled at Daisy. 'Sit down, my darling, tell me all about it, and don't miss out a thing.'

As she sat next to her mother, inhaling her familiar scent of jasmine, orange blossom and whatever Rose put on her hair, Daisy began to feel a little better.

She was at home and, even if today home was a crumbling ruin, not a British army major's splendid married quarters, she was with her parents, the people who loved her best.

Maybe her dad was right. Maybe they should give it time. Maybe England wouldn't be so horrible, after all.

If it didn't improve, however, maybe they would let her go back to India on her own? Maybe she could go and stay with Mrs Colonel Norton and her daughter Celia?

She could travel by herself, or with a chaperone. After all, in autumn she would be sixteen – grown up, if not in law, then certainly in every way that mattered.

She was getting taller and she looked more like a woman every day.

As he slouched against the wall of Mrs Fraser's little dressing room, his hands pushed deep into his trouser pockets – a stance he knew his mother hated – Ewan Fraser scowled.

'Why do *I* have to come to Dorset?' he demanded, his green eyes mutinous slits, his usually generous mouth a stubborn line.

'I can't leave you in Scotland on your own all spring and summer,' replied his mother, tartly.

'I shan't be on my own,' retorted Ewan. 'Mr Morrison and his wife are here. I could live in their cottage, and they'd keep an eye on me.'

'Darling, that would not be suitable.'

'Why not?' asked Ewan. 'I stayed there all that time you were away with Dad, when he was in hospital and you lived in Edinburgh so you could visit him, and when you had to go to see the lawyers. You don't need to worry about me.'

'Sir Michael has invited you.' Agnes Fraser looked beseechingly at her tall, broad-shouldered handsome son. 'Ewan, the Eastons are your father's cousins. They're rich, they're influential. You know you have no one else to help you make your way. Oxford will be so expensive. After you leave Oxford, you'll need contacts, friends – supporters who will get you started on a career in law, or something in the professions. Sir Michael has an awful lot of very important friends.'

'I'm going to be an actor,' muttered Ewan. 'So I don't need the help of cousins from Dorset. Anyway, you don't like Lady Easton. You've always said she's common. When my father was alive, you'd never have even talked to anybody who had been divorced, let alone gone to stay with Lady Easton, and have the woman tell you what to do.'

'Well, it's different now,' said Agnes. 'Your father didn't leave us enough money. What happened on Wall Street a year or two ago made things even worse. This place costs a fortune to maintain, and we have to live.'

'I still don't see why we should have to go and grovel to the likes of them,' objected Ewan. 'Why do you want me to go to Oxford, anyway? Why can't I leave school and get a job?'

'A minute ago, you told me you were going to be an actor.'

'Yes, I did, and acting is a job.'

'Oh, Ewan!' Agnes got up and put her arms round Ewan's waist. She hugged him tightly, laying her neat, dark head against his chest. 'You're so young and inexperienced. You don't know this wicked, wicked world.'

Ewan knew that in a moment she would start to cry. Then

he would have no option but to agree to go to Dorset. So he might as well give in right now.

'I don't have to spend the whole time fishing, do I?' he demanded, determined to salvage something.

'I'm sure Sir Michael would be very pleased if you would go with him and help him cast. When people don't have children of their own, they like to have the young around the place, and he's so fond of you.'

Agnes looked up at Ewan, brown eyes bright with unshed tears. He hoped she wouldn't actually turn the taps on, because when that happened he never knew what to do. 'I knew you'd see the sense of going,' she said.

Ewan shrugged out of her embrace and slouched out of the room.

A few days later, after Agnes Fraser had agreed with Ewan's school he could be absent for the summer because of urgent family business down in Dorset, he and his mother left Glen Grant for the long journey south.

There'd been some talk about him going back for a week in June to take examinations. All his masters had set him so much work his luggage weighed a ton. But, thought Ewan, since I don't intend to go to Oxford ...

Agnes had arranged to let their house until September, bringing in some welcome cash, but making Ewan feel even more gloomy. Now he would be stuck in rural Dorset, sponging off his father's relatives and missing the place he loved, until the best of the year was past.

They travelled down first class, which in Ewan's opinion was a waste of the money his mother said they didn't have. They had a compartment to themselves. While Mrs Fraser stared out of the window, occasionally getting out her powder compact and touching up her paintwork, Ewan lolled across three seats and read his pocket Shakespeare, a tiny copy printed on the thinnest India paper. It had been his father's, had gone with him to the trenches, and it still smelled of dirt and smoke and blood.

As Ewan read accounts of battles and tales of love, he wondered if he was ever going to live up to his father, a highly-decorated hero who had died of war wounds, even though he'd taken years to do so.

It didn't look as if another war was in the offing, or at least not yet. So he wasn't going to be able to cover himself with glory on some distant battlefield. He wondered what it would be like to fall in love.

'Ewan, what are you doing?' demanded Agnes, suddenly. 'You've got that strange look in your eyes again.'

'I'm just reading,' Ewan said, hoping she didn't want to talk to him, or rather lecture him.

'You always have your nose stuck in a book. You're always dreaming. There's life out there, child – real life!'

Yes, shooting and fishing in Dorset, and they won't compare with anything in Scotland, Ewan thought, but didn't say. He didn't want to provoke his mother into delivering yet another sermon.

Agnes rearranged her furs, peering at him over the turned-up collar of her coat, like a petulant marmoset in lipstick.

'It's freezing in this carriage,' she complained. 'I wonder where the guard can be? Maybe there isn't one on this awful train. Ewan, I don't feel well. I'm sure I'm feverish. I think I must be going to start a cold.'

Daisy had yet another cold. Since they'd come back to England, she almost always had a cold. This was not surprising, for she was always freezing, even if she wrapped herself in layers and layers of woollens, wore scratchy home-made cardigans and thick, hand-knitted socks. The spring her dad had promised them was taking its time to come.

Getting up late one morning, she found her mother in the kitchen, discussing the week's meals with Mrs Hobson, the woman from the village who helped Rose with the household chores.

Daisy liked Mrs Hobson, who had obviously decided the Denham family needed lots of jumpers, socks and cardigans, and also feeding up. She cooked them wholesome stews with plenty of suet dumplings, carrots and potatoes, and always welcomed Daisy to the kitchen with biscuits and a glass of milk.

Mrs Hobson came to Melbury House each weekday morning, and she and Rose did everything between them – dusting, cleaning, scrubbing, laundry, peeling endless piles of vegetables, and laying all the fires.

Daisy came home from school most afternoons to find her mother resting with her feet up on the sofa, pale with fatigue and looking drained.

'I thought I heard some footsteps,' Mrs Hobson said, beaming as Daisy snaked a hand across the kitchen table to grab a fresh-baked scone. 'You're not at school today, then?'

'She was up coughing half the night, so I thought I'd keep her off this morning. This old place is so damp. I'm surprised we haven't all had pneumonia this winter.' Rose brushed Daisy's fringe out of her eyes and felt her forehead. 'You're not so feverish now. If you're feeling better, you could go to school this afternoon.'

'Maybe not, it's double Latin.' Daisy grinned. 'I'll go for a walk along the beach, or into Charton and blow my germs away. Unless I can do anything for you, Mum?'

'Thank you, darling, but I think we've finished,' Rose replied, although she must have known she'd never finish, that she would never manage to run Melbury House as it was intended to be run, with a live-in staff of five or more, and extra help besides.

'If you go to the village, you must always use the road from Melbury,' she reminded Daisy. 'I know the other way is shorter, but that gated road is private. It's on someone else's land.'

'Where's my dad?' asked Daisy, pretending not to hear what Rose had said about the road.

'He and Mr Hobson are marking out a vegetable garden. Alex has lots of plans for it this year.' Rose smiled ruefully. 'I think he means to keep you children busy.'

'I'll go and see what they're doing.'

Daisy went to fetch her coat, but as she walked along the service passage the women's voices floated after her, and she couldn't help hear what they were saying.

'She's grown up very pretty,' said Mrs Hobson. 'I always knew she would.'

'She's lovely,' Rose agreed. Then Daisy heard her mother sigh. 'Of course, it's rather difficult for me, coming back here and having to see the people I used to know. I expect there's lots of gossip in the village?'

'Well, there's still a bit,' admitted Mrs Hobson. 'But not as much as when you first came home. You and Mr Denham and the children are living here so happy and respectable that I'm sure there's nothing much to say.'

'I hope you're right,' said Rose.

'Mrs Denham, I dare say it's not my business, but does Daisy know what happened all those years ago?' asked

Mrs Hobson.

'She – Mrs Hobson, look at the time, we must get all that ironing done,' said Rose.

Chapter Two

Daisy and her brothers had been taught to think of England as the mother country, and as their real home. So when they'd first been told they were going home, they had been thrilled.

Their picture books of England had shown them green fields, purple hills, romantic castles, black and white half-timbered villages, bustling cities, golden beaches, lakes and snow-capped mountains. They couldn't wait to see this paradise.

Two or three times while they were growing up, their father had been to England on official army business and to see his guardian Henry Denham, who lived in Dorset.

Alex had sent or brought back lovely things – gorgeous dolls and pretty clothes for Daisy, cricket bats and armies of toy soldiers for the boys, and lots of other games and toys from Hamley's, which from his descriptions sounded like Aladdin's cave.

Once, Rose and Alex had gone together to visit Mr Denham, who was dangerously ill. They were away three months. Mr Denham died while Rose and Alex were in England and, when they came back to India, Daisy, Robert and Stephen had never seen their father look so sad. But the presents that time had been wonderful, and they longed to see the place where all these things were made.

So, when they first arrived in England, docking in Southampton on a drizzling, dismal autumn day, everything had been a disappointment.

It was so cold and damp. They were used to cold, for

when they had spent seasons in the hills, it had been sharp and chilly on frosty autumn mornings. But they'd never known the dripping, miserable damp of cold, grey England.

'We're going to live in a beautiful old house,' Rose had explained, and got them all excited. 'Your father's guardian left it to him several years ago, but there's been no one living in it since. So it will be a little shabby now, but we'll soon get everything spruced up.'

Melbury House turned out to be a hideous old ruin, too far gone, thought Daisy, for any sprucing up, even if it was a fine example of a Jacobean mansion.

'Look at the period detail,' Rose said brightly, as she and their father took them round, pointing out elaborate plastered ceilings (cracked and green with mould, the plaster falling off in dirty, icing-sugar chunks), the Grinling Gibbons staircase (full of woodworm, so there was to be no sliding down it, for fear it would disintegrate), and the enormous, curtained beds, made on site to fit the first floor bedrooms, swagged and draped with velvet (rotting and full of spiders).

On their second day at home, while their parents shivered in the drawing room, trying to keep warm beside a smoking, choking fire, and saying they must get the chimneys swept, Daisy and the twins did some exploring of their own.

Above the second storey, the main staircase had collapsed, but they went up the service stairs and up on to the roof. They found that some of it was missing, the slates blown off or broken, the wooden beams exposed.

'We can't use that part of the house,' admitted Alex, when they'd pointed out to him that rain was getting in, and this must be the reason everything was rotten. 'The rooms on the third floor are past redemption, and nobody's used them for centuries.'

'Why don't you get the roof fixed?' Daisy asked him.

'Money,' said Alex. 'Or rather, lack of it.'

'I always thought we had a lot of money?'

'We never had a lot,' said Alex. 'But we had enough – until the Crash. The stock market, Daisy, it's a very fickle thing. You need a clever broker in these troubled times.'

'So is your broker stupid?'

'He made some very unwise investments. Listen, you fellows, don't go on the roof,' said Alex, who seemed to want to change the subject. 'It's far too dangerous.'

By the end of their first week in Dorset, they all had streaming colds. Rose was ill all winter. She had tonsillitis, followed by bronchitis, followed by influenza, followed by tonsillitis, round and round in circles.

Alex was still getting over wounds he had received in an anti-British riot the previous summer, and everyone was miserable and sluggish, unwilling to do anything but sit and dream of what they'd left behind.

'But we'd have had to come to stinking England, anyway,' muttered Robert grimly, as Daisy and the twins cleared away the breakfast things one chilly April morning.

'If Dad was in the army still, and if they hadn't lost most of their money in the Crash, you'd have gone to be finished off in Switzerland,' said Stephen. 'So you'd have been all right. But Rob and me, we'd be at some old boarding school in Kent, like the Fielding boys from our cantonment. Colin Fielding said you have to fag for older fellows, and everyone gets flogged. So we're quite glad we're broke.'

'It's Rob and I,' said Daisy.

She decided she would make the best of England. It was too wet, too cold, too dull, too quiet, but once in a while a clear, bright day made everything look better.

Then, the sky shone crystal-blue, the dew-sprinkled grass was the most brilliant shade of green, and in all the copses pale daffodils glowed yellow.

Tiny, fragile things, these Easter lilies – as the local people called them – were nothing like the gorgeous regal lilies which had grown like weeds in India. But they were pretty, just the same, and in a way she liked them better. They were modest, charming, not fleshy and demanding, shouting *look at me*.

She went to school in Dorchester, catching the early morning train from Charton. She usually walked home from Charton village along a well-maintained and gated road that went past Easton Hall, a splendid stone-built mansion. Its gleaming paintwork and new roof suggested that the people who lived there must be very rich. They must have clever brokers, she decided.

Daisy didn't know them, because they didn't mix with local people. They even had a private pew in church, with its own special entrance near the choir stalls, which no one else could use. There, boxed into a sort of holy hen house, the Eastons did their worshipping in secret, out of everybody else's sight.

Rose had told Daisy several times she mustn't go that way because the gated road was private and she would be trespassing. But Daisy took no notice. She wasn't doing any harm, and this was the short way home.

One Friday afternoon, as she was walking back to Melbury House, she saw somebody sitting on the gate that lay ahead. A boy about the same age as herself, she thought, or maybe a bit older, he didn't have a hat on, and his red-brown hair was glinting copper in the sunshine.

Most probably a poacher, she decided, a poacher or

a vagrant. Maybe that was why her mother didn't like her coming home this way. She might meet tramps and undesirables.

'Good afternoon,' the vagrant said. He looked quite respectable close up, or at least clean and decent, anyway.

'Good afternoon,' said Daisy.

'Ewan Fraser.' The boy held out his hand. Daisy didn't take it. People might look clean, but they could still have terrible diseases – living in India had taught her that.

'Daisy Denham.' Then she thought, perhaps he's not a vagrant, after all. His clothes look quite expensive. But he sounds Scottish, which is odd, considering this is Dorset. He must be one of the unemployed, come south to look for work.

'I live at Melbury House,' she added, pointing to the chimneys in the distance, hoping this would make him think again before he robbed her, and silently daring him to smirk, or make some smart remark about life in ruins.

'I'm staying with some relations here,' he said.

'Oh?' Daisy frowned. 'I haven't seen you in church.'

'I'm an atheist,' said the boy. 'So I don't go to church.' Then he looked Daisy up and down and smiled, and Daisy thought, he's got no manners, atheist or not.

'Daisy Denham, Melbury House,' he said, reflectively. 'You must be the girl my mother and Lady Easton talk about, when they think no one's listening.'

'Your mother and Lady Easton?' Daisy was astonished. 'I don't know Lady Easton, and I've never met your mother. Whatever do they say?'

'Oh, how you're very talented, and such a splendid dancer, and how it's not surprising, considering who your mother is – the usual sort of women's chat.'

'I see,' said Daisy. She thought, how very odd. She'd never known Rose was any good at dancing. In fact, she'd never seen her mother dance.

At parties, or at any other sort of social gathering in India where children were allowed, Rose had always sat and gossiped with the other *memsahibs*. She had never danced.

Perhaps she danced with Alex when the children were in bed? Maybe they wound up the gramophone and danced alone, in pale, romantic moonlight?

'I need to get across this gate,' she said.

'Where are you going now?' asked Ewan, as he moved aside.

'I don't think it's any of your business,' Daisy told him, holding down her skirt as she climbed over, and hoping she wasn't showing too much leg.

'You're right, of course,' said Ewan. 'But may I walk with you?'

'I'm sorry, I must hurry. I have lots of things to do.'

Daisy jumped down, and then she walked on briskly, feeling warm around the neck, wondering if the boy was following, and sort of hoping that he might be.

But when she glanced back furtively, she saw he was still sitting on the gate, and now he had his back to her and was staring out across the fields.

She's very pretty, Ewan thought, as he gazed towards the water meadows, which were glowing green and golden with bright yellow kingcups in the sharp spring sunshine.

He took out his Shakespeare and found *Romeo and Juliet*, which was currently his favourite play. He longed and longed to play the hero, who was his ideal of a man – a fighter who was handy with a rapier, a lover who bewitched a woman with a single sentence. *If I profane with my unworthiest hand this holy shrine* – he rolled the lovely words around his tongue.

But he'd have a girl to play his Juliet, not some wee tinker in a wig, seconded from the lower school. Daisy Denham, now, she would be perfect.

He said her name out loud, and then he whispered it. She was as young as Juliet. Or anyway, she looked it. She was certainly as beautiful. She had a grace and dignity befitting the daughter of old Capulet.

She had lovely hands, small and neat, well-shaped. He'd noticed them as she had climbed the gate.

Palm to palm is holy palmers' kiss ...

Ewan sighed, and wondered if he was about to fall in love, if love was a disease, and he had caught it.

If he had, he didn't mind. In fact, he welcomed it. Love would be a distraction from the boredom of this tedious place.

He started reading through the play again.

Daisy hurried on along the road, feeling hot and bothered.

The boy who had been sitting on the gate – he had been very handsome. She'd never seen such beautiful green eyes. They had glowed like emeralds in a maharajah's crown. Such long, dark lashes, too – wasted on a boy, of course, who had no need of lashes, anyway.

The way he'd looked at her as well, so bold and so appraising, what a cheek he'd had. But clearly he had liked what he had seen.

When she got home, she found her mother sitting in the kitchen, making one of her everlasting lists. 'Mum,' she began, 'when you were younger, did you – '

'You're very early, darling.' Rose glanced up, and Daisy saw how tired she looked, how there were lines developing at the corners of her eyes. 'Good day at school?'

'Yes, it was all right. I got a merit mark in geography, Mum, when you were younger, did you like to dance?'

'My goodness, yes. I loved it!' Rose smiled dreamily. 'In those days before the war everything was – well, I can't describe it! But we had such balls, such parties. All the men wore evening dress or uniform and, as for the women, you should have seen them, lace and silk and flowers and jewellery – gorgeous.'

'You met Dad at a ball, then?'

'No, we knew each other when we were children. Alex's guardian Henry Denham was my father's friend.'

'Why did Dad have a guardian? I've always meant to ask you. What happened to his parents?'

'I thought you were asking me if I liked dancing?'

'Yes, I was – so, did you dance with Dad?'

'I don't think I ever danced with Alex, now I come to think about it, but I danced with everybody else!'

Rose stood up. 'What about some supper? Maybe we've had too many eggs this week? I don't want everybody getting egg-bound. But it's scrambled eggs or tinned sardines with tinned tomatoes, not very inspiring, I'm afraid.'

'Sardines on toast,' said Daisy, who was sick of eggs and would have killed for chicken biryani, the sort their cook in India used to make.

On Monday afternoon, she took her usual path home, along the gated road.

As she'd sort of hoped she might, she found the boy with copper hair still sitting on the gate, reading a small, brown book.

'Have you been here all weekend?' she asked.

'Most of it,' he said, and then he smiled, and she saw he had perfect teeth.

'Why aren't you at school or work?'

'I'm on my holidays just now.'

'You mentioned Lady Easton when I saw you last. So you must be staying at Easton Hall?'

'Yes, that's correct, Miss Holmes,' said Ewan, and slipped the little book into his pocket.

'Miss Denham.'

She realised she was smiling now. She knew she must be blushing, too. She wished she wasn't, for she was so fair-skinned she looked like a tomato when she blushed.

'Where do you usually live?' she asked.

'In Scotland, but my mother wanted to spend the summer here in Dorset, with my father's cousins.' Ewan's smile died. 'I'm hating every minute of it.'

'Why?'

'All Sir Michael thinks about are field sports – fishing, guns and shooting. He lost a hand when he was in the war, and although he has an artificial one, he's very clumsy. So he likes going out with me, telling me what to do and how to do it. But I'm not interested in killing things for fun. As for Lady Easton – she's a condescending bitch.'

'Yes, they don't like her in the village. They all say she's stuck up.'

'You were too busy for a walk on Friday.' Ewan looked at Daisy hopefully, and she was reminded of a friendly Labrador who was longing to be thrown a stick. 'Let me carry your bag for you a while. It looks quite heavy.'

'Yes, actually it is,' said Daisy and, after a moment's

hesitation, she handed it to him. 'So you don't like Sir Michael, then?'

'He's pleasant enough to me, but he's a crashing bore.' Ewan kicked a stone along the road. 'At this very moment, he's anxious to become a magistrate. He talks about it all the time. He can't wait to hand down fines and floggings.'

'Mmm, he sounds really nice.'

'My mother reckons it's his great ambition to be Lord Lieutenant of the county,' went on Ewan. 'But he'll need to work at it to make the people who matter forget he married a divorcee, and she must work hard at being a lady.'

'Ewan, are you a snob?'

'No,' said Ewan. 'I'm a socialist. I believe in equal rights for all, and justice for the common man. But until the revolution comes, so-called ladies should at least be generous and kindly and polite, and grateful for their undeserved good fortune. Lady Easton's mean and rude and selfish.'

'I see,' said Daisy. 'I don't know much about them, actually. Do they have any children?'

'No, they don't,' said Ewan. 'But looking at Lady Easton, I can't say I'm surprised. She's not an appealing woman.'

'But if Sir Michael married her, surely he – '

'Oh, he was after some heiress. But she wouldn't have him, because she was in love with someone else. Chloe was about to be divorced, and she was looking out for a new husband. Sir Michael didn't like it when the heiress married this other man, and he married Chloe on the rebound. Or that's my mother's theory, anyway.'

Soon they turned off the road and took the path that led to Melbury House, skirting the cliffs and headland.

'Look, the spawn of Satan.' Daisy pointed to the twins who were skimming pebbles on the shingle beach below.

'Your little brothers, eh?' Ewan grinned. 'Lady Easton mentioned them at breakfast. Apparently they've been going in the coverts, and springing traps with sticks. If Sir Michael's keeper catches them, he's going to tan their hides.'

'They don't like seeing animals get hurt, but that's the only decent thing about them. When we lived in India, they had a whole menagerie of creatures they had rescued. Rats and bats and mongooses – you never knew what was in their pockets, waiting to leap out and bite your hand. They've probably got a new collection now. I shudder to think what's in it.'

'I had a pet white rat myself at their age. His name was Archie, and he was very clever.'

'What is it about boys and rats?' Daisy glanced at her wristwatch. 'I have to go home now,' she added. 'May I have my bag back?'

'I see I shouldn't have mentioned Archie. Why are girls afraid of things with whiskers and long tails?'

'I'm not afraid of them, but Mum is going to wonder where I've gone.' Daisy took her satchel back and slung it across her shoulder.

'See you tomorrow?' Ewan called, as she strode off down the winding path to Melbury House.

'Maybe,' she called, not looking back.

Ewan watched her go.

There was something very intriguing about Daisy Denham, which he told himself had nothing much to do with her sweet, heart-shaped face, her long, straight legs and golden hair, although of course he liked those fine.

He wondered what the mystery surrounding her could be, why his mother and Chloe were always muttering about the

Denham family, why he'd come into the morning room and find them whispering together, hissing like crones around a bubbling cauldron, brewing up a spell.

Why he'd heard Chloe laughing as she told his mother that at last the Denhams had got what they deserved, and serve them right.

What could they have done?

As the spring warmed into summer, Ewan grew on Daisy.

She wasn't overwhelmed with other friends. The girls at school were nice enough, but compared with friends she'd had in India they were boring. She missed Celia Norton dreadfully.

Celia and she had had adventures. They'd been camping and tobogganing in the foothills of the Himalayas. They'd gone into the jungle riding on the backs of elephants. They'd followed shooting parties in pursuit of tigers.

They'd explored bazaars with just their fathers' bearers to keep an eye on them, sniffing all the spices and buying penny bangles. Those girls in Dorchester, they wouldn't know an adventure if it came up and poked them in the eye.

Ewan was good-looking, wasn't stupid, and he was a socialist and an atheist, which was jolly daring. In the total absence of anyone more exciting, Ewan would have to do.

School had finished for the summer. As Ewan and Daisy lay on the headland one hot afternoon in late July, gazing towards Lyme Bay, Ewan said he was going to be actor.

'They're always out of work,' said Daisy.

'Thank you for your kind encouragement.' Ewan propped himself up on his elbows. 'You sound just like my mother. I thought I might expect a wee bit more enthusiasm from a seasoned trouper, who has not only trodden the boards herself, but has won great plaudits in the village.'

'I only mess about,' said Daisy, blushing. 'I'm just an amateur, and any professional would laugh at me.'

'You're very good, according to Miss Sefton. She's getting up a concert party soon, and she told Lady Easton you would definitely be in it.'

'She hasn't asked me.' Daisy was annoyed, but also flattered. 'Those village people,' she went on. 'I don't know what to make of them. They're chatting to you as nice as pie one minute, then gossiping behind your back the next. Making arrangements without even asking – '

'You should be familiar with their ways. After all, you're one of them.'

'No, I'm not – not really.' Daisy shrugged. 'We went to India when I was a toddler, so although I was born in England, I don't remember anything about it. When we came to Dorset, it was like coming to a foreign country.'

'Why did you come home?'

'Dad was in the army. One day there was a riot, things got nasty, and my dad got shot.' Daisy turned to Ewan. 'Indians are always having riots. You see, they want their independence, but we won't let them have it. Anyway, he was badly hurt, and when he got better, he wasn't fit enough to be a soldier any more.'

'So you came back to the old ancestral home.'

'Well, to that dump Dad's guardian left him, not that I'd have chosen it. I don't see why we can't live in a decent modern house, with proper running water and electricity, not with a well and oil lamps. It's money, I suppose. We haven't very much of it. Dad's only got his army pension. He lost most of his savings in the Crash.'

Daisy rolled over, lay on her back and stared up at the sky. 'Money, money, money, it's all Mum ever talks about.'

'It's all my mother talks about, as well. She's always going on about my school fees, about how much it's costing her to educate her stupid, lazy son.'

'Let's hope you're worth it, then.' Daisy glanced at Ewan, who wore no tie today, and whose white shirt was open at the collar. She thought she saw a glint of gold beneath the thin material. 'What's that around your neck?'

'This, you mean?' Ewan fished out a golden chain, on which there was a ring. '*It is an honour 'longing to our house, bequeathed down from many ancestors, which were the greatest obloquy i' the world in me to lose.*'

'I beg your pardon?'

'This was my father's ring. He died when I was twelve, the worms have long since eaten him, but he left me his ring. Of course, we're not allowed to wear any jewellery at school, and so I got myself a chain for it, and keep it hidden.'

'What was all that stuff you said just now?'

'It's from *All's Well That Ends Well* – but don't you know your Shakespeare?'

'Yes, I know a little, but not as much as you do, obviously.' Daisy frowned at him. 'I'm not an actress, Ewan. I only sing and dance a bit, whatever you may have heard down in the village, and not everyone can go to Eton.'

'I don't go to Eton. My mother couldn't raise the fees for Eton. I go to Blair Gowan Academy, one of Scotland's finest grammar schools. But I dare say you ignorant Sassenachs won't have heard of it.'

'If you want to act in Shakespeare's plays, you'll have to master English first,' retorted Daisy, sticking up for the England she had hated, not so long ago.

'What's that supposed to mean?'

'Well, with your accent, the only part you could play would be Macbeth.' Daisy grinned at him. 'Say worms again.'

'Worms.'

'No, not wurrums, worms!' Daisy laughed. 'You'll have to go to see Miss Sefton, ask her to give you elocution lessons.'

'Away, you saucy besom.' Ewan pushed her shoulder, and the touch of his hand through the light cotton of her dress made Daisy blush again, and made her feel hot and strange inside. 'I must go home,' she said, and scrambled up.

'Why, what have I said?'

'Oh, nothing – but Mum has lots of things for me to do.'

'Daisy, wait a minute.' Ewan grabbed her hand and pulled her down again, so she was sitting facing him. 'All right, go home and help your mother. But I'll see you tomorrow, yes?'

Then he leaned towards her, and she felt his mouth touch hers before she had a chance to jerk away.

'Tomorrow, yes?' he said again, his green eyes meeting Daisy's blue ones.

Chapter Three

Damn, thought Ewan, as he watched Daisy run off down the path, her hair a stream of radiance in the sunshine. I shouldn't have done that.

Now she'll tell her father, and this evening old man Denham will be up at Easton Hall, brandishing a shotgun and demanding satisfaction. What will it be – pistols at dawn, a public execution?

He could just imagine Daisy's father, who would be a big, fair Dorset man, the sort you saw in Dorchester on market days, purple-faced, tow-haired, in tweeds and leather gaiters.

He'd stump into the drawing room, rant and rave for half an hour, and carry on about his daughter's honour.

Agnes would turn the taps on. The ghastly poisonous Chloe would sit there smug and smirking. Sir Michael would stand before the empty fireplace, say nothing, but look disgusted. He had a talent for looking disgusted.

But Ewan couldn't regret what he had done, because today kind fate had smiled on him. He knew he'd found the girl he'd marry.

If only I'd had some warning, Daisy thought.

As she ran home, her heart was banging hard against her ribs, her face was burning, but she was laughing, too.

When Ewan kissed her, she had wanted to throw her arms around his smooth, brown neck and kiss him back, then lay her head on his broad shoulder.

So why hadn't she?

She didn't know.

But maybe it was just as well she hadn't. What if the twins had seen them kiss? They'd have laughed their stupid, horrible heads off. Then she'd have had to kill the little blighters, and she would have ended up in prison, because she wasn't old enough to hang.

Or she'd have had to get her lawyer to make out she was mad. Then they'd have put her in the local bin, with lunatics who wet themselves, who wore grey flannel uniforms and ugly, hobnail boots. She'd watched them clumping into church, where they sat and gibbered at the back, while their keepers shushed them.

She finally calmed down a little, and her heart stopped thumping. She decided she would go the long way home, taking the path that snaked through Easton Woods – which of course were private property, but she didn't care – then skirting the perimeter walls which enclosed the grounds of Charton Minster.

This was an old mansion which, the village gossips said, was a kind of prison where bad boys were locked up, regularly birched, and fed on bread and water. She often wished the brats were locked up with them.

She got home at six o'clock that evening. She went in round the back way, through the outbuildings, and there she found the twins.

'You've missed your supper,' Robert said.

'We ate all your scrambled eggs,' said Stephen.

'There's only sago pudding left for you.'

'It will be cold by now.'

'Yuck, cold frog spawn.' Robert grinned. 'Slime and slop and tadpoles.'

'I wish you were a tadpole, then you might get eaten by a pike,' said Daisy, coldly.

The twins had commandeered the stables, a group of Georgian buildings next to the big house which had stayed miraculously intact while almost everything else was falling down.

Now they were mucking out a rabbit run they'd made from bits of planking and old chicken wire, and playing with their pets.

'What are you going to do with that lot, make them into pies?' asked Daisy, eyeing a fat, brown doe with several kittens.

'They're pets, they're not for food!' Robert scooped up a black-eared heavyweight, and rubbed his nose against its furry neck.

'We got a buck and doe in the village. They were only sixpence each, and now we've got fifteen,' said Stephen, as he stroked a small, grey rabbit kitten. 'We're selling some of them to boys at school for half a crown apiece.'

'After we've checked they've got proper hutches,' added Robert, 'and they'd be safe from foxes, naturally.'

'Naturally,' said Daisy. 'Where are Mum and Dad?'

'They're in the house,' said Stephen. 'They're talking about money, and they both look pretty gloomy.'

'Now Dad's left the army and he only has his pension, we're jolly short of cash,' said Robert, putting down the rabbit. 'So, we're trying to do our bit. We told them about the rabbit farm, and how we're selling pets, and Dad said, well done.'

'But when we suggested going to the village school instead of Ryedale Manor, Mum got very weepy and said we ought to sell the house.'

'Then Dad said nobody would buy it.'

'Then Mum said it was hopeless, that Dad's broker should

be shot, and she was going up to have a bath, so that's where she is now.' Stephen looked at his sister anxiously. 'Daze, we're up the creek, or that's what Dad said, anyway.'

Daisy looked at them, saw two black-haired, grubby kids whose anxious, snub-nosed faces showed how much they wished to help, but didn't know how. They were just children, she reflected. They knew nothing about the world. Suddenly, she felt weary, sad – grown up.

'What's this one called?' she asked them, picking up a large white pink-eyed rabbit.

'Freddie, he's a buck, he's very strong, he'll kick you if he can,' said Stephen, taking the squirming animal and putting it back among its many wives.

'That brown one's Emily, she's nice, she'll let you stroke her nose,' said Robert, pointing to a pretty little doe.

Daisy picked Emily up and stroked her gently, thinking hard.

'Stokeley says he saw you on the headland earlier today,' said Agnes Fraser. Ewan had been summoned to her bedroom before dinner, and now he sat watching from the window seat as she rouged her face, pencilled in her eyebrows, and dabbed powder on her nose. 'You were with some girl.'

'Yes, with Daisy Denham.' Ewan didn't see what business it was of Albert Stokeley's, the Easton family bailiff who had once worked for the Denhams, but who had apparently been lured to Easton on Henry Denham's death with the promise of a better cottage and much higher pay.

'I don't think you should see her any more,' continued Agnes. 'You might give certain people the wrong impression.'

'We only go for walks,' said Ewan, hoping Albert Stokeley hadn't seen them kissing. Or hadn't seen Ewan kissing Daisy, and Daisy jumping up and running off.

'Well, please don't go walking with Miss Denham any more.' Agnes turned to face him. 'Sir Michael is getting up a fishing party for tomorrow, and he would like you to go along. He thinks your casting needs a lot more work.'

Ewan sighed, but then he thought that maybe he would go with the old men. It would stop his mother wittering, and Daisy had been so annoyed with him she probably needed to cool down a bit before she'd talk to him again.

'I suppose it does,' he muttered.

'You'll go fishing, then?'

'Yes.'

'Good, I'm very glad.' Agnes came to sit beside him on the window seat. 'Chloe says Daisy Denham – well, that girl's not quite the thing.'

'What do you mean?'

'Oh darling, I don't know. But there was some gossip in the war years. The usual business, I suppose. Maybe Mrs Denham had a baby rather soon after she married. Or perhaps before.'

Agnes's face grew pink. 'Dear Chloe isn't one to scandal-monger, as we know, but she wants to keep us on our guard.'

Dear Chloe, thought Ewan, sourly. Since when had it been dear Chloe? Agnes Fraser hadn't had one good word to say for Chloe when she'd first married Michael Easton. When Ewan's father was alive, Agnes had made remarks about people covering up their pasts, about how poor Michael could have had any girl he wanted, and didn't have to stoop to marrying a grasping divorcee.

But it seemed that now the boot was on the other foot, that Agnes was the pauper whose broker had invested in stocks and shares which these days were practically worthless, and

Chloe the baronet's influential wife, Agnes and Chloe were the best of friends.

I could leave school, thought Daisy. I could get a job. I could learn typing, work as someone's secretary, perhaps. Yes, I could help them out.

She left the stables, crossed the yard and went into the house. She made her way upstairs to Rose's and Alex's bedroom, where Rose took her baths in one of the old zinc tubs they had to lug up to their rooms, then fill with water from the kitchen copper, jug after tedious jug.

She could hear Alex talking, and was about to knock on the door when something made her freeze.

'I think you're exaggerating, darling,' Alex said.

'No, Alex, I am not,' retorted Rose. 'There's been so much gossip since we first came home. Someone's bound to say something soon, you know it. But Daisy should hear about it all from us, not somebody in the village.'

'You were the one who didn't want to tell her when we were in India.'

'When we were in India, she didn't need to know.'

'So do you think we ought to tell her now?'

'Well, not this evening, obviously,' said Rose. 'But soon, when the twins are out of the house, and the three of us can all sit down together quietly. Pass me that towel, please?'

'You're sure you've got the right address?' asked Alex, several moments later.

'I have that one in Leeds,' said Rose. 'If she went to America after all, maybe the people in Leeds could forward something. Alex, I need another towel now, this one's very wet. I left a pile on the landing.'

Then, before Daisy could step back, could run downstairs,

could duck into another room, Alex was suddenly there in front of her, a strange expression on his face which Daisy couldn't read.

'Oh, there you are, we wondered where you'd gone,' he said in a husky voice not like his own.

'You were talking about me,' began Daisy.

'You shouldn't listen at doors.'

'You shouldn't talk about people behind their backs!' retorted Daisy. 'Or that's what you've always told me, anyway.'

She glared at him, her offer of going out to work and helping save the family fortunes totally forgotten. 'What did Mum mean, she's got an address in Leeds? Who do you know in Leeds?'

'You'd better come in,' said Alex.

Rose was sitting on the bed wrapped up in several towels, fingering out the knots in her wet hair. She took one look at Daisy's face and sighed.

'Come and sit down, sweetheart,' she began. 'We have something to tell you.'

After she'd given Daisy the bare facts – that Daisy had been born in the East End, there'd been an air raid, her mother had disappeared for several weeks when Daisy was a few hours old, so Rose had brought the newborn baby back to Dorset – she kept saying over and over, 'Daisy, it doesn't matter who your actual parents were, you're our daughter, and we love you.'

'But you lied to me.' Daisy looked from Rose to Alex, willing herself to wake up from this nightmare. 'When I was little, and I used to have that dream, when I saw the lady with black hair, you must have known she was my mother, but you never told me.'

'You were too young to be told.'

'But now I know.' Daisy swallowed hard. 'So I'm a misfit, aren't I? You're a proper family. Mummy, Daddy, your two little boys, and I'm the cuckoo in your nest.'

'Daisy, don't ever talk like that, don't even think it!' Alex cried. 'We're your parents. You're our child. We'd give our lives for you.'

Rose wrapped one arm round Daisy. 'You're our lovely daughter, always have been, always will be. So don't you ever think you're not, do you hear me?'

'I suppose so.' Daisy shrugged. 'What's my mother's name?'

'It was Phoebe Gower. But now she's Phoebe Rosenheim, or she was going to be. I don't know if she married her fiancé.'

'So my father's name is Rosenheim?'

'No, I don't think so, Daisy. She became engaged to Nathan Rosenheim quite a few years after she had you.'

'Where does she live?'

'She came from Bethnal Green, in the East End of London, and then she went to Leeds. But I don't know where she lives today.'

'Mum, don't lie to me!'

'Daisy, it's the truth, I promise you.' Rose hugged Daisy tightly. 'She didn't keep in touch. When we were in India, I must have sent a hundred letters to that address in Leeds. I sent photographs of you. She didn't reply. Before we went to India, she told me she was going to America. I don't know if she went.'

'She didn't want me, did she?'

'It was wartime, she was very young, she didn't have a

family or a home.'

'So she abandoned me.' Daisy was still trying to digest all this, but she felt that something was stuck deep in her throat, that if she breathed too deeply she would choke.

'She couldn't keep you,' Rose said gently. 'So we said we'd adopt you, which we did.'

'How did you meet her, anyway?'

'She was the younger sister of a nurse I knew in France, during the war,' said Rose. 'Maria and I were working on the ambulance trains, and the Germans often used to bomb them. If Maria hadn't been killed, she would have adopted you, I'm sure.'

'Daisy, love,' said Alex, who was sitting on Daisy's other side, 'please don't think too badly of us. We did what we thought was best for everyone concerned.'

'I know you will be curious about her,' added Rose. 'Maybe you'll want to find her, get to know her, and we'll try to help you.'

'Why should I want to find a woman who abandoned me?' Daisy laid her head on Alex's shoulder. 'Dad, I hate her, and I don't want you to mention her again.'

'I'm sorry we didn't tell you sooner, sweetheart,' Rose said softly.

'Oh, don't worry, Mum, I understand.' Daisy shrugged and got up from the bed. 'Get dry, you'll catch a chill.'

'Where are you going now?'

'To get some supper, if the brats have left me anything.'

'Let me put on my dressing gown, and I'll come down and make you scrambled eggs.'

'Mum, I'd like to be by myself, all right?' Daisy still felt as if she was choking, that she'd swallowed something hard and indigestible. She needed to breathe some clean, fresh air.

She had to get away.

'She didn't ask about her natural father,' whispered Rose, when they were certain Daisy was downstairs, and could hear her clattering plates and saucepans in the kitchen.

'One thing at a time,' said Alex.

'She's bound to want to know eventually.'

'Let's hope she doesn't ask us yet,' said Alex. 'I don't think I could cope with it right now. Rose, come here, you're shivering. Let me dry your hair.'

'We need to find a tenant for the bailiff's cottage,' Rose told Alex. 'If we get the place spruced up and rent it out, that will bring in some cash.'

'You're right,' said Alex, as he towelled her hair. 'We should have done it months ago.'

'We've both been rather busy. But, once the place is habitable, someone from the village is sure to want it. There's an enormous garden, plenty of space to keep a flock of chickens and a pig, as well as raise a dozen children.'

'At least,' said Alex. 'I believe the Stokeleys had fourteen.'

'Alex?'

'Yes?

'Do you think we've been unfair to Daisy?'

'I honestly don't know.' Alex picked up a brush and started brushing Rose's hair with long, hard strokes. 'We did what we thought was best, and maybe we were wrong.'

'I couldn't love her any better if she was my own.'

'I know,' said Alex. 'Let's hope that after we've all slept on it, everything will settle down again.'

Daisy spent a sleepless night, turning things over and over in her mind, coming to no conclusions, hating Rose and Alex for lying, or at least misleading her, loving them still for loving her so much, then hating them again.

She got up very early, had her breakfast before anyone else was up, then left the house. She wanted to see Ewan, who would be sympathetic, she was sure, and who would understand.

She walked to the place they usually met.

She sat on a stile, waiting.

Chapter Four

Phoebe Rosenheim buttoned up her dress. She met the doctor's calm, professional gaze. 'So you don't think there's any 'ope,' she muttered.

'I didn't exactly tell you that,' the doctor said, but now he turned his head away.

'It's like I told you, I've already 'ad one baby. I didn't 'ave no bother with my labour, so why can't I have more?' demanded Phoebe. 'I'm only thirty-five, so surely I ain't past it yet?'

'My dear Mrs Rosenheim, some things aren't meant to be.' The doctor spread his clean, white hands. 'You can rest assured there's nothing seriously wrong. You have a little internal scarring, and although that can make conception hard, I wouldn't say it was impossible.'

'So just keep tryin', eh?' Phoebe put on her elegant straw hat, settled the smart, black veil over her eyes, then pulled on her new gloves. 'Nathan, he don't say nothin',' she murmured, 'an' he's very patient. But I know 'e wants kids. He's worked so hard, an' now he wants somebody to take over his business when 'e's gone.'

Phoebe's great dark eyes were full of disappointed tears. 'God knows he's done enough for me,' she cried, 'an' now I wants to give 'im somethin', too. Dr Stein, I wants to make 'im happy!'

'You say you've had one child already,' said the doctor, as he glanced at Phoebe's notes again. 'That was back in England, was it?'

'When I lived in London.' Phoebe nodded. 'It was born in

Bethnal Green, poor little devil, just like me.'

'So don't give up all hope.' The doctor coughed, clearing his throat. 'I'm sorry, Mrs Rosenheim, but did your baby die?'

'No, it was fine,' said Phoebe. 'But I wasn't married then, an' so it was adopted.'

'Do you know by whom?'

'The bloke was in the army. The woman 'ad been a nurse with our Maria – that's my sister, but she's dead – durin' the war.'

Phoebe shrugged, as if to suggest all this was ancient history. 'They was good, kind people, so I didn't mind leavin' it with them. Then I married Nathan an' we came to the States, but I couldn't 'ave brought the kid along. It wouldn't have been fair to Nathan, after all he'd done.'

'The child was not your husband's, then?'

'No, she was some soldier's.' Phoebe shrugged again. 'You wouldn't think it now, seein' me dressed up so nice, an' all respectable, but I used to go with soldiers then. It was that or starve.

'Anyway, like I was sayin' the people who 'ad the kid, they wrote to me when I was livin' in Leeds. I didn't keep the letters. I didn't want to know.'

'Where are these people now?'

'I don't know, Dr Stein.'

'It would be possible to find them, wouldn't it? You surely have their names?'

'Of course I have their names.'

'If you could be reunited with this child you lost, do you think it would help you?'

'No, it bleedin' wouldn't.' Phoebe looked Dr Stein as if he was insane. 'Sorry, doctor, 'scuse my French, but I want

Nathan's baby, not some other bloke's. I want to be a proper family!'

'Just give it time.' The doctor stood up, led Phoebe from his office and asked the receptionist to call a cab.

Ten minutes later she was in a taxi, surrounded by the noise and rush and bustle of New York City. It was still a vibrant, busy place, despite the Crash, despite the fact that these days sober-suited businessmen were standing on the sidewalks, selling stuff from trays.

But Phoebe didn't see them, because in spirit she was back in Bethnal Green. Maybe Dr Stein was right. Maybe she should try to find the baby she had lost, so many years ago? Or had she waited far too long, and was it too late now?

Daisy sat and waited the whole morning before she finally accepted Ewan wasn't coming.

She wondered if he knew.

Then she told herself, don't be ridiculous. Of course he doesn't know.

Then she remembered what he'd said the first time they had met, about how his mother and Lady Easton talked about her, how they knew her name and where she lived. They probably knew the rest of it, as well.

Now Ewan would know it, too.

The week went on, the glorious Dorset summer of blue and gold contrasting cruelly with the bitter winter that had frozen Daisy's heart. She must have looked so miserable, she realised, that even the brats were pleasant, and this was restful but alarming. Rose insisted that the twins knew nothing, but the boys were acting as if somebody had died, and Daisy was chief mourner.

Mealtimes were impossible. She was given the best of

everything, but didn't feel like eating. 'Why don't you have another pilchard, Daze?' asked Robert, one bleak supper time, on the third or fourth day after Rose's revelations. He didn't wait for Daisy to reply, but slid one off his toast, then plonked the blank-eyed corpse on Daisy's plate.

'You can have one of mine, as well.' Stephen wobbled a fish across the table on his fork.

But Daisy couldn't have eaten the wretched pilchards if she'd tried. Their blind, dead eyes stared up at her reproachfully. The thick tomato sauce looked like fresh blood. Gagging, she got up and left the table.

She knew she had to pull herself together. She was Rose's and Alex's daughter still. They'd said so, and she knew they really meant it, that they loved her dearly and would always be her mum and dad, no matter who her natural parents were.

But she was in such a muddle.

Superficially, everything in Charton was the same. The people in the village were as pleasant as they'd ever been. But now all their enquiries about her parents and her brothers seemed sarcastic, not polite. Now, she could imagine all the whispering and gossiping there must have been when the Denhams first came back to Dorset. She wondered just how much these strangers knew, when she'd known nothing.

Even dear old Mrs Hobson had become an enemy – one of the conspirators who had always known the truth, and hidden it – so Daisy had stopped going to the kitchen when Mrs Hobson was around. Sometimes, Daisy even hated Rose.

She thought, I need to get away from Charton.

But where could I go?

One hot morning, she was making for the headland,

meaning to sit on the cliffs and think the whole thing through again, when she saw Ewan coming down the road from Easton Hall.

She turned back, walking quickly. But he ran after her and caught her, falling into step beside her, hands pushed in his trouser pockets, staring straight ahead.

They walked in silence for a hundred yards. But the silence soon became so heavy and oppressive that Daisy couldn't bear it any longer. 'You never came to meet me!' she began. 'I waited hours that morning!'

'I thought you were so annoyed with me that you wouldn't come,' he muttered, scowling at the path.

'Why should I be annoyed?'

'I – because I kissed you.'

'You bashed my nose, you mean.'

'I'm sorry.'

'I should think so, too.'

'Come and sit on the beach a while?' Ewan stopped walking and met Daisy's gaze, his own beseeching.

'I've things to do at home.'

'You could surely spare an hour or two?' Then Ewan smiled, but nervously, as if afraid she'd bite him.

'Actually, I can't.'

'Please,' said Ewan humbly, obviously trying to look serious and deserving, but she could see the corners of his mouth were twitching, as if he were trying not to grin.

'Oh, all right.' Daisy realised she was smiling, too. 'Just half an hour, and then I must go home.'

'I'm sorry I didn't come that morning,' Ewan said, as they scrambled down the cliff path, all the tension there had been between them magically gone. 'But I had annoyed you. I thought you'd never speak to me again. Then Sir Michael asked me to go fishing.'

'So of course you went, and I don't blame you. It must have been more fun than kissing me.'

'No, Daisy, it was deadly, casting lines, then sitting there for hours, sticking hooks through worms –'

'Och, those puir wurrums,' teased Daisy.

'Aye, the puir wee beasties.' Ewan found he didn't mind being teased – in fact, he liked it. 'Come on, sit down a while. I promise I won't lunge at you again.'

They sat down on the shingle, underneath an overhanging rock. Daisy picked up a pretty yellow pebble. Ewan had seen it too, and as he reached for it their hands collided, and didn't seem to want to part.

Ewan walked the fingers of his other hand up Daisy's arm. She closed her free hand over them. 'You promised me,' she whispered.

'What did I promise? I've forgotten.'

'You said you wouldn't lunge at me, and now you're doing just that.'

'Daisy, I've really missed you.' Ewan gazed into her eyes and saw himself reflected there in pools of blue. 'I've missed you so much, you can't imagine.'

'I – I've missed you.' Then, as if she had been magnetised, Daisy leaned towards him. So there didn't seem anything to do but kiss her on the mouth, and hope she wouldn't pull away.

She didn't. In fact, she kissed him back, tilting her head as if by instinct, so their noses didn't bump. Then, as if he'd willed it, Daisy put her arms around his neck. So now he kissed her harder, longer, thinking how beautiful she was, how warm, how soft, how sweet, until at last he couldn't think at all.

'What else have you been doing?' Daisy asked him, when they had to take a break from kissing. 'That's apart from fishing and longing to see me?'

'Nothing else,' said Ewan, as he entwined his fingers in her hair. 'It's wonderful to be down here with you. But honestly, I've had enough of Dorset, and my mother's driving me insane.'

'Why, what's she doing?'

'She's nagging all the time. I was supposed to be studying for Oxford while I've been in Dorset, but I haven't opened any of my books. So now it's all Sir Michael this, and Lady Easton that, and let Sir Michael show you how to shoot and how to fish. Let him get to know you, worm your way into his heart, then he might leave you all his money. Aye, I thought, fat chance – he's a dozen brothers and sisters, nephews and nieces, cousins by the score. I don't want his rotten, stinking money, anyway.'

'Why is he so rich, do you know?'

'About ten years ago, some old man called Courtenay who didn't have any children left him everything – a vast estate, a pile of cash, and probably a sack of rubies, too. So now he's one of the biggest, wealthiest landowners in Dorset. These days, stocks and shares are almost worthless. But if you have acres of good farming land, you're very rich.'

'Do you have land in Scotland?'

'Yes, a little, but most of it's no good for farming, so it's not worth much. It's mainly moor and bog and heather, very bonny, but unless you shoot for sport it's useless. We have the house, of course, but in the summer it's let out.'

Ewan shook his head. 'I know fine how to shoot and how

to fish. But I do both for food, not entertainment. I'm sick of Easton Hall. I miss the Highlands, Daisy, and I miss my home.'

'I miss India,' Daisy told him.

It was true, for every day she wished she was in India, the place where she'd been happy, where there had been certainty, where she'd never doubted Rose and Alex were her parents. Where they'd had enough to live on, had a host of servants, and eaten the most delicious food, not scrambled eggs and tinned sardines and Mrs Hobson's stews.

'What do you miss most?' asked Ewan.

'Our bungalow, our friends, the colours, smells and hugeness of it all, the heat, the snow.'

'You had snow in India?'

'Yes, of course we did.'

'I thought it was always hot in India.'

'It's always hot in Delhi, where we lived in winter. But in summer we went to Simla. It's a town up in the hills. We could see the Himalayas from our bedroom windows.'

'What, you've seen Mount Everest?'

'No, Everest's in Nepal, and that's a long way from Simla! But I've been trekking in the Himalayan foothills.' She laughed at Ewan's goggle-eyed astonishment. 'Some years, we stayed in Simla just for summer, but other years we stayed until the autumn. When it got cold, it snowed. Then we all went tobogganing.'

Daisy sighed. 'I don't suppose there's ever any decent snow in Dorset. Last winter, there was some in January, but it melted. It turned to slush and mud.'

'I know what you mean about the snow,' said Ewan, nodding. 'A winter landscape of freshly-fallen snow – it lifts your spirits. It makes you feel alive. I wish I could see some now. If I were at home, of course, I could.'

'But surely there won't be any snow in August, even up in Scotland?'

'There'll still be a little on the highest peaks, and in the northern corries.' Ewan took Daisy's hands and held them, looked into her eyes. 'Daisy, why don't we go and find some snow?'

Chapter Five

'Where can she have gone?' asked Rose. She'd poured out glasses of mid-morning milk for Daisy and the twins, and now she watched the boys gulping it down. 'I wanted her to help me with the bedrooms.'

'She's probably with that man from Easton Hall,' said Robert, reaching for a biscuit.

'What man from Easton Hall?'

'You know, the tall one, with red hair.' Stephen took one of Mrs Hobson's scones. 'We saw them on the beach this morning.'

'They were kissing,' added Robert.

'Yuck.'

'They were what?' said Rose, and frowned. 'I think I'll need to have a word.'

'You mean you didn't know?' Robert sighed and shook his head.

'Daze has been messing around with him all summer, Mum,' said Stephen. 'May I have her milk?'

'We can't just disappear,' said Daisy.

'I don't see why not.'

'Ewan, don't be ridiculous. Our parents will wonder where we've gone. They'll worry.'

'If we tell them what we're doing, they're bound to say we can't,' objected Ewan. 'In my experience, parents always do. You could leave a note.'

'What would I say?'

'You're going away for a couple of days, that's all. Come

on, Daisy. Let's do something, shall we, before we die of boredom? Let's go to Scotland. Let's go and get the train.'

Daisy was very tempted. Since Rose's revelations, she'd been dying to leave Charton. 'What shall we do for money?' she asked. 'I've got about ten shillings, and that won't get us far.'

'If we go third class, I have enough to get us to the rail head. After that we'll walk, or find a wagon going up the glen.'

'All right, we'll do it.' Daisy made her mind up. 'I'll meet you at Charton station in an hour. But don't buy tickets for the express. We'll tell them in the ticket office we're going into Dorchester.'

'Why should we do that?'

'So Mr Larkin doesn't get suspicious and telephone our parents. When we get to Dorchester, we can buy our tickets for the train to Scotland.'

'My, what a canny plotter!' Ewan grinned. 'I see I've underestimated you.'

'You meant it, didn't you?' Daisy asked him, suddenly feeling anxious. 'You want to go to Scotland?'

'Aye, I want to go to Scotland.' He pulled her to her feet. 'So come on, get up. I can't show you anything to touch the Himalayas,' he added, as they climbed the cliff path. 'But we'll find some snow. Away and pack your bag now, and don't let anybody see you leave.'

Daisy ran home to Melbury House. She grabbed an oilskin shopping bag from a hook behind the kitchen door, then ran upstairs, hoping she wouldn't meet Rose.

What should she take to Scotland? She'd never packed for herself before and didn't know how to do it. In India, her ayah had looked after her clothes. Since they'd lived in Dorset, she hadn't been away.

A change of things, she told herself, shoving a clean cardigan, a dress and various bits of underwear into the oilskin bag. Soap and a flannel, hairbrush, toothbrush, money ...

She scribbled a hasty note to say that she was going to Scotland for a week or two. But Rose and Alex mustn't worry. She'd soon be home again.

Then she sneaked down the service stairs, went out the back way past the stables, and she was on her way.

They caught the train at Charton, changed at Dorchester, and two hours later they were on a fast express to Glasgow.

In all her haste to get away, Daisy hadn't had time to think or worry. But, as she sat and watched the scenery speed by, she suddenly felt sick.

Whatever was she doing? What would her parents think, and would they be furious when she got home again? Whenever Celia Norton misbehaved, she got a beating from her father. She didn't think Alex would ever beat her, but ...

'What is it, Daisy?' Ewan leaned towards her, his green eyes solicitous.

'Nothing, I was just looking at those cows.' Daisy forced a smile. 'They're Jerseys, aren't they?'

'Yes, I think so, but why are you interested in cows?'

'Dad's borrowing some money from the bank to buy a herd of Jerseys. Mum says she's going to manage it. She'll run the dairy, and sell the cream and butter. She's going to get some laying hens and sell the eggs, as well. How long is it going to take to get to Scotland?'

'All day and half the night,' said Ewan. 'Talking of eggs, I'm starving, so let's go to the buffet and have some lunch.'

'Buffets are expensive, aren't they?'

'We'll have something cheap.'

But Daisy's stomach was in knots, and she couldn't force down anything. So Ewan ate her glutinous brown soup and ham and eggs, and polished off her pudding.

Their journey went on for ever, with everlasting changes after Glasgow as they zig-zagged up into the Highlands. When they reached the halt that served Glen Grant, it was pitch dark and raining hard. Luckily Ewan had thought to bring a torch.

'You can have my jacket.' He took it off and draped it round her shoulders, turning up the collar against the downpour.

'But you'll get soaked,' said Daisy.

'Oh, it's just a shower.' Ewan grinned. 'We Scots are no' afraid of a wee drop of rain.'

'This is a monsoon.'

Ewan was delighted to be home, and certainly wasn't bothered by the rain. As he and Daisy squelched along the rutted gravel track, he took her hand, shaking his wet hair out of his eyes, and talking about what they were going to do.

At last, they reached the Morrisons' little cottage, which as he'd expected was in darkness. This was not surprising, since it was well past midnight.

'We'll have to wake them up,' he said.

'I do h-hope they won't be angry,' stammered Daisy, who he could see was shivering and shuddering with cold.

'Oh, they're used to me.'

'You mean you often turn up in the middle of the night?'

'It has been known,' said Ewan, and started hammering

on the door.

Mrs Morrison didn't seem annoyed or even very surprised when she saw him and Daisy standing outside her cottage in the rain in the small hours of a Wednesday morning.

A comfortable, pleasant-looking woman in her fifties, she wore her usual flannel nightdress and woollen dressing gown, and her hair was hanging down her back in a long plait.

'Oh, it's you,' she said, and shook her head reprovingly. 'I said to Donald only yesterday, we haven't heard from Ewan for a while, so perhaps he's on his way back home.'

'You were right, and here I am,' said Ewan.

Ewan always thought of Flora Morrison as a second and much more motherly mother. Now, as a proper mother should, she clucked a bit, but then she hustled them inside.

'I expect you're hungry?' she said calmly, as she stirred the fire into a blaze.

'Yes, we're starving,' Ewan admitted. 'Daisy, come and get warm,' he added, sitting her down next to the fire, and feeling guilty now because she couldn't stop her teeth from chattering.

Mrs Morrison made hot drinks and sandwiches, towelled Daisy's hair, and then she sent them both to bed.

'You must phone your parents in the morning,' Ewan heard her telling Daisy, as she lit a candle to take her up the stairs. 'Mrs Gordon at the post office will let you use her phone. She'll put the cost on Mrs Fraser's bill, I have no doubt.'

Daisy more or less fell into bed, and went to sleep immediately, waking to the smell of frying bacon, and to see sunshine streaming through the window of her attic room.

She found a dressing gown on her bed, and so she put it on and went downstairs, where everybody else was up and dressed.

'It's a lovely day,' said Mrs Morrison, as she filled their breakfast plates with bacon, eggs and slices of peculiar brown sausage. 'Daisy, your clothes are here beside the fire, and they're dry again.'

'You say you're going climbing on Ben Grimond, Ewan?' Mr Morrison, who was sitting at the kitchen table and shovelling down his breakfast, mopped his military moustache with a big yellow handkerchief. 'I don't know if that's wise.'

'Oh, don't worry,' Ewan told him. 'We'll be fine.'

'There've been a couple of landslips recently, so go up the south side, keeping to the paths and tracks.'

'We'll do that,' promised Ewan.

'The wireless says we'll have more rain,' added Mrs Morrison. 'So, if you're going out, we must find your friend some proper waterproofs. We'll have a coat and boots to fit, I'm sure. But is this young lady used to climbing mountains?'

'Daisy's been trekking in the Himalayas,' Ewan told Mrs Morrison. 'So she won't be impressed by our wee Scottish hills.'

Daisy wasn't so sure.

'You mustn't forget to go and phone your people,' Mrs Morrison reminded Daisy, once she was satisfied that her borrowed mackintosh and boots would keep her warm and dry.

So she and Ewan walked up to the post office, where – like Mrs Morrison – Mrs Gordon didn't seem at all surprised to see them.

'So you're home again,' she said, and smiled. 'I was in Dorset once myself. It's pretty, but it doesn't compare with Scotland. You'll have to wait an hour or so before you get a call to England.'

Daisy knew that she would be told off. But when Mrs Gordon finally managed to put a call through to her parents, she was almost deafened as Alex told her what a thoughtless, selfish beast she'd been, how her mother had been beside herself, and how she was to come home straight away.

Then he hung up.

Daisy shook her head to clear the ringing in her ears. 'I've never heard my father shout like that,' she said, as Ewan took the phone and hung the mouthpiece up again.

She had forgotten about the snow. Now, she was desperate to go home, see Rose, give her a hug, and to apologise.

'My turn now,' said Ewan.

'Sorry?'

'I need to put a call through to my mother, and let her shout at me.'

'I bet she couldn't shout as loud as Dad.'

'Aye, well, we'll see.'

'I tell you what we'll do,' said Ewan, when he'd finished being shouted at or rather whimpered at by Agnes Fraser. 'Now we're here, we'll go and climb Ben Grimond. We'll see the snow, and then go back to Dorset.'

'You don't have to come with me,' said Daisy. 'You wanted to come home again, so stay. I'll get the train back by myself.'

'I think I need to come to Dorset. I need get between you and your father.'

'I can deal with Dad.'

'You're sure?' said Ewan, frowning. 'I don't know about that. Chloe says Mr Denham's very aggressive.'

'Chloe's wrong.'

'Perhaps,' admitted Ewan, doubtfully.

'So is this all yours?' she asked, as they set off across the expanse of moor which lay in front of Mr and Mrs Morrison's little cottage, and headed for the mountain.

'It would have been,' said Ewan, gazing round. 'But when my father died, my mother had to sell a lot of land to pay our debts. What's left is land she couldn't sell for various reasons – entails, covenants and stuff. I don't pretend to understand it.

'See the house,' he added, pointing. 'The big Victorian house, I mean, with all the gables and the barley-sugar chimneys, not the little cottage where we're staying?'

'Yes.'

'If you follow a curving line from there down to the burn, then look towards the mountains on your right, what you can see belongs to us.'

'You're very lucky. The mountains and the river and the moors – they're beautiful.' Daisy turned to him. 'Ewan, you love it, don't you?'

'Yes, I do.'

'Why don't you want to live here all the time, then?'

'How do you know I don't want to live here all the time?'

'You said you were going to be an actor.'

'I am indeed,' said Ewan.

'So you're going to entertain the sheep?'

'I'm going to entertain the world. But I shall have the summer seasons off, and spend them in Glen Grant.'

'You'll be a very successful actor, then?'

'Of course I shall,' said Ewan, willing Daisy not to laugh

as Agnes would have done. 'But in the summer, I'll be a laird as well.'

They reached the foothills of Ben Grimond, which loured over them like some great crouching monster, its summit hidden by clouds.

'What do you think?' asked Ewan. 'Shall we go up and find some snow?'

'Yes, all right,' said Daisy.

'It's going to rain.'

'I've got a coat.'

'Come on, then – take my hand.'

'*Blow winds*,' cried Ewan, as he dragged her up the mountain track. '*You cataracts and hurricanoes, spout!*'

'Ewan, please don't go so fast,' gasped Daisy, as she felt the first fat drops of freezing rain go trickling down her neck, and was glad of Mrs Morrison's heavy mackintosh.

Ewan hauled her like a bag of washing up a bank of scree, then let her have a rest. She watched with awe and dread as lightning forked on a bare ridge a mile or two away.

'My God, you are unfit,' said Ewan, who was breathing normally himself.

'You don't believe in God,' said Daisy, shuddering. But, God – this was ridiculous, she thought, climbing a Scottish mountain with a boy she'd known five minutes, hardly able to get her breath, and terrified the storm would hit them, blow them off the crag.

'It's all right, it's going the other way,' said Ewan, and he smiled reassuringly.

'I don't much like lightning,' she confessed.

'You mustn't worry, I'll look after you. Do you want to go back down now?'

'What about the snow? I want to find some snow.'

'All right,' said Ewan. 'Then we must get on. We can't be on the mountain after dark.'

They reached the top of the mountain, but they didn't find much snow – only a little tucked deep in a corrie, left there by the blizzards that had scoured and carved the landscape.

'Here,' said Ewan, scooping up a crystal handful and offering it to Daisy.

'It smells of the North Pole,' she said. She licked it, and he watched as the white flakes dissolved on her pink tongue. 'It tastes of winter.'

'You're so lovely, Daisy.' Ewan couldn't believe that anyone or anything could be so beautiful. '*Chaste as the icicle that's curdied by the frost from purest snow, and hangs on Dian's temple.*'

Daisy blushed. 'More Shakespeare?' she said lightly, and Ewan felt the electricity flickering between them. 'More *King Lear*?'

'*Coriolanus.* He's one of my heroes. I mean to play him one day.'

'Then I'm sure you will.'

'I'll play Romeo, Orlando and Benedick, as well.' Ewan tipped up Daisy's chin and made her look at him. 'You could be my Juliet, my Rosalind, my Beatrice.'

'I – *tis an honour that I dream not of,*' said Daisy, laughing.

'You'll be my Juliet,' said Ewan.

Then he kissed her, and it didn't matter when their noses bumped, because she kissed him back, their passion rising as the stinging rain came down.

'We should go home,' he said, five minutes – or it could have been five hours – later. 'Daisy, hold my hand.'

He shouldn't have brought her up the mountain, he realised that now. As they slipped and slithered down he held on to her tightly, terrified they'd be benighted by the worsening storm.

'At least we found some snow,' she gasped. She clearly didn't understand the danger she was in, as they forded torrents that hadn't been there when they climbed the mountain earlier that morning, and as they slid down gullies, grazing their bare hands.

'Come here, and hold on to me down this bit,' Ewan said, as Daisy slid and scrabbled down a rocky apology for a path. 'It's this way now.'

'Do you know where we are, then?'

'Yes, of course,' he said, and grabbed her hand just as she started sliding towards a sheer drop and certain death.

To Ewan's huge relief, although he'd never have admitted it to Daisy, Mr Morrison came to look for them. Daisy was all in, and they had to carry her home between them.

'You two need your heads examined,' Mrs Morrison scolded, wrapping Daisy in a thick grey blanket, and making her sit down beside the fire. 'Just you stay there, miss, and sip your broth. Well, Ewan, how far did you go?'

'To the top, of course.'

'You'll be the death of Mrs Fraser, and of this young lady's mother.'

'You'll be doing jigsaws and playing cribbage for the next few days,' added Mr Morrison. 'The weather's turned. Some of the railway line's been washed away. I don't know when you're expected back in Dorset. But you've no chance of getting away this week.'

They had to go for walks. There was no other way they

could be alone, and kiss, and talk, and kiss again.

In Wellington boots and hats and mackintoshes, they went for rainy hikes all round Glen Grant, sheltering under rocky outcrops, darting into empty bothies, hiding under the warped and rotting eaves of ruined sheep folds – anywhere they could kiss.

Mrs Morrison gave them severe, old-fashioned looks, but didn't say anything.

Daisy was in love. She knew it. There could be no other explanation for this delicious warmth that made her glow, for the smile she couldn't keep from curling round her mouth. All she wanted was to be with Ewan.

'I love you,' he whispered as they sheltered from another downpour in a shepherd's hut.

'I love you, too,' she told him.

Ewan took the chain on which he wore his father's ring from round his neck. 'Daisy, will you wear this chain?' he asked.

'What about the ring?'

'I'll have the ring, you have the chain.' Ewan fastened it round Daisy's neck, and then he kissed her lightly on the lips. 'Promise me you'll never take it off?'

'I promise,' Daisy said. 'I'll always wear it, and I'll always keep you in my heart.'

They waited for the storm to die away and for the railway line to be repaired, and then went back to Dorset on the early morning train. The journey took forever, but it wasn't long enough for Daisy, who was hoping it would never end.

The little local train pulled into Charton, and she saw the sight she'd dreaded. Alex was standing waiting for them on the station platform, looking beyond grim.

'I'm for it now,' she said.

'He can't kill you, it's against the law.'

'I doubt if that would bother him,' said Daisy, who felt sick.

'Good luck,' said Ewan.

'Thanks, I'll need it. Daisy stepped down from the train. 'Dad, I'm really sorry,' she began.

'Where is this man?' demanded Alex.

'Good evening, sir,' said Ewan, holding out his hand to Daisy's father, who wasn't a red-faced, leather-gaitered, tow-haired Dorset man. He was tall and dark, and didn't look anything like Daisy.

Ewan remembered he had been a soldier. He still looked like one – everything about him said authority. He didn't rant and rave or carry on. Instead, he looked at Ewan as if he was something nasty on the bottom of his shoe.

'Ewan Fraser, is it?' He didn't take Ewan's proffered hand. 'I suppose you realise Mrs Denham and your mother have been frantic?'

Every word was like a blow, and Ewan flinched, but he refused to drop his gaze. 'I'm sorry to hear it, sir.' He knew his face was scarlet, but he tried to stand up straight and tall. 'Mrs Denham will be happy to have Daisy home,' he added, lamely.

'Yes, I'm sure she will.' Mr Denham turned and strode towards the car, and Daisy scuttled after him, much to the interest of the ticket man, who didn't dare ask Daisy for her ticket.

Ewan didn't blame him.

Alex didn't say a word as he drove back to Melbury House.

But the very moment Daisy got out of the car, the twins came hurtling out of the front door, and launched themselves at her like small torpedoes.

'Daze, you've been so wicked!' Stephen cried. 'Dad's been so angry! We haven't dared to cheek him for a week!'

'A boy in the village said you were a hoyden,' Robert added, grinning. 'We had to look it up, it means a rude and ill-bred girl, and so we thumped him. He's got two black eyes.'

'Daze, we've got some cows.' Stephen started pulling her towards the ruinous cowshed. 'Come and see them, they're – '

'Daisy, go and see your mother,' Alex said, and Daisy followed him into the house. 'She's waiting for you in the drawing room.'

Daisy was expecting tears, reproaches and some kind of punishment. But Rose looked calm and placid. 'Sit down,' she said, and patted the place beside her on the ancient, sagging sofa.

'Mum, I'm sorry,' Daisy said, and meant it.

'At least you left a note, and rang us up to tell us where you'd gone.' Rose took Daisy's hand. 'Daisy, love, this man you went with, he and you – '

'Oh, don't worry, Mum,' said Daisy, reddening. 'Ewan and I are friends, that's all.'

'Why did you go away?'

'When you told me what happened about my real mother, I thought everyone in Charton must be whispering and laughing at me behind my back. I had to get away.'

'I understand,' said Rose. 'But please don't run away again. Your father and I were so upset and worried. When we realised you had gone with the boy from Easton Hall,

Alex had to go and see Sir Michael and his wife. I believe it was an awkward meeting. He's never liked Sir Michael.'

'Ewan says Lady Easton is a bitch,' said Daisy, nodding. 'As for Sir Michael, he's – '

'I think we should forget it,' interrupted Rose. 'Darling, will you promise me something? Don't upset your father, and remember Alex loves you.'

'I'll remember,' Daisy promised, getting up.

It wasn't until she went up to her bedroom that Daisy realised Rose herself hadn't said anything about loving Daisy.

So didn't she think of herself as Daisy's mother, after all?

The following morning, Alex went to Easton Hall again, and came home looking blacker than the last time.

'What exactly did you say to Michael?' Rose asked gently later on that evening, when she was sure the children were in bed, the doors were shut and nobody could hear them.

'I told him to see that Fraser fellow doesn't come near our daughter,' muttered Alex. 'Chloe then reminded me that Daisy's not our daughter.'

'I hope you didn't rise to that?'

'Rose, it's fine for you to sit here being calm and reasonable! It was different for me to have to walk into their den, to see them sitting there so rich and smug.'

'Darling, I made my choice,' said Rose.

'A bad one, wasn't it?' Alex shook his head and looked away. 'Easton said he'd heard we'd bought some cattle, and that dairy farming was a waste of effort on land as poor as ours.'

'But you didn't comment?'

'I didn't give him the satisfaction of seeing I was riled, or that I thought he might be right.'

'What about the Fraser boy, did Michael say he'd speak to him?'

'He said that Ewan, or whatever he's called, is seventeen, that he's not a child, and he has no authority over him. The mother sat there snivelling and dabbing at her eyes. I didn't see the boy. I suppose he was avoiding me.'

'What do we do now?'

'We must appeal to Daisy's common sense – that's if she has any common sense.'

'Alex, we need to tell her the whole story.'

'So we do, and open a can of worms to stink out Dorset?' Alex turned to look at Rose. 'We don't know if Phoebe told the truth, and we could never prove it if she did. So why spoil everything for Daisy, and maybe even lose her?'

'It wouldn't come to that, she knows she's ours.'

'Why did she run away, then?' Alex grimaced. 'Easton said his keeper's seen the twins going in the coverts. He suspects they're springing traps. So he's told Stokeley he may thrash them if the keeper catches them.'

'What did you say to that?'

'I told Easton that if any of his servants touch my children, I will personally thrash *him*.' Alex's grin was humourless. 'You should have seen his face – and Chloe's.'

'Alex, it wasn't wise to make such threats.'

'Well, that's too bad, I've made them now.'

'Do you think we ought to tell the children about you and Chloe? Or at least tell Daisy?'

'No, I don't.'

'All right, we'll leave things as they are for now.'

'I'm sure that will be for the best.' Alex got up and stretched. 'I asked Mr Hobson to get the cows into the cowshed, so they'll be ready for the vet when he comes first thing tomorrow morning. I'm just going to check he's shut them in. We don't want them wandering round the yard.'

Alex left, but a few minutes later he came running in again, followed by the scent of wood smoke on the summer night. 'Ring the fire brigade!' he cried, as he burst into the drawing room, his clothes begrimed with smoke. 'The cowshed is on fire!'

Rose was on her feet at once. 'What about the Jerseys,' she began, pulling on her shoes.

'I've let the cows out. They're running round the paddock. I hope the gate's shut and they don't get on the road. Rose, forget the cows. Go and wake the children. The wind is blowing the fire towards the house!'

Chapter Six

Luckily the well was deep and full, but though they threw buckets of water at the blaze, though they dragged out bales of smouldering straw and tried to contain the fire inside the cowshed, the wind was blowing off the sea that night, and drove the smoke and flames towards the house.

The sparks from burning timbers danced and flew like wicked fairies. The beams in the roof of Melbury House, exposed to all the elements and tinder dry from three or four weeks of glorious summer sunshine, soon caught fire.

'We'll go up on the roof, Dad,' offered Stephen. 'We'll beat out the flames.'

'You'll do no such thing!' cried Rose, and she grabbed each twin by his pyjama jacket collar to stop her children running into the blazing house. 'Oh, Alex, where's the fire brigade?'

'It's on its way,' said Daisy. 'I can hear the bells.'

'Come on, you chaps,' said Alex, wiping his arm across his soot-streaked brow. 'Now we've got the straw outside, a few more bucketsful should get the fire in the cowshed out.'

But although the cowshed was gradually damped down until it became a steaming, blackened ruin, the Denhams could do nothing to stop the house from burning down.

Daisy, Robert and Stephen, still in their bedraggled pyjamas, stood with their parents as the firemen – who had finally arrived, but admitted they were far too late – failed to do anything but contain the blaze, and stop it spreading to the stables, too.

Mr and Mrs Hobson and other people from the village

had smelled smoke, had seen the flames, and they came running across the fields to help put out the fire. But although they made up bucket chains, the old house burned like matchwood, defying all attempts to stop it turning into its own funeral pyre.

The water from the firemen's hoses completed the destruction of the lower floors. By morning, Melbury House and most of the range of outbuildings behind it were reduced to one great, smoking ruin.

'It's just as well we haven't yet let the Stokeleys' cottage,' Rose observed, as Alex stared shell-shocked at the soot-stained walls and charred oak timbers of his childhood home. 'We can move in there for the time being.'

'We've still got the cows, Dad,' added Robert.

'The rabbits are all right as well,' said Stephen, who had been to check.

'It's just a house,' said Daisy.

'Yes, it's just a house, but it was mine.' Alex turned to Rose. 'This is down to Easton,' he growled, through gritted teeth. 'He'll never let me forget I took you from him. Although he got his filthy hands on everything that's yours, he still can't allow us to be happy.'

'Dad, what do you mean?' asked Daisy. 'Did Sir Michael want to marry Mum?'

Alex put his arm round Daisy. 'Yes, he did,' he muttered. 'A long time ago.'

'A very long time ago, love,' Rose said quickly. 'I never wanted to marry anyone but your father, and Mike Easton doesn't like being thwarted. But Alex, I can't imagine he'd do anything like this.'

'Oh, Mrs Denham!' Mrs Hobson loomed out of the early morning mist. 'What will you do now?'

'We'll manage, Mrs Hobson.' Rose's tired, pale face looked bleached and ghost-like in the misty morning light. 'We'll move into the bailiff's cottage.'

'But Mrs Denham, dear, you can't live there! It's miles from the big house, the stables, everything you need.'

'It's half a mile at most,' said Rose. 'As I said, we'll manage. We're going to have to build another cowshed anyway, so we could build it there, close to the cottage.'

'I still don't think it's right that you should live in Albert Stokeley's cottage,' muttered Mrs Hobson.

'It will have to do.' Rose smiled wearily at the other villagers clustered round. 'Thank you, everyone, for all your help.'

'We'll find you sheets and blankets,' promised Mrs Hobson. 'Me and Mrs Dale, we'll get our brooms and soap and buckets. We'll sort the cottage out.'

'We'll get you food, bring up some bread and milk,' announced Miss Sefton.

'There are some tins of cream distemper in the village hall,' went on the parish clerk. 'I'll go up and fetch 'em.'

'You'll need some firewood,' said the postman.

'I don't think so, Mr Tranter,' Rose said wryly. She turned to look at Melbury House, at the fallen timbers that were smoking in the dawn. 'We already have enough of that.'

'I'll kill him,' muttered Alex, who was still standing with his arm round Daisy, staring into space. 'I'll finish him. I'll deal with Chloe, too.'

'What did Mr Denham say?' asked Mrs Hobson, peering curiously at Rose.

'Oh, nothing important – he's upset.' Rose put her arm round Alex. 'Come along, my love, there's work to do.' Rose led him away, leaving Daisy standing there alone, still unable to believe the evidence of her eyes.

'It must have been a cigarette,' said Robert, as he and Stephen came out of the cowshed, carrying various trophies like blackened, twisted pieces of metal, and interesting bits of charcoaled wood.

'Yeah, I 'spect you're right,' said Stephen, nodding. 'It was one of Dad's butt ends, I reckon. He chucks them everywhere. Or it was Mr Hobson's stinking pipe.'

'Listen, brats, don't share your thoughts with Dad,' said Daisy, rounding her little brothers up like lambs, then shepherding them towards their parents. 'He won't want to hear them.'

'But why didn't I know?' demanded Ewan, when he eventually found out what had happened, and came running over to see what he could do to help.

'The wind was coming off the sea, blowing the smoke away from Easton Hall.' He found Daisy in the cottage kitchen, still in her pyjamas which were covered in black streaks, unpacking a box of plates. 'There's a hill between us, so you wouldn't have seen the flames.'

'But you could have all been killed.' Ewan shuddered feverishly. 'My God, if you'd been hurt – '

'I wasn't, luckily – nobody was hurt.' But now Daisy's eyes filled up, and soon the tears were coursing down her cheeks. 'Oh, Ewan, it was horrible!' she sobbed. 'The house went up like tinder, and my dad is so upset – '

'Daisy, love, come here.' Ewan pulled her close to him and kissed her on the forehead, tasting smoke and ashes, feeling sick as he imagined what might so easily have happened.

She laid her head upon his shoulder, he wrapped his arms around her and he would have kissed her more, but Rose walked in just then, and she was very cool with him.

'Mr Fraser, is it?' she said, tartly. 'What are you doing here?'

'I came to see if I could help.' He supposed he shouldn't be surprised by Mrs Denham's attitude. 'Does Mr Denham need anyone to help him with the cows?'

'I don't think so,' Rose said crisply. 'They're all traumatised enough already. If Mr Denham needs anybody's help, he has the twins.'

Rose had a posse of village women sorting out the cottage, scrubbing floors, and clucking like so many broody hens. 'Daisy, dear,' she added, 'if you want to be useful, go and sort through the stuff the firemen managed to pull out. It's piled up on tarpaulins in the stable yard. See if you can find us all some clothes.'

'I'll come and help you,' Ewan said.

'Be careful, though, and don't go in the house,' continued Rose, as if he hadn't spoken.

But then she turned to Ewan, grey eyes cold. 'Mr Fraser, I'm sure your mother must be wondering what's become of you. I don't think she'd be pleased to know you're here.'

'My mother wants me to go home to Scotland,' Ewan told Daisy, three days later.

'Well, that was what you wanted, wasn't it?' she asked, as they walked or rather skulked along the shingle beach, close to the overhanging cliffs, unwilling to attract the attention of the twins, of Stokeley, or of anyone from Easton Hall.

'I want to be with you.' Ewan took Daisy's hand. 'I've written to lots of touring companies, I've made a list of theatres in the district, and I'm going to see their managers. I'm sure I'll find a rep to take me.'

71

'You're going to walk into a theatre and say you're going to act?'

'No, I'll be an ASM, paint scenery – do whatever it takes to get me started.' Ewan made her meet his gaze. 'Listen, you don't have to go to school. Your parents need your help. Why don't you – '

'Run away again? My dad would kill me.'

'I was going to say, why don't you join a rep with me? Daisy, I know I'm going to be a star. I'm going to be Hamlet, Romeo, Mark Antony, I'm going to play them all. I want you to come with me. I want you to be my leading lady. I want you to be my Juliet.'

Daisy looked at him and saw he meant it. She felt a great surge of affection, realised that she wanted most of all to be with him.

Although her life was such a mess, although she'd lost her home and almost everything she owned, being with Ewan made her feel alive, made her believe she could do anything – with him, she could be happy.

'I'd love to be your Juliet,' she said. 'I'll talk to Mum and Dad tonight.'

She found her parents sitting in the kitchen of the bailiff's cottage, poring over catalogues of farm machinery. 'So if I leave school, and earn some money, that will help,' she said, looking from her mother to her father, hoping they would see the sense of it.

'What about your General Certificate?' said Rose. 'Darling, you don't need to find a job. We'll get the insurance money soon, then we'll be on our feet again, you'll see.'

'You'll need that money for rebuilding Melbury House.' Daisy looked at Rose, her blue eyes bright. 'Mum, Dad, I don't need to pass exams, not for the kind of work I want to do.'

'What *do* you want to do?' asked Alex, looking up from drawings of trailers, photographs of tractors.

'I was wondering if I could join a rep?'

'You mean you want to be an actress?' Rose's look of horror was almost funny. 'No, I'm sorry, Daisy. That won't do at all.'

'I don't understand.' Daisy frowned at Rose. 'When we were in India, I was always in productions. You encouraged me to sing and dance. You even sent me to have drama lessons with Mrs Abercrombie.'

'Yes, I know, but that was amateur stuff,' said Rose, and looked down at the table. 'You were just performing for our friends. You didn't do it for anyone who had a spare half crown.'

'So if I do it for nothing, it's all right, but if people pay me, it won't do at all? Mum, you're a snob.' Daisy looked at Alex. 'Dad, do you agree with Mum?'

'If you're serious, Daisy, maybe you could go to drama school,' said Alex carefully, but it was obvious he was hedging.

'You don't have any money for drama school!' Daisy glared at him. 'Listen, I want to help! I want to work!'

'You'd meet some very peculiar people in the theatre,' said Rose.

'You mean they would be common.'

'Let's think about it, shall we?' Alex looked at Rose and then at Daisy. 'Your mother's right, you know. You'd meet all kinds of people in the theatre, not all of them agreeable.'

'Talking of agreeable, I'm not very happy about you seeing so much of that Fraser boy,' said Rose.

'I'm going to see a manager in Weymouth,' Ewan told Daisy. 'I wrote to the man who's running the company in rep there for the summer season, and he said he would talk to me.'

'That's wonderful,' said Daisy, and he could see she meant it. 'What did your mother say?'

'She and Chloe and Sir Michael, they got the heavy guns out, didn't they? The Eastons made a speech about ingratitude and about how I had to do my duty. "If you don't go to Oxford, I'll disinherit you," my mother told me, and wept into her wee lace handkerchief. Mum missed her vocation. She should be on the stage herself.'

'But could she do it?'

'No, she isn't versatile enough, she couldn't play anything but weeping widows.'

'I meant could she disinherit you?'

'I suppose she could.' Ewan shrugged, at that moment feeling he didn't particularly care. 'I don't know. I'd have to ask the lawyers. When my father died, he left the whole estate to her, assuming she would pass it on to me. But maybe she could leave it to the local orphanage, if she chose.'

'But Ewan, you love Scotland.'

'Yes, I do,' said Ewan. 'But I want to be an actor far more than I want to be a laird.'

'What happened next?'

'Sir Michael and his ghastly other half stood up for Mum, of course. Lady Easton told me that if I went to see this chap in Weymouth, I would not be welcome at the Hall.'

'What did you say?'

'I told her I had money to pay for digs in Weymouth for a month, and if I didn't get into a rep, I'd find a job. Then Sir Michael said that maybe I was not aware there were about two million unemployed.'

'What will you do now?'

'I'm still going to see this chap on Wednesday, so will you come with me?'

'Yes, of course I will.'

'I want to do the balcony scene for him. So you'll have to be my Juliet.'

'Oh, that's fine,' said Daisy. 'I'll be very happy to feed your lines to you.'

'Thank you, you're an angel.' Ewan hugged her, relieved that Daisy at least was always on his side.

But Daisy found that Ewan didn't want mere feeding.

He wanted passion and commitment, too. He found some copies of the play in the library at Easton Hall and then he set about directing Daisy, making her repeat her lines until she spoke them naturally, breaking her of the histrionics Mrs Abercrombie had fostered in her pupils, and making Daisy feel she *was* Juliet.

They spent the rest of the week on a deserted beach holidaymakers never used because it was miles from any road, and totally submerged by the high tide. An overhanging rock made a balcony for Juliet. They played to an audience of seals and gulls.

Ewan was finally satisfied with Daisy and, as she watched Ewan, she could see he was born to be an actor. When he spoke Romeo's lines, he wasn't Ewan any more. He was Romeo.

'*At what o'clock tomorrow shall I send to thee?*' asked Daisy, as they reached the stile where they parted every evening.

'*At the hour of nine,*' said Ewan, kissing her goodnight.

'*I will not fail,*' said Daisy.

'See?' said Ewan. 'You can do it now. You speak the verse as naturally as breathing. But maybe we'd better make it eight o'clock, at Charton station. I don't want to keep this fellow waiting.'

Wednesday dawned cold and dull, with a sea mist hanging over everything. After a lovely summer, autumn was on its way.

'You're up bright and early. Where are you going?' asked Rose.

'To Weymouth,' Daisy said. 'I need to buy some things for school. A new geometry set, some pencils, stuff like that.'

'You could get those in Dorchester,' said Rose. 'Your father's going there this morning, he needs to see the bank. He'll give you a lift.'

'I know, Mum, but I fancy going to Weymouth. I've saved my pocket money, so I've got the fare.' Daisy put on her jacket. 'I should be back by lunch time.'

'I'll need you to help me with the ironing, don't forget!' called Rose, as Daisy left the house.

She and Ewan caught the train to Weymouth. 'My mother isn't speaking to me now,' said Ewan, as they settled down in a third class compartment. 'She's been having breakfast in her room for the past week. She has the vapours every evening. She told Lady Easton she can't believe how I've turned out, and that my father must be spinning in his grave.'

'Mine knows I'm up to something,' Daisy said.

The theatre was in a side street near the sea front. It was a tiny little playhouse whose faded plush, unpolished brass and threadbare, dirty carpets had all seen better days.

It had an end-of-season, tawdry air. Its posters were all

faded, and its piles of programmes sat yellowing and curling in the dusty foyer.

Ewan walked in confidently. Daisy was close behind him, breathing in the familiar scents of dust and sweat and greasepaint she remembered from the garrison theatres in India, where she had played fairies, elves and maidens. 'Ewan, are you nervous?' she whispered.

'Terrified,' he replied, but she could see his eyes were bright.

'You must be Mr Fraser?' A middle-aged man with mutton-chop whiskers, a huge belly and tiny feet in spats suddenly materialised out of nowhere, like the ghost in Hamlet. 'I'm Alfred Curtis, pleased to meet you. Your letter was most timely. One of my juveniles has just walked out on me. His understudy broke his arm last week, so we've been doubling up the parts. But that's not very satisfactory, as you will understand.'

He hadn't seemed to notice Daisy, but as he led Ewan into the dark and silent theatre, she tiptoed after them.

'Let's get some lights on. Tom!' the manager shouted, to some invisible being. 'May we have a spot or two down here? Thank you, that's much better. Now, Mr Fraser, what have you prepared?'

'A scene from *Romeo and Juliet*.' Ewan turned to Daisy. 'This is Miss Denham, she'll be Juliet.'

'We could have got a lady from the company to be your Juliet,' said Mr Curtis, plumping himself down like a cigar-scented, hound's-tooth-suited walrus in the front row of the stalls. 'But since your friend is here – oh, very well, then. Off you go.'

Daisy's first few lines came creaking out, and sounded false and artificial. But Ewan spoke so naturally, so earnestly, that soon she started to relax, and speak only to him.

She forgot about fat Mr Curtis, forgot she was in a musty English theatre on a damp September morning, balanced on some rickety wooden steps which had to be her balcony. Instead, she was in Verona, on a warm, velvet night, and she'd just fallen desperately in love ...

'Mr Curtis?' Ewan snapped out of being Romeo, and walked downstage.

'Yes, Mr Fraser, that was very good.' Mr Curtis grinned. 'I have a bit of trouble seeing Romeo as a Scot, but – yes, you're hired, my boy.'

He rubbed his several chins and looked at Ewan sideways, as if measuring him. 'Actually, we won't be doing Shakespeare,' he continued. 'The bard is wasted on the Midlands and the North of England, which is where we'll be this winter.'

'Oh,' said Ewan, frowning. 'But – '

'But you'll be fine for general modern drama. You've got that look about you. All the lady patrons will fall in love with you. Do you have a suit of evening dress, some casual flannels, cricket whites, a Fair Isle pullover?'

'Yes, I can find them,' Ewan told him, wondering where the hell he'd look. He'd outgrown his cricket whites, and although he was a Scot he'd never owned a Fair Isle pullover.

'You'll need to supply your make-up too, of course. You must work on your accents.' Mr Curtis grinned again. 'On the English stage, you see, you need to sound as if you come from Surrey, not from Aberdeen.'

'I can do English accents,' Ewan said, and rattled off some lines from one of Noël Coward's plays. 'Mr Curtis – er – what would you pay me?'

'Three pounds ten a week until next March, and then we'll see.' The manager glanced at Daisy. 'What about your lady friend? Where is she working now?'

'I'm not working,' Daisy told him. 'I still go to school.'

'Two pounds a week?' suggested Mr Curtis, doing his measuring-up look once again.

'Doing what?' asked Daisy.

'Mostly walking on. Maids and cooks and nurses or whatever, but a bit of understudying, too.'

'I'm not sure if my mother – '

'Mrs Curtis chaperones the ladies, so you can tell your mother she doesn't need to worry about you getting into trouble. All our digs are proper boarding houses, they only take theatricals. I'm happy to meet your mother, if you wish.'

Ewan took Daisy's hand and squeezed it, pleading with her, willing her to hear him.

'Thank you, Mr Curtis.' Daisy met the manager's gaze. 'I accept your offer.'

Daisy walked into the bailiff's cottage feeling very nervous – far more nervous than when she'd been on stage, which in a curious way had felt like home.

'You can't,' said Rose, at once. 'You're far too young.'

'Rose, let's talk about it,' Alex said. 'You know you weren't much older when you went to nurse in France.'

'There's no comparison,' snapped Rose. 'You may recall that it was wartime. I was needed.'

'Where are these people based?' asked Alex.

'They travel round the country. They've been in Weymouth for the summer, but this winter they'll be in the Midlands and the North of England.'

'Birmingham, Wolverhampton, Manchester – dirty,

dangerous places,' said Rose shuddering. 'Alex, listen to me – in case you have forgotten, this girl's not yet sixteen.'

'I will be soon,' said Daisy. 'Dad?'

'Maybe we should go and meet these people?' Alex looked enquiringly at Rose.

'Mum, I'll be with lots of other people,' continued Daisy. 'Mr Curtis says he'd like to meet you. He can tell you what goes on. You can meet Mrs Curtis, too. Listen, Mum,' said Daisy, desperately, 'it's what I really want to do.'

'This is all ridiculous,' said Rose. 'You're still a child. You need to go to school. I'm going to bed.'

Daisy met Ewan on the shingle beach the following day. 'What did your parents say?' he asked.

'My mother's definitely against it. She's being absolutely horrible. She doesn't want me to have any fun. She thinks I should do my General Certificate, then be a clerk, or something. But Dad might be persuaded.'

'Shall I have a word with him?'

'Yes, if you want him to put his foot down, and forbid it after all. You might not have noticed, but you're not very popular with Dad. What about your mother, what did she have to say?'

'Oh, nothing much, but she'd be spitting pins and throwing carving knives if she had any handy.' Ewan grinned. 'I'm leaving Easton Hall tomorrow morning.'

'Where will you go – to Weymouth?'

'Yes, I'll find some digs.'

'Ewan, will you do something for me?' Daisy looked at him, into his eyes. 'I'm not sure if I should ask you this – '

'What do you mean? Daisy, I'll do anything for you.'

'You'll help me find my real mother?'

Chapter Seven

'The next thing we know, she'll say she's going to America, to find her real mother,' Rose told Alex, as she crashed and banged around the kitchen.

'I think that's very likely.' Alex was sitting at the kitchen table reading *Farmer's Weekly*, and now he calmly lit a cigarette. 'She's always been adventurous. I remember when we were in Simla that first summer – '

'What's wrong with you?' Rose slammed a saucepan down on to the table. 'Alex, she's a child! She knows nothing of the world. What if she meets lots of awful people?'

'Rose, the world is full of awful people.' Alex stood up. 'She'll have to meet them some day.'

'What do you mean by that?'

'What I just said.' Alex sighed. 'We can't protect our children from everything for ever – can we, Rose?'

'What do you mean?' asked Ewan.

'It's obvious, isn't it?' Daisy looked down at her hands and wished she didn't bite her finger nails. It didn't look very grown up, and she must stop.

'Well, it's not obvious to me.'

'I was adopted when I was a baby. My mother came from the East End of London. She wasn't married. They only told me a few weeks ago.'

'After the fire, you mean?'

'No, just before we went to Scotland.'

'Oh, I see – that's why you were so keen to get away.'

'Do you blame me? Ewan, everyone in Charton knew, but

Mum kept it from me.' Daisy looked up at Ewan, challenging him. 'Go on, say you're disgusted.'

'Of course I'm not disgusted.' Ewan put his arm round Daisy's shoulders and pulled her close to him. 'Your mother had a love affair in wartime. I think that's very romantic. I'll help you find your mother, of course I will.'

'I don't have much to go on.' Daisy cosied up against the Harris tweed of Ewan's jacket, inhaling the delicious smell of him, of shaving soap and boy. 'All I know is that her name was Phoebe Gower, and now she might be Mrs Rosenheim. She could still be in England, or she might be in the USA.'

'Well, that's just two countries out of dozens, and she's not called Anne Smith or Mary Brown. So don't worry, we'll soon find your mother.' Ewan kissed Daisy's nose. 'Now, what about the other matter? Do you think your parents are going to be persuaded? Or shall you have to run away again?'

'I can usually get my way with Dad. It sometimes takes a while, but if I keep on at him, he generally gives in. But Mum's determined to spoil everything.'

'Let me come and talk to her, perhaps?'

'No, don't you dare! She'd throw you out, and then she'd lock me up for ever.'

Daisy realised her best bet was Alex.

While he was always strict with the two boys, he was lenience itself with Daisy. Or he had been up to the time he'd yelled at her and ordered her to come back home to Dorset.

In India, she and Celia Norton had enjoyed a degree of freedom girls who lived in England could only dream about. She knew this freedom had a lot to do with being the daughters of British army officers. In colonial India, if anybody hurt, attacked, molested or annoyed the daughter of a *burra sahib*, the repercussions would be dire. But, having tasted freedom, it was very hard to accept she might not always have it ...

Alex became her project. While Rose was still adamant the whole scheme was ridiculous, and wouldn't talk about it, Alex was persuaded to go with Daisy into Weymouth to meet the manager and his wife.

Daisy now imagined what her father must be seeing – a pair of oddly-dressed, Micawberish small-time actors. Mr Curtis's white spats were silly, his loud check suit was grubby, and he had a pointless little monocle round his neck.

Mrs Curtis wore a calf-length dress of faded purple velvet, with some oddly puckered-looking segments in the skirt, making Daisy wonder if it had been a curtain. She also wore a horrid orange wig, a huge amount of rouge, and lots of rings with diamonds which were obviously fakes. She had the stubble of a grey moustache.

They were both well into middle age. Their dreams of thespian glory must have faded long ago. Nowadays, they eked out an existence in the sticks, putting on shows for easy-to-please provincials, and hoping to save enough for their retirement.

She shook her head, and looked at them again. Now she saw two people who could help her realise a dream. Or Ewan's dream, at least, and Daisy knew how much it meant to him.

Yes, said Mrs Curtis, she would see Miss Denham wrote home once a week, at least. She would make sure Miss Denham had good lodgings – ladies only, definitely. She and Mr Curtis had a daughter of their own. Mr and Mrs Denham needn't worry about a thing.

Please, Dad, don't say anything, thought Daisy, as Mrs Curtis gushed on like a geyser, now and then reaching out to pat his hand, which made him flinch.

'Thank you, Mrs Curtis,' Alex said politely, as she finished her monologue and stuck a hairpin back into her wig.

'So we'll look forward to Miss Denham joining us,' said Mr Curtis, baring yellow dentures that would have looked more natural inside a tiger's mouth.

'Well, Dad?' said Daisy, as they walked along the street towards the railway station.

'Well, Daisy – is it what you really want?'

'I'd like to try it, Dad.'

'If it doesn't work out, if you get stuck, if you're in any kind of trouble, you tell me straight away.' Alex stopped walking, looked at Daisy, took her by the shoulders and made her meet his gaze. 'I'll come and fetch you. Whatever you've done, wherever you are, it makes no difference, I'll be there.'

'I know you will.'

'I'm getting a telephone put in the cottage. The men are coming to do the wires next week. So promise me you'll phone, and you may go.'

'I promise, Dad,' said Daisy.

'I didn't know Mum knew words like that,' hissed Robert.

The twins and Daisy were sitting on the staircase while their parents argued in the kitchen. 'Daisy,' whispered Stephen, 'she sounds really angry. Do you think Dad will be all right?'

'Of course he'll be all right.' Daisy scowled at him. 'Shut up, I want to listen to what they're saying.'

'Look out, here they come!'

The three of them ducked back as Alex walked out of the kitchen and left the house, slamming the door behind him.

'What are you children doing there?' Rose had followed Alex, and now she glared upstairs, hands on her hips, dark hair a wild halo, grey eyes flashing fire. 'I dare say you were listening?'

'You were shouting at Dad so loud we couldn't help but hear,' retorted Daisy. 'Mum, I know it wasn't like this in your day. I know girls stayed at home and did embroidery, then married the first man who came along and had a dozen babies.'

'Don't you dare talk to me like that,' snapped Rose. 'You're still a child, you know!'

'You can't afford to keep me. Since we came back from India, we've been paupers. We're camping in a hut, Mum. We never have new clothes. We live on turnips. So let me help, why don't you?'

'I can't think what's come over you,' said Rose. 'You used to be so sweet. You were a charming little girl.'

'Maybe I've grown up. Mum, I need to start to live my life, do what I want, and you need to accept it.'

'I've spoiled you, haven't I? I've let you have too much of your own way, and this is the result. You've turned into a selfish, rude, ungovernable young woman. I've nothing more to say to you.'

Rose stalked into the kitchen, and started banging pots around as if she meant to break them into tiny little pieces.

Robert and Stephen glanced at one another, melted into the shadows and went to bed.

'So may I go, or not?' Daisy asked Rose, at breakfast the next morning.

'If I say no, you'll only run away again, or do something else absurd.' Rose wouldn't look at Daisy. 'Apparently, your father says you may. So I've been overruled in any case.'

'I'm not a baby, Mum.' Daisy wanted desperately to make her mother smile and say that everything would be all right. 'Most girls in England start going out to work when they're fourteen. I know that actors are often out of work, but so are lots of other people these days. Mum, I need a job. You know I love to act, and now I'm grown up I want to make a career on the stage.'

Rose didn't comment, so Daisy looked at Alex. 'Dad, say something, please!'

'You'd better go and pack your things,' said Alex. 'I'll run you into Weymouth. Does that Fraser fellow want a lift?'

'No, he's already there, he's living in a boarding house,' said Daisy. 'Lady Easton made him leave the Hall.'

'Ladies and gentlemen, may I present Miss Denham and Mr Fraser?'

Alfred Curtis had summoned the whole company to meet the new arrivals. 'Mr Fraser's kindly taken over Mr Atterbury's roles, and he'll be understudying Mr Morgan, Mr Reed and Mr Kenton,' the manager continued, gazing round portentously. 'Miss Denham's going to take some smaller parts and female walk-ons. She'll also understudy Miss Hart and Mrs Nightingale.'

Mr Curtis pointed to a pile of scripts lying on the piano in the wings. 'The new stuff came this morning, so we'll have a read through in ten minutes.'

Daisy looked nervously at Miss Hart and Mrs Nightingale, who were lounging against some flats and eyeing Ewan Fraser. They were clearly pleased with what they saw.

Two divinely dressed and made-up creatures in their twenties, their scarlet lips curved into smiles when Ewan glanced their way. One of the actors was grinning at him matily, while another offered him a light.

Daisy felt a pang of loneliness. She wished she was in the kitchen of the bailiff's cottage, shoving books into her satchel, ready to go to school.

In spite of what Mrs Curtis had told Alex, her digs in Weymouth weren't exactly homely. The whole house smelled of mice and onions. The mattress on her bed was stuffed with straw. Last night it had been freezing in her attic, and she hadn't slept a wink, but a tiny attic was all she could afford.

'Miss Denham?' Alfred Curtis tossed a script her way. 'Do wake up, my darling. You're the office girl, and later you'll be the woman at the bus stop. My loves – Act 1, Scene 1!'

'Miss Denham?' said Miss Hart, catching Daisy as she left the stage. 'You're the girl who's got the attic room in Westbury Drive, and didn't come down to breakfast. But you don't need to be afraid of us.'

'I'm not afraid,' lied Daisy, who couldn't have eaten anything that morning, even to save her life.

'You're terrified. But you don't need to worry, we won't bite.' Miss Hart lit up a Craven A, then offered the pack of cigarettes to Daisy, who quickly shook her head. She had never smoked a cigarette. She would ask Ewan for one of his, she thought, and practise it in private before risking a coughing fit in public.

'I'm Julia,' said Miss Hart, 'and Lady Muck is Amy Nightingale. She has the room right under yours, so don't go thinking it's me who snores all night. We're going to the pub. Do you want to come?'

'I can't, I'm under age.' Rose was right, thought Daisy. She was still a child. She ought to be at school.

'We'll sneak you in,' said Julia, grinning. 'Stand tall, stick your chest out, put on a bit of lipstick, and you'll pass.'

'I left my make-up at my digs,' said Daisy. 'I didn't think I'd need it in the daytime.'

'Jesus and Mary, child – never go anywhere without your war paint, didn't your mother ever tell you that? Here, borrow mine.' She handed Daisy a pretty little compact and a lipstick. 'Come along, my love. We're wasting drinking time.'

The men were nice, thought Daisy.

George Reed and Francis Kenton were middle-aged, immaculately dressed in well cut barathea suits, silk shirts and multi-coloured ties. They were inclined to treat her like a child, but not in a condescending, patronising way.

'If you want advice or need a little private coaching, you pop along and see your Uncle George,' said Mr Reed.

'Or your Uncle Frank,' said Mr Kenton. 'We'll soon sort you out. Do you like liquorice allsorts?' he added, offering her one.

Mr Morgan was a little younger, much flashier in looks and manner, and Daisy wouldn't have trusted him with sixpence. But with his thin moustache, his snap-brim trilbies and his two-tone shoes, he was a somewhat comically obvious seducer, an end-of-the-pier romancer. The kind of man who'd always be a joke, thought Daisy, and nothing like her handsome Ewan.

Julia Hart was usually friendly, but she often drank too much, and then she could be waspish. Amy Nightingale was rather frosty, curling her lip disdainfully when Daisy fluffed her lines, and making loud remarks about certain people who should be in kindergarten, not on the stage.

'She's jealous,' whispered Julia. 'She's always wanted to be a natural blonde. She spends a fortune on peroxide. She likes your gorgeous boyfriend, and she thinks you want her roles. She's getting on a bit, and wishes she was young again.'

'I wish I was older.' Daisy looked at Amy wistfully, wishing she could afford to buy silk stockings, lovely velvet hats and jackets trimmed with astrakhan.

'You mustn't wish your life away,' said Julia. 'I couldn't wait to be grown up, and now I wish I was sixteen again.'

Julia told Daisy she'd been born in Manchester. She was the eldest in a family of nineteen. 'I never had a mother,' she added, sadly. 'Well, I did, but she was always pregnant, and she never had any time for me. I hate the sight of babies. I don't want any of my own.'

So Daisy didn't say that at the moment one of her favourite fantasies was of being married to Ewan, and of having half a dozen pretty children – blonde-haired girls, of course, and copper-headed, handsome boys like him.

She wrote to Rose and Alex to tell them she was well and happy, that everyone in the company was lovely, and she was having fun. She added that she hoped they'd come and see her in a show before the company left Weymouth.

Rose didn't come, but Alex came and brought the brats, and to Daisy's huge relief the twins were well-behaved, and didn't make any remarks about the smallness of her roles.

'Mum said to give you all her love,' said Robert, reddening as he always did when he was telling lies.

'Send us some postcards, Daze?' said Stephen. 'We're

collecting picture postcards of the British Isles. It's our form's project for the term.'

'I'll send you lots,' said Daisy.

'Look after yourself,' said Alex, kissing her on the cheek, and making her want to go back home, to tell Rose she was sorry, and she'd made a big mistake.

'I'll look after Daisy, Mr Denham.' Ewan came up and put his arm round Daisy. She saw Alex wince, but he seemed to hear her silent pleading, and was polite to Ewan, shook his hand and wished him well.

The following day, the company packed up, got out, and caught the train to Walsall.

'You'll be playing the daughter of the vicar in the new three-acter,' Julia told Daisy, lighting up although it was no smoking. She told the others this compartment was girls only, and made the middle-aged couple who were already sitting in it glare. 'I heard old Alfred telling Mrs C last night.'

'But don't go getting a swollen head,' said Amy Nightingale, who'd set out all the equipment for a manicure, and now began to file her long, sharp nails.

'It's really stuffy in here,' she added. 'There's a bit of a pong as well, like last night's fish and chips or unwashed socks. I wonder if we should have a window open?'

The couple got up and left.

'Good riddance to them,' said Julia, putting her feet up on the seat. Opening her case, she took out several paper bags. 'Daisy, have a cheese and pickle sandwich, then tell me all your secrets. Where did you find your lovely boyfriend?'

'He was on holiday in Dorset.' Daisy blushed. 'I met him walking home from school one day.'

'He's quite delicious, isn't he?' Amy Nightingale began

to paint her nails with scarlet varnish. 'I've always had a weakness for dashing, handsome Scotsmen with red hair and emerald eyes.'

'Leave him alone, you harridan,' said Julia, and then she turned to Daisy. 'Angel, don't look so worried. I mean, a painted-up old tart like Amy here, against a fresh-faced little beauty – she wouldn't stand a chance.'

'I don't know about that,' purred Amy, smirking. 'In my experience, most young men are more than happy to respond to smarter, older women who have seen a bit of life.'

Daisy looked at Amy, whose immaculately made-up face was striking if not beautiful, and she felt a tremor of unease.

She didn't think Ewan would go after other women. But she hadn't thought about what might happen if other women went after him.

Ewan thought he was in paradise.

He was doing what he'd always wanted and, even if he wouldn't be playing Romeo for Mr and Mrs Curtis, he was sure one day his chance would come. He'd made some wonderful new friends, and – best of all – he was almost permanently in the company of the girl he loved.

Whenever they arrived in a new place, he and Daisy got the gazetteer from the public reference library and looked up all the Gowers and Rosenheims.

They checked electoral registers, and even knocked on doors, alarming several Gowers and Rosenheims, who were usually very nice about it, but who couldn't help.

They never found a Phoebe Gower or Phoebe Rosenheim. 'She might be in America,' said Daisy, at the end of yet another fruitless afternoon, when everybody else was at the talkies, and they'd been annoying or perplexing various strangers.

'We'll be going there one day.'

'We'll never find her in America.'

'We might, you never know.' These days, Ewan was confident he could do anything. 'Look on the bright side, eh? We're doing well, we're getting good reviews. So things are going our way.'

'Nathan, I don't think it's goin' to happen.'

Phoebe was sitting at the breakfast table in the newly-fitted-out apartment in the Lower East Side, drinking coffee and smoking Lucky Strikes. 'I'm bein' punished for givin' Daisy up. I reckon God don't want me to 'ave more children.'

'My dear, it's nothing to do with God.'

'Well, it ain't nothin' to do with me. I told you I went to see doc, and all he said was keep on tryin'.'

'So that's what we'll do.' Nathan took Phoebe's hand, and smiled his usual reassuring smile. 'Phoebe, you're still young. There's plenty of time to have another child. Do you remember Sarah Goldman, Harry's wife? She was nearly forty when she had her twins.'

'I won't see thirty-five again.' Phoebe sighed. 'I know you're trying to cheer me up, but time is runnin' out.'

'We won't give up just yet.'

'I'd better go to work.' Phoebe stood up and smoothed her smart, black dress over her hips. 'We're gettin' a delivery of ostrich feathers this morning, an' I want to check they haven't sent me rubbish like they did the last time.'

'Your shop is doing very well,' said Nathan. 'The country might be in a state of chaos, but it seems people still need hats. I was looking at your books last night. You're going to make a handsome profit this year.'

'That's something, I suppose,' said Phoebe, shrugging. 'If I'm not goin' to be a mother, I need something else to do.'

'Phoebe, listen to me a moment.' Nathan pulled her down on to his lap. 'I'm not saying I don't want children. Of course I do, it would be wonderful. But if it never happens, we mustn't let it blight our lives.'

'You're far too good for me, you know that?' Phoebe kissed his cheek and forced a smile. 'I tell you what we'll do. We'll give it another couple of months, all right?'

'All right, but then?'

'If nothin' happens, I'm goin' back to England. I'm goin' to find my daughter.'

'Do you want me to come with you?'

'No, I know you 'ate the place, an' I can't say I blame you. England ain't done much for you, or me. But I gotta go.' Phoebe looked anxiously at Nathan. 'I promise I'll come back. So don't you go divorcin' me?'

'I won't divorce you,' Nathan promised. 'You're my life.'

Daisy had just come in. Ewan had walked her home as usual, told her she'd been excellent this evening, and that she'd made him proud. They'd spent a pleasant hour saying goodnight.

So she was tired but happy.

Julia and Amy looked anything but happy. They hadn't had a curtain call, and none of their regular gentlemen who followed the company from town to town had sent them flowers or chocolates tonight. They were busy grumbling, drinking gin and getting maudlin.

'So when I got divorced, my parents said they didn't want to know me any more. It was just as well I could my earn my living on the stage,' Amy Nightingale was saying, in a cut-glass accent which Daisy thought was probably authentic, even though Amy used a range of other accents too, and might decide to be a Scouser in the morning.

'Daisy, you wouldn't know it, but our Amy used to be a swell,' said Julia, pouring out another glass of gin. 'She was married to an honourable.'

'Who had a string of mistresses, so I had an affair, but he found out.'

'So it was the divorce court for old Amy, who ended up with nothing. She'd be beggin' in the streets if Alfred Curtis hadn't come along.'

'The woman always loses everything.' Amy stared into her empty glass. 'You watch young Fraser, Daisy May.'

'Yeah, don't you get too serious with Ewan.'

'We've met his kind before.'

'Good-looking boys, they're always trouble.'

They were wrong, thought Daisy. Someone as sweet as Ewan couldn't be trouble if he tried. But she didn't argue. She just said goodnight and went to bed.

Amy and Julia started to reorganise her wardrobe. They lent her clothes which Ewan often said he didn't like because they made her look too old.

'He means you'll start attracting other men,' said Julia, as she buttoned Daisy into a very flattering black jacket with a smart fur collar that set off her blonde hair.

'You ought to get a permanent wave, you know,' continued Amy. 'It would make you look grown up. You need to get your ears pierced, too. We'll do it with a needle and a cork. Then you can wear my rhinestone earrings. This old chain you always wear – it's very plain, you know. I think you need a bit of sparkle.'

Daisy heard Rose's voice inside her head saying rhinestone earrings would look vulgar, permanent waves were common, and using corks and needles would lead to septicaemia ...

'No matinee today,' said Ewan, as he and Daisy shrugged into their coats after a morning read-through in the back room of a pub in Scarborough. 'What would you like to do?'

'She can't do anything with you, she's under age – and anyway, she's going to the talkies,' Julia told him, smirking. 'So you run along, and go and play with the other boys.'

'Did you hear Alfred telling Mr Morgan that Daisy will be playing his girlfriend in the new three-acter?' Amy purred, grinning like a cat and running her scarlet nails down Ewan's chest.

'So Daisy will be kissing him,' said Julia.

'On the mouth,' said Amy.

'I won't mean it, Ewan,' said Daisy hurriedly.

'I know you won't,' said Ewan, who wasn't bothered about Bryn Morgan. 'Anyway, ladies,' he continued, 'I have news for you. Mr Morgan's leaving us. He's going to do some concert parties, and he's got a season in Torquay.'

'How do you know?' Julia demanded.

'More to the point, why didn't we?' Amy scowled and narrowed her mascaraed eyes suspiciously.

'Bryn told George this morning. George told Frank and me. Bryn will be telling Mr and Mrs Curtis later on today. George says they'll have fits.'

'He's right, they will,' said Amy.

'Daisy, shall you and I go for a walk along the prom?' suggested Ewan

'Yes, that would be lovely.' She tucked her arm through his and smiled at him.

'You told me you wanted see a talkie, Daisy May,' said Julia, frowning.

'I've changed my mind. I can see a talkie any time.'

'Come on, darling.' Amy took Julia by the arm, her crimson nails like spots of blood on Julia's pale sleeve. 'Let these babies go and have their walkies. You and me, we'll find some grown-up fun.'

'What a pair of harpies.' Ewan watched Amy and Julia saunter off, arm in arm and sniggering. 'I can't stand spiteful women.'

'They're all right,' said Daisy. 'They're very kind to me. They just like making mischief. Actually, Amy's got her eye on you.'

'God, you must be joking!' Ewan was horrified.

'No I'm not, she thinks you're very handsome, and she's always pointing out most men like older women.'

'She's wrong,' said Ewan, firmly. 'The woman should be younger than the man. Daisy, do you find other men attractive?'

'No.' Daisy put one arm round Ewan's waist and pushed her hand into his trouser pocket. 'I don't want anyone but you.'

'I was thinking, Daisy – if I'm lucky, I might get Bryn Morgan's roles. It might be me who's kissing you on stage.'

'Let's get some practice, then.'

'Have you written to your mother lately?' Daisy asked him half an hour later, as they strolled along the promenade.

'Yes, I wrote last week. I got a postcard in reply. So she must be speaking to me again.'

'Where is she, still in Dorset?'

'No, she's gone back to Scotland. Daisy, do you think Mrs Denham has forgiven you?'

'I don't know. But I hope she has, I hope she's not still cross or worrying. I write home often. I send them cuttings, programmes, handbills, postcards for the twins. I tell them where I'm going, what I'm doing. I remind them you're looking after me.'

'Then she shouldn't be worrying at all.'

Chapter Eight

Daisy had noticed Julia wasn't well, but Amy told her not to worry. Julia was a moody cow who had her ups and downs, and she'd snap out of it.

But there were downs and there was hitting rock bottom, Daisy thought, and since they'd left Scarborough Julia had been missing cues, getting on stage with seconds to spare or even seconds late, and making Alfred Curtis tear his hair out or what remained of it. She was drinking gin from thermos flasks and smoking like a pot bank.

Then, one Sunday morning, Daisy caught her coming out of the bathroom at their digs, as green as Banquo's ghost, and carrying a mysterious parcel wrapped in pages from the *Daily Sketch*.

'Goodness, what's the matter?' she demanded. 'Julia, you look awful! Why don't you go back to bed? I'll make you some toast.'

'I couldn't eat any toast, and for God's sake keep your blooming voice down, Fairy Fay. I don't want that hideous old bag who owns the place up here.'

Julia glanced over the banisters to see if anybody was lurking in the hall. 'Do you know if she's gone to church, or to her coven, with the other witches?'

'She had her prayer book, so she must have gone to morning service. She won't be back for ages. Julia, do you need – '

'I need a fag,' said Julia. She thrust the parcel into Daisy's hands. 'Do me a little favour, love? Go and shove that in the dustbin, eh? Make sure you push it right down to the bottom, so the cat can't get it.'

'Yes, of course, but what – '

'You know that chap I picked up in the pub in Wolverhampton, a couple of months ago? The one with the cheeky grin and Oxford bags and Brylcreemed hair?' Julia scrabbled in the pocket of her dressing gown, found her cigarettes and lit one, drawing greedily. 'Well, the bugger got me up the duff.'

She tottered back into her bedroom and sank down on her bed. 'But now I've dealt with it, so everything is tickety-boo again. Be a little angel and don't say anything to Lady Muck, or any of the others? I don't think I could stand a flipping chorus of I-told-you-so.'

'I won't say anything.' Daisy could almost feel the parcel writhing in her hands. Although she knew she must be just imagining movement, it was certainly still warm.

She shuddered as she realised she could have been a parcel, if her natural mother hadn't been too – what, too ignorant, too religious? She hurried off down the stairs and did what Julia had asked, still shuddering. She slammed the lid back on the bin.

'What's up with Fanny Anne this morning?' When Daisy went back into the house, she found Amy at the breakfast table, smoking and eating kippers and feeding titbits to the cat.

'She – she's not feeling well. She's going to stay in bed this morning.'

'I saw you sneaking something to the bin. She wants to watch it. She takes too many chances, does our Fanny Anne. If I've told her once, I've told her half a million times. She needs to make the blighters use a thing. But her religion says you can't, or something daft like that.'

Amy leaned back and blew a perfect smoke ring. 'You want to watch it too, young Daisy May. I've seen the way your Ewan looks at you, his eyes undressing you, tongue hanging out. He'd have you in the pudding club as quick as winking. Then, of course, he would blame you.'

Amy watched as Daisy put the kettle on. 'I'll have another cup,' she said, 'and if you're going back upstairs, make sure that trollop hasn't left the evidence in the bathroom.'

'Evidence?' said Daisy.

'Yeah, like knitting needles, messy towels. We don't want the landlady to find them, the old bag would throw us out, and anyway I want to have a bath.'

Bryn Morgan's concert party offer was too good to refuse. He needed to leave the company even earlier than expected, making Alfred Curtis curse and say he'd never again employ a Welshman. There'd be penalty clauses in all contracts from now on.

'Alfred's been on the telephone all week,' said Amy, as the ladies got made up and ready for a matinee in Stoke. 'He can't find anyone at all, so Mrs C was telling me. Of course, there are the usual drunks and layabouts, people with one leg or half a brain that no one wants to work with any more. But everyone who's any good appears to have a job.'

'I reckon he's going to have to promote your boyfriend,' Julia told Daisy. 'So you two will be kissing in the spotlight after all. Alfred's got someone coming along tomorrow,' she added, as she lit a cigarette. 'I heard him telling Mrs C – name's Jessie something.'

'Why do we need another girl?' Amy rolled on her stockings. 'What's the old devil up to now?'

'Maybe he's bought a play with a few decent roles for

women?' Julia slicked on lipstick. 'It would make a pleasant change.'

'It would make for more rehearsals, too. Daisy, love,' said Amy, 'lend me your number 5, and pay attention when I'm on this afternoon. I've got a bit of a sore throat, so I might be indisposed this evening, and you'll have to go on as Sarah Drew.'

Daisy was working hard at understudying, and at being a useful member of the company.

That evening, she was very tired after two performances in which she'd played a dozen little parts in a half-empty theatre, something which always left the cast low and dispirited.

'Nobody's got any money in the Potteries, they're all on the dole,' said Julia, creaming off her eye paint. 'I dunno why Alfred took these lousy bookings, anyway.'

'The premises are cheap,' said Amy, scowling round the dressing room in which the paint was flaking and which smelled of ancient sweat and tomcats. 'Come on, girls, let's go and have a drink or several, try to drown our sorrows.'

'See what we can find,' said Julia, winking.

'All right, miss holy innocent, don't look at us like that,' said Amy, catching Daisy's eye. 'We can't keep ourselves in gin and knickers on what that skinflint pays us, and a girl needs company now and then, in any case.'

'That bloke who kept me in drink and fags last night, he was a proper gentleman,' added Julia, smugly. 'A travelling salesman, so he said, and it might be true, he had a case of samples.'

'I bet he's married, though,' said Amy. 'He had that look about him. You can always tell.'

'Married, single – as long as he's a man, he'll do for me,' said Julia, smirking. 'If he's in the saloon bar of the Lamb and Flag tonight, I'm getting off with him. He should be worth a few more gin and tonics, and something else as well. But if he turns out to be a very naughty boy, I could always threaten to tell his wife.'

'I think I'll go home,' said Daisy, yawning. 'I need to write to Mum and Dad before I go to bed.'

'Oh, don't be such a little goody two shoes.' Julia had at last re-done her make-up, and now she checked her lipstick one last time. 'Come and have a gin with us. It's time you learned to drink.'

Daisy had a dandelion and burdock, which tasted very unpleasant and medicinal, then told Amy she was going home.

Amy wouldn't be going back just yet. Julia was wrapped around her salesman, and Ewan was rather obviously reluctant to tear himself away from beer and darts. But he said Daisy couldn't go home alone.

'I'll be all right,' she said. 'I'll get the bus, there's one in fifteen minutes from the station.'

'I promised Mr Denham I'd look after you.' Ewan told the others he'd be back, and they waved him and Daisy off with several crude remarks.

They caught the bus back to the boarding house where Daisy meant to make herself some cocoa, eat whatever sandwiches the landlady had left for them, then have an earlyish night.

'What's the matter, Daisy?' Ewan asked, as they walked down the road towards the ladies' lodging house.

'Nothing, I'm just tired,' said Daisy. 'Thank you for coming home with me. What will you do now?'

'I was beating George at darts, so maybe I'll go back to the pub.'

'All right,' said Daisy. 'Ewan, have you heard any more about who might be playing Mr Morgan's roles?'

'I hope it will be me. I don't think I could stand to watch if Frank or George kissed you.'

'They're both to old to play Jack Grove.' Daisy stood up on tiptoe and kissed Ewan. 'So it's almost certain to be you.'

'Let's hope you're right,' said Ewan, as he gave her one last hug. 'Sleep tight, and dream of me.'

Daisy put her key in the lock, opened the door and walked into a scene.

'I don't care what the manager told you, I'm not going anywhere else this evening,' said the owner of a broad, strong back and head of coal-black hair. 'We'll sort it out tomorrow morning. I'm sleeping on the sofa in your sitting room tonight.'

'This house is ladies only,' said the landlady. 'I never have any men.'

'My dear Mrs Fisher, whatever do you think I'm going to do?' the person with the coal-black hair demanded, in a low and drawling voice that sent delicious shivers down Daisy's spine. 'Fry your canary, rape your parlour maid?'

'I'd be very grateful if you wouldn't use that sort of language in my house,' said Mrs Fisher, who looked flushed and cross. 'Good evening to you, Miss Denham. I didn't see you standing there. Your Mr Curtis, he called round last week to ask me if I could put up a Jessie Trent. He told me all the other boarding houses were full up, so he was desperate. I agreed, of course, because I thought he meant a lady. But here's this man, instead.'

The man turned round and looked at Daisy. 'It's J-e-s-s-e,' he said, and sighed resignedly. 'Jesse, as in the outlaw Jesse James and father of King David.'

Daisy gazed into a pair of dark brown eyes, in a face which wasn't hard or heavy – which was in fact fine-boned and delicate, but definitely a man's.

'M-Mrs Fisher,' she began, painfully aware that she was stammering, but unable to do anything about it, 's-surely you won't mind if Mr James here – I mean Mr Trent – sleeps on your sofa, just tonight?'

'I do mind, as it happens.' Mrs Fisher grimaced. 'I never have any men here,' she continued irritably. 'I don't like men. I never have, they leave a bathroom in a shocking state, bits of bristle stuck all round the basin, whiskers in the plughole, scum around the bath. They never lift the seat – '

'I'm house-trained, Mrs Fisher,' Jesse Trent assured the landlady, in his lovely, slightly mocking voice. 'If you let me stay, I promise on my honour I'll behave myself.'

'You'd better, Mr Trent.' Mrs Fisher turned to Daisy. 'Well, Miss Denham, if you and the other ladies wouldn't object? I suppose it's late – '

'I don't object at all,' said Daisy.

'Very well, I'll find a couple of blankets,' muttered Mrs Fisher. 'But tomorrow, Mr Trent – '

'I'll leave at crack of dawn.' As Mrs Fisher bustled off, Jesse Trent smiled gratefully at Daisy. 'Thank you for sticking up for me, Miss Denham.'

Daisy couldn't speak. She stared at Jesse, hypnotised. *Whoever loved*, she thought, *that loved not at first sight?*

She finally stammered her excuses and went to bed. But, though she was so tired, she couldn't sleep. When she got up next morning she was feverish, hot and cold by turns. She was hungry, but couldn't have eaten anything at all.

She heard Amy and Julia stirring in the rooms below, but she stayed in bed until she heard the front door slam, which she hoped meant the newcomer had gone.

'He was here when I arrived – talk about an early bird – and he sounds as if he comes from Yorkshire,' Amy told the rest of the people standing or sitting in the damp rehearsal room above a dirty spit-and-sawdust pub. Jesse Trent himself was closeted downstairs with Mr Curtis, sorting out his contract.

'Anyway,' went on Amy, 'it seems his company was flooded out of its last place. They couldn't find other venues, and so they've all dispersed. He found us because that miser Curtis was desperate enough to put an advert in *The Stage*.'

'So aren't we glad he did?' Julia put on yet more lipstick, even though they were only doing a read-through, and the cast all wore old slacks, old skirts, old jumpers, and most looked very morning after a heavy night before. Ewan was especially pale, and so were Frank and George.

'All right, people, settle down.' Mr and Mrs Curtis came in with the newcomer, who looked bright and cheerful, not hung over in the slightest – unlike the other men.

'This is Mr Trent, who's kindly agreed to join us at short notice,' Mr Curtis told them.

'He'll be replacing Mr Morgan, who as we all know has managed to find himself a far superior engagement,' added Mrs Curtis waspishly.

Jesse Trent smiled genially all round, and Daisy's heart did somersaults.

'So Mr Trent will be Jack Grove in our new drama *Blighted Blossoms*,' continued Mr Curtis, 'and he'll be David Masefield in our new light comedy *Down the Drain*.

All right, boys and girls, pick up your scripts and walk.'

They began the read through. In the new drama *Blighted Blossoms*, Daisy played the innocent girl corrupted by her brother's devious friend, and every time she glanced at Jesse Trent she could understand how this could happen. Jesse was attractive, handsome, charming, worldly-wise – a fatal combination ...

'How old, do you think?' hissed Julia, as they watched Jesse and Ewan who, to his great and obvious disappointment was playing the girl's brother, read a scene.

'Let me see, now. Twenty-eight, perhaps, or maybe thirty?' Amy stubbed out a cigarette. 'Older than you and me, my love, but none the worse for it.'

'A charmer, but a bastard, too. Plenty of experience, I'd say. But I always like that well-worn look, and I – '

'Miss Hart, if you don't mind!' Mrs Curtis glared at Julia, and then at Daisy. 'Miss Denham, have you lost your place?'

'No, Mrs Curtis,' Daisy fibbed, and started turning pages rapidly.

'We're on Act 1, Scene 3,' snapped Mrs Curtis. 'Do wake up, my dear – and concentrate!'

Daisy found it hard to concentrate on anything but Jesse Trent's dark eyes. Julia was right, he looked well-worn, but he was also so good-looking that he made her think of fallen angels, tarnished but still beautiful and bright.

He wasn't as tall as Ewan, but he was well made and didn't carry any fat. He moved like a dancer, lithe and light upon his feet.

He smoked, of course – and so, like all the other men, he smelled of cigarettes. But, since he smoked Sobranies, the scent was quite a novelty. Everybody else smoked British gaspers, Capstans, Woodbines, Craven A.

Then it was time for Daisy's opening scene. 'Ready, Miss Denham?' Jesse's voice was low, caressing, husky without being harsh, warm without being suggestive.

'R-ready,' whispered Daisy, and choked out her first line.

When they reached the kissing scene, the tension in the room became electric. She was aware of Ewan's gaze – proprietorial, jealous. 'Relax,' said Jesse, as he held her in his arms and tipped her back a little, but not enough to make her feel off balance. 'You're doing very well.'

But Mr Curtis didn't think so. He didn't like the way that Daisy moved. She was supposed to be girl of twenty, he said crossly – supple, graceful, yielding – not a crone of eighty with lumbago and a buggered hip.

He said although she had to be an innocent, he wanted her to be much more flirtatious. She tried to be flirtatious, but then he told her not to look so arch. She wasn't the Christmas fairy in a blasted pantomime.

She ended up kissing Jesse Trent a dozen times or more, and every time she kissed him she was aware of Ewan's angry glare. It was burning through her cardigan and scorching holes into her back.

'Miss Denham, please don't look so worried,' said Jesse, several hours and many kisses later, as they were all packing up to leave. 'Everyone knows kissing on the stage is difficult, especially when you don't know the kisser very well.'

Jesse's dark eyes sparkled, Daisy noticed, and his smile was warm, appealing and sincere. 'Miss Denham, is there any particular problem, anything I can do to help?'

'I haven't kissed anyone on stage before.' Daisy felt the blush creep up her neck, and hated herself for being so gauche and young. 'But I dare say I'll get used to it.'

'I'm sure you will.'

'I hope you've got your digs fixed for tonight?'

'Yes, thank you. I'm staying with the other boys. The landlord's found an attic room for me.' Now Jesse's smile was gently mocking, wry and confidential. 'So,' he added softly, 'all you ladies will be safe.'

'Coming for a little snifter, Daisy?' George Reed came bustling up and put his arm round Daisy's shoulders. 'I should think you need it, after all that effort! Alfred's so pernickety. You'd think we were playing Drury Lane, not the Alhambra, Stoke. Mr Trent, it's opening time, so what about a beer or two?'

'Frank just asked me, thank you, George.' Then Jesse grinned, revealing sharp, white teeth, and Daisy's heart did handstands. 'I think he said the Hope and Anchor, didn't he? I need to talk to Alfred for a moment, then I'll be on my way.'

'Mmm, look at those shoulders,' Amy said to no one in particular, as Jesse strolled back across the room to talk to Mr Curtis.

Look at him move, thought Daisy. He's so graceful. I'd love to see him dance. Or dance with him, a little voice inside her head said speculatively.

'Frank and George and Alfred,' whispered Julia. 'He's only been here twenty minutes, but you'd think he runs the show.'

'We'll have to keep our eye on Daisy May.' Amy lit a cigarette and sniggered. 'Look at her, standing there all goggle-eyed. I'd say that girl's been smitten, and I can't say I'm surprised.'

'What the hell did you think you were doing?'

Ewan's anger took him by surprise. He'd stood there watching closely as Trent had kissed his girlfriend, and he had seen their lips had merely touched, that there had been no inappropriate groping or grabbing on the part of Trent.

Daisy had been nervous. She'd clearly hated being scrutinised as she was playing something as intimate as a love scene, but as a professional actress she had tried to get it right.

So why was he so furious?

The others had all gone, determined not to waste a single moment of precious drinking time. But he'd hung back, and Daisy had hung back with him, making a performance of doing up her coat and winding a woollen scarf around her neck.

They'd walked into the street in silence.

The monster had appeared from nowhere, like a genie spooling from a bottle, and everything had spun out of control. He'd meant to talk – just talk, not shout, not lose his temper. He wanted to explain how he was feeling, let Daisy know how much it had upset him to see her kiss another man. He didn't want to yell, he didn't want fly into a rage, he didn't want other pedestrians to stop and ask her if she knew this man.

But the monster didn't want to talk.

It wanted to pick a fight.

'I wasn't doing anything,' she faltered as the monster ranted, so then he was ashamed, because she looked so small and frightened. 'I was acting, Ewan. I didn't mean it.'

'You looked as if you did!' the monster shouted, and waved his arms about.

'Ewan, don't be silly.'

'Silly?' howled the monster, growing angrier by the second. 'My girlfriend stands there kissing another man, and obviously enjoying it, then tells me I'm silly?'

'Ewan, stop it.' Daisy touched his sleeve. 'Please don't shout at me. People are looking at us and pointing.'

'I don't care,' the monster growled.

'If you're going to carry on like this, I'm going to join the others.'

'Go, then – I'm not stopping you.'

'Why don't you come, too?'

'I'm going for a walk.' The monster jerked away from Daisy, turning on his heel and striding off, uncomfortably aware that she was standing staring after him. He wanted to go back. He wanted to apologise for shouting, to say of course he knew she had been acting.

But the monster wouldn't let him do it, and he kept on walking.

'We have a letter from Daisy, Rose!'

As he'd come out of the brand new cowshed, built a hundred yards from the bailiff's cottage across the cobbled yard, Alex had met the postman at the gate.

One day, he thought, Rose would have to accept it. Daisy had been right to go with Mr and Mrs Curtis. Rose and he had brought her up to think for herself, be strong and independent. So they couldn't complain because she'd turned out dogged and determined. Now she was doing what she loved, and – it would seem – doing it well, working with a professional company. If anything, they should be proud.

He put the other letters on the kitchen table and picked up the *Farming Times*, from which he was trying to teach himself to be a dairy farmer. He hoped that using most of the insurance money to build a modern cowshed and a dairy had been the right decision, and his herd of Jerseys was going to prosper, whatever Michael Easton said.

'Goodness, what a pile.' Rose lugged a basket full of washing over to the copper. 'I hope it's not all bills. I always seem to be paying bills. Cattle feed and visits from the vet and school fees for the boys, it's never ending.'

She turned to shout upstairs. 'Stephen and Robert, up you get!' she called. 'Your father needs you to do some jobs for him before you go to school. Come on, I shan't tell you again!'

'You also have a letter from America,' said Alex, as he started sifting through the brochures, catalogues and all the inevitable bills. 'Who do you know there?'

'I don't think I know anyone. Unless...'

Rose picked up the foreign-looking envelope, and saw the childish writing. She slit it open, scanned it quickly, then sat down, looking winded.

'Oh my God,' she whispered. 'I never thought we'd hear from her again. She – she wants Daisy back. She says – '

But Rose didn't finish, because the twins came thundering down the stairs and burst into the kitchen fighting and demanding breakfast. So it was impossible to discuss the matter any more.

More than anything, Ewan wanted Daisy back.

As Trent and Daisy rehearsed their scenes together in *Blighted Blossoms*, he tried to tell himself they were acting, that it seemed so real because they were so good at it.

The monster didn't agree. The monster wanted action and a showdown. Ewan found if he didn't keep a tight grip on himself, the fury would start building up inside him, turning him into somebody he didn't recognise, and definitely didn't want to be.

It had been such an easy conquest. The bastard didn't even have to try. He only had to look at Daisy and her eyes lit up. Daisy was so good at playing the part of an infatuated girl because she was infatuated herself.

In some ways, he was happy to be playing Daisy's furious brother because he was so angry anyway, and it was a good way to let off steam. He was only sorry the stage directions didn't demand he took a swing at Trent. But maybe it was just as well – he'd probably have knocked out half his teeth.

I've got her, haven't I, said Trent, but only with his eyes. What are you going to do about it, eh?

Ewan didn't know.

Chapter Nine

The company moved on, playing to half-empty theatres all around the Midlands.

When they arrived in each new place, Julia and Amy got painted up and went round all the shops to hand out playbills and a few judicious complimentary tickets, dragging Daisy along with them, and hissing at her to stick her flipping chest out, and to stop looking thirteen.

The men were sent out after dark to stick up posters on fences, walls and hoardings, on lamp posts and where there were signs which said *no bill sticking here*.

Today it was the morning of the dress rehearsal for the drama *Blighted Blossoms*. The only rehearsal on a stage, in fact, so everyone knew they'd have to get their moves right, cues right, props assembled, entrances and exits all worked out, while Tom the dour stage manager had to sort out the scenery and lighting, in a few short hours before they opened for the paying public that same Monday night.

Daisy had meant to get in before everybody else, to see how big the stage was, or how small, to see what kind of dressing room she'd have – the usual sort of horror with peeling paintwork, grubby washbasin and splintering matchwood furniture, or something even worse, ankle deep in pigeon droppings, with no running water and no electricity, up four steep flights of stairs.

But she found Jesse there already, sitting on the edge of the stage, swinging his legs and looking as if he'd grown there.

'Good morning,' she began, aware that she was blushing

scarlet, which she always did whenever Jesse was around.

'Hello, Miss Denham.' Jesse smiled, and his smile made Daisy's heart turn cartwheels. 'Where's everybody else?'

'I don't know.' Daisy shrugged. 'Amy and Julia must be on their way, but I expect they've stopped at a corner shop for cigarettes. Where are the other boys?'

'George was in the bathroom when I left, and Frank was having breakfast.'

'What about Ewan?'

'He's gone for a run,' said Jesse, shuddering. 'He's started running every morning now. Gets up at crack of dawn, puts on his old school plimsolls, off he goes. I see him from my bedroom window. Maybe he's having so much fun he's lost all track of time.'

Jesse lit a cigarette and blew a stream of fragrant Russian smoke across the stage. 'When I look at Fraser,' he continued, in a husky drawl, 'I can't but help remember how wonderful it felt to be so young, so full of energy. I'm such a slug myself. I hate all outdoor exercise, although of course I like to dance.'

Daisy glanced at Jesse, at his narrow waist, broad chest and well-developed shoulders. She thought that if he took no exercise apart from dancing, he was an extremely lucky slug. 'You can't be very old,' she said.

'Alas, I won't see twenty-five again.'

Jesse stood up and stretched, and then began to pace around the dimly lit and dusty stage. Daisy was reminded of a panther she had seen in India, a dark and dangerous thing. She stared in fascination, then realised he had noticed she was staring, and that his dark chocolate eyes were bright.

At that moment, Julia and Amy came bustling in, lighting up and giggling. 'Ooh, are we interrupting something?' Julia demanded.

'No,' said Jesse, and turned to her to smile his lazy smile. 'Why would you think that?'

'Our mistake, I'm sure,' said Amy. 'Only it looked to us like you were showing off to Daisy here, and we can't allow it.'

'You want to watch that fellow, sweetheart,' murmured Julia, as she brushed past Daisy. 'Stick with the baby boyfriend, that's my advice to you.'

'Come on, Daisy May,' said Amy, taking Daisy's arm. 'Sadly, it's time to tear yourself away from Mr Gorgeous here. You need to put your frock on and to get made up, or Alfred will be after you.'

Ewan didn't want to believe that it was happening, that Daisy was becoming more besotted with each passing day.

But he had no choice but to believe. The evidence was there in front of him. What could he do, how could he warn her, and would she listen, anyway?

After the dress rehearsal, which had gone very badly – but everyone said this was a good sign, a dreadful dress rehearsal meant a brilliant opening night – he tried to get her on her own.

But it proved impossible. Although most of the others, including Trent, had gone off to the pub, Julia and Amy seemed to have decided they had to be on permanent sentry duty. On reflection, he supposed he should be grateful – the bastard couldn't do anything with that pair of painted harpies hovering around.

'Daisy, I need to talk to you,' he said, while the two harpies sat doing their nails and nattering in the stalls, and Daisy was going over her own moves for one last time.

'You mean you want to shout at me,' she said, and wouldn't look at him.

'I don't want to shout.' Ewan locked the monster in its cage and threw away the key. 'What's gone wrong between us?'

'You're behaving like an idiot, that's what, and well you know it.'

'I thought you loved me?' Ewan didn't know what else to say. 'I thought we loved each other?'

'Ewan, I do – we do.' Daisy stopped her pacing, sighed and shook her head. 'But you stifle me.'

'What's that supposed to mean?'

'I don't want you following me around all the time, and always checking up on me.'

'I told your parents I'd look after you.'

'But you didn't offer to be my jailer.'

'I've never tried to be your jailer.'

'No?' Daisy moved downstage, turned round and checked the distance to the wings. 'Ewan, we can go out together sometimes, go to places on our own. But I'm happy for you to go and play football with the boys – and you should be happy for me to go out with the others, go to the talkies, go out dancing, possibly.'

The monster stirred and growled. 'Go out dancing with that bastard Trent, you mean,' it muttered.

'Of course I don't,' said Daisy, but she reddened. 'You're being very stupid about Jesse. I don't know why you hate him. But everyone has noticed, and it's got to stop.'

'How did Phoebe find us after all this time?' asked Rose. She'd put the letter away, more than a week had passed, but she knew that sooner or later she was going to have to

116

answer it.

'She must have kept a note of our address,' said Alex. 'She sent the letter to Melbury House, and so of course the postman brought it here. She stayed there once when Henry was alive, don't you remember, during that hot summer? Daisy was living with Mrs Hobson then.'

'Yes, of course, you're right. We were about to go to India. Phoebe said she couldn't take Daisy to the USA, so you suggested we adopt her, and we did.'

'May I see her letter?' asked Alex, who had waited patiently for Rose to let him read it, but was now tired of waiting.

'Yes, I suppose so.' Rose took it from the dresser drawer, handed it to him and watched him read.

My dear Rose

I'm sorry it's taken me so long to write to you again. I'm not too smart at putting things in writing, like you know. So please forgive mistakes, and also sorry for the blots. My pen don't work too good.

I thought you'd like to know that me and Nathan have settled down very well in New York City. He's got some cousins here, and when we come they made us very welcome straight away.

Now we got a swell (that's an American word, it means it's good) apartment. It's got a bathroom and a sitting room and a lovely kitchen with hot water and a little balcony. We got spare bedrooms, too. We're in the Lower East Side, that's where all the garment factories are, and Nathan's cousin took him into wholesale, and now he's gotten his own business.

Me, I got a hat shop, and it's doing fine.

But we don't got us any kids. Nathan and me's been trying for years, and nothing's ever happened. So, Rose, I need to see my little girl. You been her mother, and I'm sure you been a good one, but I want to see her, get to know her, and surely that's not much to ask?

I hope this finds you, Rose, and finds you well. I hope whoever is living in your house (if it's not you) will send my letter on. Rose, I haven't forgot about all what you did when I had Daisy. You was a friend in need.

I'll wait for you to answer this before I book my ticket on Cunard.

Give my best to Alex, and hope to hear from you.

Phoebe (Rosenheim)

'What shall we do?' asked Rose.

'You must write back inviting her to visit us, of course,' said Alex. 'Daisy is Phoebe's daughter, and Phoebe has a right to know what's happened since she saw Daisy last.'

'Alex, Phoebe didn't care tuppence about what happened to her daughter! If it hadn't been for us, Daisy would have ended up with foster parents – baby farmers, probably, people who take children in for money – or in some awful orphanage, where it's very likely she'd have been neglected, beaten, starved. What earthly right has Phoebe – '

'She is Daisy's mother. Rose, we have to welcome Phoebe. What else can we do?'

'I could pretend I didn't get the letter, couldn't I?'

'I seem to remember telling Daisy that if she ever wanted to find her mother, we would help her look.'

'Alex, you've forgotten Daisy said she hated Phoebe, and didn't want us to mention her again.'

'She was angry and upset.'

'I don't know what to do.' Rose's own emotions were in turmoil. 'I know it must be your decision, too. But let me think about it for a while? Phoebe wouldn't want to cross the Atlantic in the winter, anyway. She'd do much better to wait until the spring.'

Daisy was getting better and better. Everybody said so. She was getting flattering notices in all the local papers, and even the most curmudgeonly of the provincial critics – a bunch of ignorant old drunks who couldn't find the way to their own arscholes, as Mr Curtis eloquently put it when they trashed a show – were complimentary to Daisy.

'*Although the play itself was somewhat plodding, and the end predictable, the entire production was enlivened by the presence of a charming juvenile,*' announced the *Stafford Echo*.

'*The casting of the beautiful Miss Denham in a tiny part gave life and spirit to a tired evening,*' said the *Hanley Chronicle*.

'They mean they liked your legs,' said Amy sourly, one afternoon before a matinee that looked like playing to an almost empty house. 'So don't get too big-headed and think you're going to be a star.'

'Give the girl a break, she's doing fine,' said Jesse Trent, and Ewan scowled at him.

'Daisy, darling, come over here a minute.' Julia motioned Daisy to the wings, then handed her a package nicely wrapped in clean brown paper. 'I got you this. It's a little thank you for helping out that time, know what I mean?'

'What is it?' Daisy asked, remembering the last time Julia had given her a parcel, and not especially keen to open this one.

'It's for your notices. You're the only one who's getting any, after all. Go on, open it.'

So Daisy did, and she was pleasantly surprised.

'It's lovely, Julia – thank you!' she exclaimed, leafing through the leather-covered album, delighted with its pastel-coloured pages and pockets tied with ribbon, all waiting to make a record of her professional life. 'I'll paste the first ones in tonight.'

'Come along, Miss Twinkletoes, you're on,' hissed Amy Nightingale. She yanked the album out of Daisy's hands, plonked it down among the props, then almost dragged her on. 'You mustn't disappoint your fans,' she added, acknowledging the applause that greeted Daisy through clenched and gritted teeth.

Ewan knew he wasn't doing well. His heart was just not in it, and it showed. He hated the new plays, the vacuous, stupid comedy *Down the Drain* and the idiotic *Blighted Blossoms*. He wanted to play Romeo, Mercutio, Benedick, not a succession of idle bounders, tennis-playing chumps, disgusted brothers and hero's friends.

'I'd like you two to stay behind for a moment, dearest boys,' Mr Curtis said to George and Ewan, after a bad rehearsal for the comedy *Down the Drain*. 'Mr Fraser, you've got the voice at last, the gods of drama all be praised. But this is supposed to be a farce, and quite frankly you're not going to get a single laugh.'

Ewan was almost certain he heard the bastard Trent begin to snigger.

'You must work on your moves, as well,' continued Mrs Curtis. 'You clump around the stage like some old carthorse, and you get in everybody's way. You masked poor Mr Reed through one whole scene. Darlings, we can't afford a bad review. We're going to have our work cut out making any money at all in this godforsaken little town. So let's run through Act 2, Scene 3 once more.'

Ewan started to protest, but Mr Curtis jammed his monocle in his eye and fixed him beadily. 'Position please, dear boy.'

'Daisy, if you could wait ten minutes,' Ewan called, as the rest of the company started heading for the doors.

'It's all right, I'll walk Daisy to the pub,' Jesse called back to him, as he helped Daisy with her coat.

'Or we could wait for Ewan,' suggested Daisy.

'I don't want Mr Fraser being distracted by Miss Denham, he needs to get this right.' Mr Curtis waved them off. 'He'll see you later, girls and boys.'

Daisy and Jesse left the rehearsal room, walked down the stairs and out into the street.

Julia and Amy weren't hanging around and waiting, as they usually did. Daisy assumed they must have gone ahead – Julia had mentioned having a navvy's thirst on her today – but this meant she had Jesse to herself.

It made her nervous, but excited, too.

He had a new trilby, Daisy noticed, with a very up-to-date soft brim. It shaded half his handsome face and made him look impossibly romantic, she decided. Like Clark Gable, or maybe Ronald Colman, somebody like that.

'It seems so strange to come out of rehearsals or a performance when it's light,' she said. 'Somehow, I always think it will be dark.'

'Yes, and for most actors daylight's far too much like real

life, with all its boredom, pain and irritation.' Jesse smiled. 'You and I, we're creatures of a brighter, sharper, more exciting world. We only come alive when we're on stage, in the glare of artificial light.'

'Yes, you're right, we do.'

'But we probably shouldn't be in darkness all the time. So let's go through that little park and get a bit of air.' Jesse took Daisy's hand and held it as they crossed the road, but then forgot to let it go again, and she didn't like to pull away. 'How long have you been with Mr and Mrs Curtis?' he enquired.

'I joined the company last September.' Daisy blushed and stared down at the gravel path, aware of Jesse's fingers stroking hers, his pressure on her hand. 'I've done a lot of amateur work, of course – singing, dancing, one act plays – but this is my first professional engagement.'

'I never would have guessed.' Jesse laughed, but warmly, not unkindly. 'I'm sorry, I didn't mean to laugh,' he added. 'You do very well, Miss Denham.'

'Thank you, Mr Trent,' said Daisy, primly.

'Jesse, please.' Jesse sat down on a bench and, since his hand still held hers prisoner, Daisy had no option but to sit down beside him.

'Where do you come from?' Daisy asked him, staring straight ahead. 'I mean, where were you born?'

'In Yorkshire.' Jesse stroked her fingers gently, slowly, thoughtfully. 'My father is a minister, so you could say acting's in my blood.'

'You're a son of the vicarage, then?'

'Good heavens, no!' Jesse sighed and shook his handsome head. 'Nothing as respectable, I'm afraid. My parents are members of a strict and frankly outlandish non-conformist sect. They disowned me when I started acting in return for money.'

'Really?' Daisy warmed to Jesse as a kindred spirit. 'My mother isn't a member of a sect,' she told him, confidentlally. 'But she feels acting and getting paid for it is vulgar, too.'

'You didn't have a happy childhood, then?'

'I had a lovely childhood, but – '

'Mine was horrible. I've had the devil beaten out of me so many times that – well, see for yourself.' Jesse turned back a cuff to show a pattern of angry purple welts encircling his wrist. 'My father used to tie me up and thrash me.'

'But that's awful, surely there are laws?' Daisy had never been so much as slapped, and suddenly her heart contracted as she imagined Jesse as a frightened, lonely child, loomed over by a monster of a father. 'I'm so sorry.'

'Oh, don't be sorry, at least I got away.' Jesse pushed his cuff back down, stood up. 'Let's get going, shall we? The others will be wondering where we've gone, and we don't want to get them talking.'

'Why would they talk?' asked Daisy. 'All we're doing is sitting chatting in a public park, and where's the harm in that?'

But, as she said it, she felt her heart beat faster, and she knew that in a public park with Jesse was the only place she wished to be.

Ewan came out of the rehearsal room to find Amy hanging around outside it, but the other harpy Julia was nowhere to be seen.

'How did it go?' she asked.

'I suppose I'm getting there,' said Ewan. 'Mr and Mrs Curtis seem to think so, anyway.'

'But you're not in the mood for comedy, are you, Mr Fraser?' Amy looked at him with mournful, deeply-shadowed eyes. 'Hamlet, yes – I think you'd make a perfect gloomy Dane. You'd be in your element playing melancholy mad. Any London manager would sign you up for Hamlet straight away.'

'I doubt it,' muttered Ewan, who at that very moment didn't believe he had enough acting talent to play the back end of a horse. So, as for Hamlet, that was just a joke.

'Darling, I'd put money on it,' Amy told him, 'and I'm not a betting girl. I don't believe in paying taxes on stupidity. But anyway, enough chit-chat, have you got a light?'

'Yes, of course.' Ewan took out his matches and lit Amy's cigarette, carefully so as not to singe her eyebrows or set her blonde spun-sugar hair on fire.

'Thanks,' she said and smiled, but then she sniffed. 'I'm sorry, but I think I'm going to blub.'

'Why, what's the matter?' Since he was so miserable himself, Ewan was more than ready to sympathise, even if it meant he'd have to watch a woman cry.

'I've had some rotten news. My mother's dying, but she doesn't want to see me.'

'I'm sorry.' Ewan thought, I'd better write to mine, it's been a while.

'It can't be helped.' Amy slipped her arm through Ewan's. 'So come on then, walk me to the boozer, and I'll drown my sorrows. You're not very happy these days, are you?'

'What do you mean?'

'Oh, come on, my darling, don't play the innocent with Auntie Amy, you know very well.' Amy moulded herself against him, glancing up at him occasionally and puffing cigarette smoke in his eyes.

'Listen to me, sweetheart,' she continued. 'I've been watching you since you and Daisy May first joined this company. I can tell you now you're worth a dozen Jesse Trents. You're ten years younger, you're much nicer-looking, and you're a better actor – or you could be, if you took the trouble.'

'Do you think so?' Ewan shook his head. 'These past few weeks, I must admit I've wondered.'

'You're just preoccupied. You're worried sick about your Daisy May, and I can't say I blame you.'

'I don't know what to do,' said Ewan, and now he thought, Amy's not a harpy, after all. In fact, she's very kind and, for an older woman, she's quite attractive, too.

'Just be patient, darling,' Amy told him, shrugging, and Ewan could feel her bosom pressing close against his side. 'She'll come to her senses, see the error of her ways. Or Mr Smarmy Smartarse will overreach himself, and Mr and Mrs C will have to sack him.'

'If that bastard so much as touches her – '

'I know, you'll punch his horrid head in, his beauty will be ruined, and you'll end up in prison. So calm down, let matters take their course, and in the meantime think about your own career.'

'I don't seem to have one nowadays.'

'Ewan, don't be ridiculous. But you're a serious actor, not a lightweight. When you get a chance to play a part that's got some meat on it, you shine. Audiences in the Midlands don't want serious stuff. They want melodrama, or light, escapist comedy, and comedy isn't really you, my sweet. You're too intense for comedy.'

'Amy – Mrs Nightingale – it's all very well for you to say I should be playing Hamlet, but where should I be playing him?'

'Somewhere like Manchester or Glasgow. The City Players or the Comrades would be perfect companies for you.'

'I've heard about the Glasgow Comrades.'

'I know one of its backers.' Amy glanced up at Ewan and smiled conspiratorially. 'If you like, I could put in a word?'

'That would be very kind of you,' said Ewan. 'But I can't leave Daisy. I told her parents I'd look after her, and I can't break my promise.'

'She might break it for you,' Amy told him, grimacing. 'Look, can you see them – straight ahead?'

Ewan looked, and saw the bastard Trent walking with Daisy, and they were hand in hand.

Chapter Ten

'I'd love to see you dance.' Jesse moved Daisy's lemonade to make room for his pint of bitter, and then sat down beside her on the wooden bench.

Ewan caught Amy's eye and saw her shake her golden head – don't rise to it, she was saying, don't gratify his vanity, don't give him ammunition.

'You have the perfect body for a dancer,' continued Jesse. 'You're slender, not too tall, and you have nice, long legs.'

'I do like to dance,' admitted Daisy, going red as Jesse came out with words like legs and body, which seemed a bit too intimate for general conversation in a pub.

'Ballroom, ballet, tap?' asked Jesse.

'Anything and everything,' Daisy told him, smiling.

'We'll go dancing, then,' said Jesse. 'On the next rest day, we'll try out the local palais, shall we? Give the regulars some entertainment? Show them how to do it?'

Jesse looked round the table to see half a dozen pairs of eyes all goggling at him. 'All of us,' he added hastily, as the others stared.

'Oh, I thought you and Daisy May were fixing up a private outing,' Amy told him caustically.

'Good of you to let us tag along,' said Julia, taking out her compact, then starting on her mouth.

Ewan didn't say anything. He put his arm round Daisy's shoulders, and then he pulled her close. He glanced at Amy, who nodded her approval and smiled covertly at him.

That evening, Daisy looked at herself in the spotted wardrobe mirror. She thought that yes, she did have nice long legs, that her still childish figure was perfect for a dancer.

She'd been inclined to envy Julia's and Amy's generous curves. But now she thought, who needs a bosom like a bolster, anyway?

Jesse made her feel attractive – even beautiful. When he smiled, she felt so warmed, so bathed in radiance, that it was as if the sun shone even on the dullest, rainiest day.

She couldn't wait to dance with him.

'You and Mr Smartarse, you should be in revue, that Mr C B Cochran doesn't know what he's been missing,' Amy said sarcastically to Daisy, as the three of them straggled to the bus stop on another wet and windy morning, after they'd all been dancing at the local palais the previous Tuesday night.

As they had arranged, on their rest day the whole company had gone dancing. Mr and Mrs Curtis had floundered round the hall like walruses, but looked as if they were having a good time. George and Frank had danced a bit with Julia and Amy, but the four of them had soon got tired of this unwonted exercise, and settled down at the bar.

Ewan had been taught to dance at school. But he wasn't naturally graceful. Strong and athletic, rather than lithe and sinuous, he was no Fred Astaire.

After he'd watched Ewan and Daisy dance a fairly competent but wooden foxtrot, Jesse had found he couldn't stand to watch them any more. He'd disentangled her from Ewan, who couldn't punch him in a public place, and then he took Daisy in his arms. They'd shown the other dancers how it should be done, with style and flowing grace.

'Where did you learn to foxtrot like a pro?' Jesse had demanded grinning, when they finally took a break and went to get a drink.

'In India,' Daisy told him, aware that she was glowing and feeling gloriously alive, lit up with the happy satisfaction of doing something she did well. 'My father was in the army there, and Mum sent me to dancing lessons. Singing lessons, too.'

'Sing for me, then?' Jesse had whispered, slipping his arm round her waist and pulling her close to him again.

Daisy had been aware of Ewan watching, of Amy screwing up her face and scowling, but she was enjoying herself so much she didn't care.

As the band struck up again, she'd sung for Jesse Trent, keeping perfect time with the middle-aged, over-made-up dance hall vocalist, her sweet soprano ringing true and clear.

'You're very good, you know.' As she'd sung to him, Jesse had pulled back a little, so that he could gaze into her eyes. When he'd smiled, her heart turned joyous cartwheels. 'You need more lessons to teach you how to move and how to breathe. You're not too well co-ordinated yet, and when you're dancing you must learn to follow, while the man should lead. But your voice is lovely, and you float like thistledown. Adele and Fred Astaire had better watch it when we get to London!'

'We're going to London, are we?' Daisy breathed.

'You bet we are,' said Jesse.

'When are we going?'

'Soon, my angel,' whispered Jesse, and he winked at her as if she were a fellow plotter. 'You try to save a bit of money, sweetheart – then we'll see.'

As Amy, Julia and Daisy fought their way on to the crowded bus, a trundling, dirty vehicle full of people spitting, coughing, arguing and shoving their elbows into one another, she realised she couldn't wait to see him.

She couldn't wait to get her frock on, get her make-up on and be on stage that night. When Jesse kissed her, she could feel he meant it, and for just a few short, precious moments she could forget the audience noisily sucking boiled sweets, rustling their boxes of cheap chocolates half-filled with shavings, bran or crinkly paper, forget old ladies coughing, fidgeting and whispering to their next door neighbours.

Every night, under the glare of spotlights, she fell in love again.

Chapter Eleven

The company was going north to Yorkshire.

'You're going home,' said Daisy, as they all piled on the Sunday train to Doncaster.

'What do you mean?' asked Jesse, who was struggling with a suitcase he wasn't quite tall enough to heave on to the rack. So Amy had to help him, which she did with a sarcastic grin.

'You're going to Yorkshire, where you come from, don't you?'

'Yes, of course,' said Jesse, grimacing. 'But I'm from Wakefield, miles from all the places we'll be going.' He lit a cigarette and slumped down in his seat. He stared out of the window, making it clear he wasn't in the mood for conversation.

Daisy realised she'd been very tactless. Of course he wouldn't be happy to be going back to Yorkshire, the scene of all his childhood misery.

Monday morning saw the company members trooping from their various chilly lodgings to a shabby theatre in a rough part of the town, where they would spend the next two weeks giving twelve evenings and four matinees to a hopefully receptive audience of shop assistants, mill hands, clerks and general tradesmen and their wives.

'All right, girls and boys, less gossiping!' Alfred Curtis strode on to the stage, his monocle in place and white spats gleaming – they'd obviously been Blancoed recently. 'We've three hours to get everything set up. The property and costume skips will still be at the station. So, Mr Trent and

Mr Reed, could you please go and fetch them? You may take a taxi, gentlemen. If you can find one in this godforsaken town.'

Then Mrs Curtis, clad as usual in regal purple, and wearing an amazing hat that looked as if she had a chicken nesting in her wig, came up to join her husband.

'Ladies, your dressing room leaves quite a lot to be desired,' she told them, all her chins a-wobble with disapproval. 'There's no basin, the flipping roof is leaking, and there's an inch of water on the floor. I've asked the management to find duckboards, but God knows if they will. You've got facilities down the passage.

'Gents, you've got a khazi in the yard, and it looks disgusting. But there are chamber pots in all the cupboards.'

When they scanned the local papers after their first night, Daisy found she'd got some decent notices again. She cut them out to stick them in her album.

Then, to her surprise, she got a pay rise, to three pounds two and six a week. She would soon be earning enough to send some money home.

'It's not your acting, it's your legs, my darling,' whispered Julia, as they stood waiting in the wings that evening. 'Alfred can't resist a pair of pins, neither can the audiences, and of course yours are up there with the best. If I had legs like yours, I'd walk around in knickers all the time, so everyone could see.'

'But he's still exploiting you, like he exploits the rest of us,' said Amy. She shot a poisonous glance at Alfred Curtis, who was standing on the opposite side and arguing with a lighting man who seemed both daft and drunk.

'You're only jealous.' Julia elbowed Amy in the side.

'Daisy, darlin', I don't like to ask, and you'll get every penny back, I swear, but lend me a quid till Friday?'

'I wouldn't if I were you,' warned Amy. 'She'll spend it all on gin and fags and lipstick, mark my words.'

'Who asked your opinion?' Julia looked beseechingly at Daisy. 'Sweetheart, fifteen bob?'

'Yes, of course,' said Daisy. 'Just remind me after we come off tonight.'

'You're far too soft, young Daisy May.' Amy Nightingale hitched up her stockings, smoothing out the wrinkles at her knees. 'This leech will bleed you dry. Come on, love, we're on.'

Ewan was determined to be cool with Daisy, to give her space to breathe, to hope that if he didn't stifle her she'd get sick and tired of being smarmed at by the devious bastard Jesse Trent.

'Who's your letter from?' he asked one lunch time, sitting down beside her on the edge of the apron stage. They'd come back early from the pub and were made up and costumed for the matinee, in plenty of time before the audience came in. Daisy was swinging her legs and reading, shaking her head and laughing now and then.

'My mother,' she replied, not looking up.

'Oh, which one?' said Ewan.

'I beg your pardon?'

'As I remember, you have two.'

'Yes, I suppose I do.' Daisy folded the letter up and put it in her pocket. 'It's from Dorset,' she explained. 'Mum sent it to the last address but one, so it's been following me around, and it's all old news now. But it's so nice to hear from them and find out what they're doing, especially the twins.'

'It wasn't so very long ago we were searching every street directory in England for Phoebe Gower or Rosenheim,' said Ewan. 'I would be happy to start again while we're in Yorkshire.'

'I don't know if there's any point.'

'Maybe, maybe not. But, as I say, if you want to knock on doors, look at electoral registers, or anything like that, I'll be glad to help you.'

'Thank you, Ewan, you're very kind.'

Then Daisy looked at him, and suddenly she was wistful and soft-eyed, and Ewan saw the Daisy that he loved.

He saw the glint of gold around her neck. So she still wears my chain, he thought, she must still feel she's mine. They would find their way back to the place where they had been so happy, and everything would be all right again. He reached out, touched her lightly on the shoulder. 'Daisy?' he whispered.

'Yes?' She leaned towards him, red lips parted, blue eyes wide.

'I'm sorry I've been a stupid, jealous fool.'

'You haven't, Ewan,' said Daisy. Then she put her arms around his neck, and he was about to kiss her when there was a thump, a curse, the unmistakeable sound of someone dropping something heavy, probably on a foot.

They heard the audience gathering in the foyer, buzzing like a swarm of happy bees. The auditorium doors crashed open, and the spell was broken. Daisy scrambled to her feet to duck behind the curtain, and Ewan did the same.

Amy and Julia skittered up behind them, chattering and laughing at some private joke.

'All right, you two?' said Amy. She gave Ewan a big grin, a saucy wink, and then she kissed him on the cheek before she scurried off to fix her make-up.

Just about all right, he thought, and smiled. I hope we're almost home and dry. He'd have to try to think of somewhere he and Daisy could go together on their next day off. Somewhere the others wouldn't follow them.

'I've been wanting to ask you, Ewan,' whispered Daisy, as they joined each other in the wings, 'why are you so thick with Amy these days? Why are you always following her around?'

'I don't know what you mean,' said Ewan, genuinely astonished.

'I think you do,' said Daisy. 'She's always nodding at you and smirking. She was doing it just now. It's as if there's something private going on between you.'

The monster, who'd been lying dozing, suddenly woke up. 'Why do you see so much of Jesse Trent?' demanded Ewan. 'You seem to spend every daylight hour with him!'

'If I do, why shouldn't I?'

'You're my girl, that's why!'

'So I can't have a conversation with another man? I spend time with George and Frank, as well. You don't mind that.'

'George and Frank aren't interested in girls.' Ewan scowled at Jesse, who'd just walked on to the stage with George and started to do stretches, while George made sure the chairs and tables and various other props were where they ought to be. 'George is not like Trent.'

'Ewan, hadn't you better make sure you know where all your things are for this afternoon?' asked Daisy coldly. 'You couldn't find your boots last week, and don't forget you're going to need the violin today. You won't be able to do Scene 3 without it.'

'Less chattering, now,' hissed Mrs Curtis, bustling up behind them. 'Darlings, if could you possibly save your lovers' tiff till later, I'd be very grateful. The audience is coming in, and they've paid their money to see the play, not hear Mr Fraser carrying on.'

Ewan went to find his violin.

'There's not a bad old crowd out there today,' said Julia, as the beginners for *Blighted Blossoms* huddled in the wings.

'Jolly good,' grinned George, patting first his padding and then his crêpe moustache.

'Daisy, I must have a word.' Jesse Trent took Daisy's arm and pulled her to one side, turning his back on George and Julia. 'It's no good,' he whispered. 'You must know how I feel about you. What are we going to do?'

'We can't do anything right now, we're on in thirty seconds.' Daisy didn't know what else to say.

'Oh, Daisy, don't be such a flirt!' cried Jesse, making Julia turn and stare at him. He glared at her until she finally shrugged and looked away. 'You and I, we're not meant for this dull provincial stuff!'

'Ten seconds, boy and girls,' said Mrs Curtis, who was stage manager that afternoon. 'Miss Denham, you look flustered, are you well?'

'Yes, Mrs Curtis, I'm all right.'

But Daisy was confused. What was Amy up to, why was she vamping Ewan, and why did he seem to like it?

Well, two could play at that game, she decided, as she glanced again at Jesse Trent.

All the time they were in Doncaster, Jesse stuck to Daisy like a debt collector's runner, appearing out of nowhere when

Ewan was rehearsing, squashing himself down next to her when Ewan went to the bar, making use of any opportunity to talk to her, or smile a secret smile.

One evening in the pub, Daisy happened to remark to no one in particular that she had ambitions to play Juliet one day.

'You can't be a tragedienne with a name like Daisy Denham,' Jesse told her, laughing.

'I could change it, couldn't I?' retorted Daisy crossly.

'No, my love, don't change your name, or anything about you.' Jesse's hand caressed her shoulder, stroking away an errant strand of hair. 'You could be wonderful in a musical comedy, you know. Or I can see you in revue. Gertrude Lawrence, Daisy Denham in *Good Evening, London*.'

'Or *Hi There, New York*,' said Daisy dryly.

'Yes, that's it!' cried Jesse, as Ewan came back carrying some drinks, and glowered to see Jesse sitting in his place. 'They'd love you in New York.'

'How do you know?' Julia asked him, pursing scarlet lips. 'You've been there, have you?'

'No, but I'll be going one day,' Jesse said, as Ewan forced himself into the space between them and sat down next to Daisy. 'Daisy, you and me on Broadway, eh?' he added, leaning forward to catch Daisy's eye.

'Maybe.' Daisy smiled and drank some lemonade.

'But in the meantime, the Majestic, Doncaster.' Amy took her glass of gin and lemon. 'Thank you Ewan darling,' she added, in a carrying whisper. 'You're a gentleman. You stand your round and pay your way.'

After Christmas, when almost every theatre in the land was doing pantomime, and so the company had no bookings,

Mrs and Mrs Curtis gave them all a few days off.

Ewan said he should go and see his mother, and would Daisy like to go to Scotland? 'Come with me?' he said, his green eyes soulful and beseeching. 'Let's go and see some proper snow?'

But Daisy said she didn't think that she and Mrs Fraser would get on, and in any case she should go home and see them all in Dorset.

She found Rose in a most peculiar mood, distracted but affectionate, interested in everything Daisy said about the company, but still preoccupied. Daisy was sure that if she tested Rose on what she'd just been told, Rose would not remember anything.

'It's money, I suppose,' she told the twins, as they dragged her off to see the cows, who were warm and dry in their luxurious new cowshed.

She was pleased to find that Rose and Alex had spent a bit of the insurance money on the bailiff's cottage, too. So now it was a comfortable if cluttered little home, with bright new curtains, modern furniture, and a decent kitchen with an efficient range which was nothing like the old Victorian horror they'd had at Melbury House.

All the same, they surely couldn't mean to live in it forever? One day, they'd move back to the big house?

'It's always money these days.' Robert stroked a golden, docile cow, who gazed at him with liquid, dark brown eyes. 'Dad's spent a fortune sorting out this place. Mum's always going on about the bank, and saying how are we ever going to pay the interest on the loan.'

'There's something else as well,' said Stephen.

'What?'

'I was in the kitchen one Sunday morning and they were

coming across the yard. Dad told Mum she'd have to do it some time.'

'Do what?'

'I don't know.'

'What did Mum say then?'

'She told him she'd get round to it eventually, and there was no hurry. She'd waited long enough already, and a few more months would make no difference.'

'Then what happened?'

'They saw me at the window and clammed up.'

'Do you think she's ill?' asked Daisy, thinking back to when the family first arrived in Dorset, and Rose had been in bed most of the winter.

'She isn't ill,' said Robert. 'Well, she doesn't cough or anything. But we can see she's worried.'

When the twins had gone to bed that evening, Daisy asked Rose if anything was wrong.

'I don't think so, darling.' Rose looked up from her everlasting mending, shook her head and smiled. 'The twins are doing well at school, you're happy acting, and your father's sure he's going to make it as a farmer. So I'd say everything is fine.'

The middle of January saw the company on tour again, fighting off the coughs and colds picked up on crowded trains and draughty stations, making their way through snow and slush and wondering aloud why anybody chose to be an actor.

When asked what he'd been doing on his break, Jesse said he'd been to see his parents, and Daisy thought how sweet and how forgiving. 'I saw mine as well,' she said.

'I'm sure that made their day,' said Jesse in his usual

mocking drawl. 'So we've both done our duty, haven't we?'

One evening, they stood together watching Ewan from the wings. 'Fraser's yelling at them again,' said Jesse, as his right hand lay on Daisy's shoulder, idly massaging her collar bone. 'Listening to him, you'd think this audience was deaf as well as stupid. They might be, I suppose. All mill hands have cloth ears. But Fraser should be playing in a field, not on a stage.'

'I think he's very good,' said Daisy, not adding that in her opinion Jesse often mumbled, that she had heard old biddies in the front row of the stalls complain they couldn't hear him.

'He could be good,' said Jesse. 'But he doesn't watch, he doesn't learn. He thinks that since he was the star of all his school productions, he knows it all already.'

'What about me, should I be in a field?'

'I don't think so, Daisy.' Jesse leaned towards her and looked deep into her eyes. 'You're a natural – even that old idiot Curtis says so – watching you lifts everybody's heart.'

'Thank you.' Daisy looked away, blushing red beneath her number 5.

'When this season's over, and I've got a bit of cash saved up, I'm going to go to London, try to get into revue,' said Jesse. 'Why don't you come with me?'

'You're going to do a song and dance act? I didn't know you could sing?'

'Oh, I can sing,' said Jesse. 'I can do all the serious stuff as well, but that's not what people want today. This country's in a deep depression. Millions are out of work or on short time, absolutely everyone's fed up, so when they go out they want to have a bit of fun. You and I could make their hearts grow lighter. At the moment, musical comedy's the coming thing.'

'I'm on now,' said Daisy, straightening her skirt.

'So take it fast,' said Jessie, 'then we can all go to the pub.'

As Daisy lay in bed that night she wondered – could she go to London, and could she go with Jesse Trent? As for revue, she'd love to do revue. She'd love to sing and dance like Ginger Rogers.

But if she went with Jesse, what would Ewan say?

Their next engagements were in theatres in Birmingham and the Midlands, but after that the company would break up.

Frank and George were going to Skegness to do a concert party season, in boaters, Oxford bags and stripey blazers. 'All the old widows love us,' they told Daisy. 'We do the ragtime standards, and they sing along.'

Mr and Mrs Curtis said they hoped to get hotel work – comedy sketches, piano duets and poetry recitals in palm courts in places like Torquay and Bognor Regis. Julia and Amy would be unemployed. Jesse was wearing Daisy down about trying her luck in London.

Yes, she said, to shut him up and stop him buzzing round her like a hornet, she would definitely like to go. Yes, she'd be his partner. Yes, they'd put an act together. Yes, they'd try to get into revue.

But, if she went with Jesse, she'd have to break the news to Ewan, and she didn't quite know how to do it.

It was a rest day, and Ewan was determined to have Daisy to himself.

So, since he knew she needed shoes – he'd heard her saying so to Julia – he suggested going shopping in Birmingham city centre.

Daisy said she'd love to, in fact she'd been so sweet to him just recently that he had begun to hope she'd got over Trent, and everything would be all right again.

The devious bastard had casually announced the previous evening that he was going to Cheltenham to see a family friend, and he'd cleared off at crack of dawn. Frank and George had gone to see a manager in Walsall who might have some casual work for them, work which they would definitely need, because a run of concert parties wouldn't make them rich. Mr and Mrs Curtis were doing the accounts, so that just left Julia and Amy. He hoped they wouldn't decide to tag along.

Luckily, they didn't. They said they were going to get their hair done, to try one of those softer, less unpleasant-smelling permanent waves.

'Go on, take her out to lunch,' Amy had added, grinning at him and winking. 'Then go and see a talkie, kiss her in the dark and tell her all about your Scottish plan.'

'You think she might come with me?'

'I reckon it's a certainty.'

So now they were in Rackham's restaurant, eating shepherd's pie and watching as the rain poured down on Birmingham, making it look even more depressing.

But Ewan was feeling happy and relaxed. They'd bought the shoes, and Daisy had let him also buy a beautiful silk scarf, provided he let her buy a tie for him.

Then, as they started on their pudding, she dropped her bombshell.

'You're going to London?' Ewan stared. It was as if she'd told him she was going to the moon. 'You're going with him?'

'I'm going with Jesse, certainly,' said Daisy, reddening. 'But it's a professional arrangement, nothing more.'

She reached across the table, took his hand. 'I'll still see you, Ewan,' she promised. 'I'll still be your girl. Why don't you come to London, too?'

'I can't,' said Ewan, and jerked his hand away.

'Why, what will you be doing?'

'I'm going back to Scotland to join a company in Glasgow. It's called the Comrades. I'll be doing Shakespeare, and some modern drama, too.'

'You never said!' cried Daisy.

'You never asked,' retorted Ewan.

'When did you go to Glasgow?'

'When we had those few days off in January, and I went to Glen Grant to see my mother. I wrote to the manager of the Comrades and asked if I could meet him. I read some stuff for him, and he engaged me on the spot.'

'Oh, I see,' said Daisy, looking winded. She pushed away her pudding. 'I think you might have told me.'

'You've been so busy with Mr Jesse Trent that you've not had time to speak to anybody else.'

'So there'll be five hundred miles between us.'

'Yes, so it would seem.' Ewan felt a miserable sort of satisfaction. 'What do your parents have to say about this London scheme?'

'I haven't told them yet.'

'I'm not surprised. I don't suppose they'd be delighted to hear you're going to London with a man.'

'Maybe not,' admitted Daisy, fiddling with a teaspoon. 'Ewan, will you write to me?'

'If that's what you want,' said Ewan, looking for the waitress to ask her for the bill.

143

'I don't want us to part like this,' said Daisy.

'What do you mean?'

'You're angry with me.'

'I'm not angry.'

'So why are you scowling?'

'You want it all ways, don't you?' The monster opened one red eye and grinned. 'You want both me and Trent dancing attendance. Well, make your choice. It's him or me.'

'There's no choice to make!' cried Daisy, standing up and throwing down her napkin. 'You're the man I love!'

'It looks like it,' said Ewan, and now he caught the attention of the waitress. 'Miss, may I please have the bill?'

'Ewan, you're impossible!' Daisy turned and stormed out of the restaurant.

The monster winked and said, I told you so.

Alex had decided Phoebe must be asked if she would like to come to Dorset, and said that if Rose didn't write, he'd do it anyway.

So Rose gave in and wrote to Phoebe, inviting her to visit them in Charton. Phoebe sent a wire to say she'd booked her ticket on Cunard.

After Rose had panicked quietly for a day or two, she went to see Mrs Hobson in the village, and told her what had happened.

Mrs Hobson said while she wasn't bothered about what Mrs Rosenheim might think, they couldn't let young Daisy down, could they, Mrs Denham?

'She'll have Daisy's bedroom, will she?' added Mrs Hobson.

'There's nowhere else,' said Rose. 'I don't imagine she'd want to bunk up with the twins.'

'Maybe not,' said Mrs Hobson, grinning. 'Mrs Denham, please don't look so worried. You've made that old cottage look so nice. Anybody would be pleased to stay there, even somebody from New York City.'

'I'm not so sure,' said Rose.

They polished and they painted. They cleaned up bits of furniture they'd taken from the ruins of Melbury House. They washed and starched and ironed. They went to Dorchester and bought some pretty bedclothes and a fat, pink eiderdown. They managed to make Daisy's bedroom look like something from a magazine.

Or so Rose hoped.

Daisy couldn't decide what she should do. Go with Jesse to London? Go with Ewan – not that he had asked her, so she'd have to talk him round, and hope this Comrades lot would offer her a job as well? Or – as a last resort – go back to Dorset?

'What's the matter, Daisy May?' asked Amy, as Daisy frowned and fretted, trying to decide what she should do. In spite of what she'd said to Ewan, and what she'd said to Jesse, it wasn't too late to change her mind.

While she'd been in Dorset, she had seen how hard her parents worked, and she had mucked in, too. Alex had Mr Hobson and the twins to help him with the cows, and Mrs Hobson came up every day to help her mother, but Daisy felt she ought to help them, too – either she should be there, or she should be sending money home.

She found three bits of paper. London, Dorset, Scotland – she wrote one place on each, and then asked Julia to pick one.

'What is this, a raffle?' said Julia doubtfully. 'What am I

going to win? I don't want any bath salts.'

'Just choose a bit of paper!'

'Oh, all right, the pink one.'

'Thank you,' Daisy said. 'I'm going to London.'

'Yeah, I thought you might be.'

The guest arrived in Charton, but instead of being delighted by the bailiff's cottage and saying it was cute, she was appalled.

'Rose, whatever 'appened?' Phoebe stared round the kitchen open-mouthed, as if she couldn't believe her eyes. 'This place is a slum! You look like some old cleanin' woman in that jersey two-piece! It's all saggin' round yer arse! Rose, what are you doin', dressed up like a charlady, an' livin' in a slum?'

'There was a fire at Henry's house, and we lost almost all our things.' Rose had been brought up to be a lady, and now she did her best to smile politely as her visitor ranted on.

But having Phoebe standing there and wailing about charladies and slums, when enormous efforts had been made to make the cottage bright and welcoming – Rose was mortified.

'There was some insurance money, of course, but we're ploughing that into the farm,' she went on, gamely. 'If the farm does well, we'll think about rebuilding Melbury House.' She glanced down at her cheap brown knitted skirt, 'and buying some new clothes.'

'But Rose, you was so rich!' cried Phoebe. 'You 'ad all them things! All them silk dresses, all them jewels, all them furs!'

'But then she married me.' They hadn't heard Alex come into the kitchen. As they turned, he smiled in welcome, bent

146

to kiss Phoebe on the cheek, and then stood back to take in all her splendour.

'You're looking very well,' he said. 'That's a most extraordinary hat! You're quite a bobby-dazzler these days – wouldn't you say so, Rose?'

' 'Ello, Alex, love. It's good to see you.' Phoebe preened and smirked, smoothing the expensive, soft material of her smart, black coat. 'I – listen, you wasn't meant to 'ear me goin' on. I don't mean no offence.'

'I know you don't,' said Alex. 'What about some tea? Or coffee, as you must drink nowadays?'

'A cuppa would be wonderful.' Phoebe sat down and started to unskewer all her hat pins. 'I takes it strong an' black, two sugars, please. They don't know 'ow to make a decent cuppa in the States. They just pours warm water over teabags. God, I ask you!'

Rose moved Phoebe's feather and net creation to a safe place high up on the dresser. She put the kettle on the hob. 'Where did you get your gorgeous hat?' she asked. 'One of those expensive New York stores?'

'No, I got a hat shop of me own, didn't I say?'

'Oh, yes, you did,' said Rose, remembering. 'I hope it's doing well?'

'Not 'alf it's doin' well!' Phoebe grinned delightedly. 'Listen, I got four girls in the workroom, an' a lady in the shop itself. She speaks so nice, she does the business with the toffs like I could never do.'

'I was just thinking, you haven't lost your accent.'

'Well, you know what they say. You can take the girl from the East End, but you'll never take the East End from the girl! So where's my Daisy, Rose? One of your letters said she was goin' to dancin' classes, didn't it? Must 'ave been a while back now? I'd love to see her dance.'

'She's not here at the moment. She's followed in your footsteps, actually.'

'She – Rose, you don't mean to say she's 'ad a kid?' demanded Phoebe, looking shocked and horrified.

'No, she's on the stage,' said Rose. 'She's very talented. She can act and sing and dance. Do everything, in fact. She's had some lovely notices. I'll go upstairs and get them.'

'Later, Rose,' said Phoebe. 'She don't take after me,' she added, in a smaller voice. 'Yeah, I wanted all the glamour, people lookin' at me and clappin', but I didn't 'ave no talent, not a stick of it. Took me years to admit it to meself.'

'But Phoebe, you enjoyed it, you were probably very good.'

'You never saw me, Rose.' Phoebe shook her elegantly-coiffed head. 'All I did was stand there, twitch me arse and show me drawers, get those poor buggers up on stage to take the shillin'. Rose, I could use a drop of brandy, if you got it.'

Jesse was delighted. 'You won't regret it,' he told Daisy, grinning.

'How do you know?'

'I feel it in my bones. You and I, we're heading for success.'

'I hope you're right.'

'Of course I am, my love, I'm always right.'

He'd bought himself new clothes, she noticed, probably in anticipation of the bonus Mr Curtis said he would be paying everybody with their final wages.

The houses hadn't been very good of late, but the manager was apparently confident he'd make a decent profit. So, he'd added graciously, it was only fair to share it with his dear hardworking boys and girls.

'Get yourself some decent clothes,' said Jesse, as he flicked some lint off his new jacket which Daisy noticed had the latest wide lapels.

'I'll wait until I get there,' Daisy told him. 'I'll have a lot more choice.'

'Go shopping in London often, do you?'

'No,' said Daisy. 'I've never shopped in London. But when we lived in India, my mother ordered clothes from shops in London, and they were always wonderful.'

'You're all excited, aren't you?'

'I must admit I am. But I'll miss the others,' added Daisy, thinking I'll especially miss Ewan, because from now on I won't be seeing much of him at all.

'Do you see much of 'im?' asked Phoebe, as she sat and smoked and drank her brandy, as she fiddled with her rings and teaspoon. Alex had gone to see a neighbouring farmer, the twins weren't back from school yet, so the women were alone. 'I mean, I thought you said 'e lived round 'ere? Or used to, anyway?'

'Oh, he's still in Charton. May I?' Rose took one of Phoebe's cigarettes. She lit it and inhaled, coughing because she wasn't used to it, but needing to do something with her hands. 'His father died a couple of years ago, so he's Sir Michael now. He lives about three miles away from here, at Easton Hall.'

'What about that other 'ouse?' Phoebe stuck the knife in deeper, twisting it round and round inside the wound. 'The place you showed me when I come down 'ere to visit you, after the war? Charton Minster, wasn't it?'

'My father wanted me to marry Mike. I married Alex, so

Daddy left the Minster and the whole estate to Michael.' Rose shrugged. 'He didn't want to live in it, of course, so now the Minster is a school for wayward children.'

'Your father never left you nothin'?' Phoebe looked aghast. 'Rose, for God's sake, how could he?'

'It was his house and his estate.'

'Oh, Rose!' wailed Phoebe. 'This stuff that's 'appened to you, it's all because of me!'

'Phoebe, it's nothing to do with you.' Rose stood up. 'Look at the time. I need to get the supper on.'

'I'll 'elp you, if you'll let me?' Phoebe shrugged off her coat. 'I could make a puddin', peel the spuds?'

'You'll stay with us? It's not at all luxurious, I'm afraid, not like your apartment in New York.'

'Oh, I been in worse,' said Phoebe. 'Actually, lookin' round, it ain't too bad at all. It's small, of course, but it's as smart as paint. It's cosy, and it's – '

'Mum?' Robert came bursting into the kitchen like a small tornado, closely followed by Stephen in a flurry of coats and boots and bags.

They were stricken speechless, something Rose had never thought to see, and for twenty seconds they simply goggled at the scented, gorgeous vision that was Phoebe Rosenheim.

'Hello,' managed Robert, who recovered first.

'Good afternoon,' said Stephen.

'Blimey, you never said you 'ad two boys!' Phoebe beamed at Rose's tousled sons. 'What 'andsome boys, as well! A regular pair of lookers! They'll break all the ladies' 'earts!' She turned to Rose. 'Takes after Alex, don't they?'

'Who's this lady, Mum?' asked Stephen.

'This is Mrs Rosenheim,' said Rose.

'I'm Phoebe, Daisy's mother.'

Ewan opened the big manila envelope postmarked Glasgow, and a pile of scripts fell out.

As he sifted through them, he saw they were exactly what he wanted – challenging roles in Shakespeare and interesting parts in modern drama. He couldn't have asked for more, and he blessed Amy Nightingale for suggesting he should try the Comrades.

He knew he was going to be tested, but he was confident he could do it, and this was his big chance.

He supposed he ought to do his packing. Listening to George and Frank, who were nattering away and sorting out their masses of belongings in the room they shared below, he realised he was lucky to be young and have his life before him.

The country must be full of middle-aged and elderly actors who had once dreamed of fame, and who had once been hopeful, but who had ended up in companies like this one, playing to provincials, trudging through tedious tripe like *Blighted Blossoms* night after weary night.

But it wouldn't be like that for him. He'd make his reputation on the stage, then he would go to Hollywood and get into the talkies.

As for Daisy – he wished more than anything that she was going with him up to Scotland. But it looked as if she'd made her choice.

He told himself it didn't matter, because he'd finished running after women, anyway. She'd asked him to write, and he supposed he might. Well, now and then.

'Why don't you write to Daisy?' Rose asked Phoebe.

Phoebe was still in Charton. Now she had settled down, and made herself at home in the best bedroom of the bailiff's cottage, to Rose's great surprise it looked as if she meant to stay.

'I'm scared,' said Phoebe. 'What if she don't want to know me, eh? What if I goes up to 'er, if I says, 'ello, darlin', I'm your mum, an' then she smacks me one across the gob?'

'She won't do that,' said Rose.

'Give me another day or two, an' then I'll make me mind up, yeah?' said Phoebe.

'No hurry,' Rose replied.

'You 'aven't told her that I'm 'ere, then?'

'No,' said Rose. 'It's not my news to tell, and anyway I wondered if you might not come to England, after all. Or, if you did, you might decide it would be better not to meet. I didn't want to raise her hopes, then see her disappointed.'

'Yeah, I suppose I ain't very reliable – or not where she's concerned, at any rate.' Phoebe looked enquiringly at Rose. 'You often go an' see 'er, do you? In them plays, I mean?'

'No, I've never seen her act in England. Since she went away on tour, Alex and I have had no time to spare. But I think – I hope – she understands.'

'When was she down 'ere last?'

'She had a break in January, she came to see us then, and that was lovely. I write once a week, and so we manage to keep in touch.' Rose shook her head. 'I must admit she's not a very regular correspondent, or not recently, in any case. Sometimes, weeks go by. But she's with the company, I know she's being properly chaperoned, so I try not to worry.'

'She takes after me then, don't she, Rose? I didn't take weeks to write, though, I took years. I'll make me mind up soon, I promise. You'll be wantin' to see the back of me.'

But Rose was in no hurry to see the back of Phoebe. Since Daisy had left home, she'd been so busy that she hadn't realised quite how lonely she'd become, and just how much she missed her friends.

Now she was back in Dorset, she'd lost touch with the other army wives. She hadn't time to write the long and newsy letters they demanded, and in any case she didn't have much to say that didn't turn on cows or hens. She didn't know about the latest fashions, who was seeing the Prince of Wales, if diamond clips were out or in.

The women of Rose's age who lived in Charton remembered her when she had been Miss Courtenay, the spoiled and cosseted daughter of the squire, whose parents had never let her mix with any local children. So, although the women were polite, there was too much history dividing them and Rose, and they could never be her friends.

She didn't wish she'd never met Alex, and she loved her boys. But she knew she must keep busy, must not think too much. Or the black dog of melancholy would get her, drag her down.

'I could get used to livin' in the country,' Phoebe said, as they stood together at the kitchen table one bright morning, mixing up a mash for Rose's hens. Rose was hoping that now the longer days were coming, the hens would start to lay again.

The twins thought Phoebe was amazing. She was from America, the land of jazz and honky-tonk, where anyone could become a millionaire. In fact, her Nathan, he'd started out with nothing, and these days he was practically a millionaire himself – so Phoebe said. She knew the latest songs, and sang them like a proper entertainer, doing all the actions, bumps and grinds.

When Rose explained to them that Phoebe was Daisy's

natural mother, but it had been wartime and she hadn't been able to look after a baby, the boys accepted everything, and didn't seem to think the worse of Phoebe.

'Well, Mum, Daze is very blonde, but you and Dad are dark,' said Robert, sagely. 'So Daisy's actual father was probably fair-haired.'

'Or a redhead,' added Stephen.

'It's sort of obvious that you and Dad – '

'Well, if you mate a dark one with another dark one – '

'If you take a white one and a black one – I'm talking about rabbits, Mum, don't look at me like that – you don't get many white ones in the litter,' went on Robert.

'Most of them are black or grey. It's like Rob and me, we're dark, so obviously we're yours. But it would be very strange if you and Dad had bred a Daisy.'

'Oh, I see,' said Rose, who'd never thought the rabbit farm would be so educational.

Daisy knew she ought to write to Rose and Alex to tell them she was going to London.

But she was aware there would be ructions, and so she put it off, and then she put it off again. They'd said she could go on tour with Mr and Mrs Curtis, not go gallivanting round the country in the company of a man they'd never met.

They'd both met Ewan, and they'd appeared to trust him. Perhaps they hadn't warmed to him, but at least they hadn't seemed to dislike him. They hadn't met Jesse, though, and Daisy would put money on Alex hating Jesse Trent on sight.

She'd write when she arrived, she thought, when she had an address, and preferably an acting job as well. Jesse seemed very confident they'd find work straight away.

She bought a picture postcard of Birmingham's town hall

and wrote a three line message, telling them the Midlands tour was going very well – she was getting lovely notices – and they still had a few more dates to go. She added she was happy and very busy, and would soon write again.

She stuck a stamp on and took the postcard to a letterbox. Now, she thought, the twins would have another card for their collection, and she'd have done her duty.

'They're lovely boys,' said Phoebe, as she watched the twins set off for school one sunny morning, running across the field like two young animals, pushing each other, trading punches, laughing, skipping, gambolling like lambs . 'You an' Alex, you must be very proud of them.'

'Of course,' said Rose and thought, I'm very lucky.

'I never 'ad another kid.' Now Rose saw Phoebe looked despondent, and there was tragedy in her big brown eyes. 'The doc says give it time, but I don't think it's goin' to 'appen.'

'It might,' said Rose, and felt how rich she was, in spite of living in what Phoebe called a slum and dressing like a charlady.

'Do you think I ought to go an' see Daisy?'

'Yes, I suppose I do,' said Rose. 'Well, you can't come all this way and not meet Daisy, can you?'

'When I was in the States, it all seemed simple. She was 'ere, an' I was there, an' all I 'ad to do was book my passage. But now I'm actually in England, it don't seem so obvious what to do.'

'It must be your decision.' Rose picked up a bag of kitchen scraps to add them to the chicken bin. Nothing was wasted in the bailiff's cottage, and when she thought about her privileged childhood at the Minster, she was appalled by how much waste there'd been. 'I'm sure she'd like to meet you. She's in Birmingham at the moment. I've got the tour dates somewhere, so I'll go and look them up. Phoebe, why don't you go and see her there?'

'You'll come with me, Rose?'

'I can't, I've far too much to do in Charton. Anyway, I think you should go and see her by yourself.'

'I'll sleep on it,' said Phoebe. She bit her lower lip. 'I'll let you know. Look, 'ere's your mailman.'

'Good morning, Mrs Denham – a lovely one, as well.' The postman handed Rose her letters. 'You've got a postcard from Miss Denham.'

'Thank you, Mr Lock.' Rose read it quickly, and then passed it to Phoebe. 'There,' she said, as the postman walked off down the road. 'Your daughter's still in Birmingham. I think you ought to pack a case, don't you?'

Chapter Twelve

The tour wound up on Friday evening, with a barely half capacity house in one of Birmingham's seediest, dirtiest theatres.

But Mr and Mrs Curtis didn't complain about the miserable takings. In fact, they seemed very pleased with the way that everything had gone, praising all the actors to the skies, and congratulating them on having had a splendid season. All things considered, this tour was a success.

After the show, they told the actors they'd see them in the local, where it would be drinks all round, all night. Or until closing time, at any rate.

'Mrs C and I, we're going to take a little break,' said Mr Curtis, leaning on the beer-swilled counter, monocle jammed into place, and offering the barman three more one pound notes. 'We want to visit our daughter down in Reading. Maudie's not been well just recently. Some sort of women's trouble, I believe. We'll be doing our summer shows and concerts, obviously, but we won't be putting together another tour like this one until autumn.'

'If we do it at all,' said Mrs Curtis, leaning against her husband and wheezing like a pair of rotten bellows. 'It's getting hard on the old bones.'

Then she squashed the bones and all the rest of her vast velvet bulk into a seat by Daisy. 'We might retire,' she added, as she picked up her glass of port and lemon. 'Alfred and I, we've saved a little bit. I tell you, girls and boys, the thought of a country cottage somewhere on the Berkshire Downs is quite appealing.'

'Drink up, fellow acolytes of Thespis,' Mr Curtis urged, as the white-aproned waiter set down a loaded tray. 'Mr Fraser, you don't look too happy. I'd have thought you would be looking forward to having Romeo in your sights at last?'

'Come round to our digs and get your money, let's say about ten o'clock tomorrow morning,' Mrs Curtis told them, as the pub was putting up its shutters, and everyone was saying their affectionate goodnights. 'Alfred will have sorted things out with the theatre management by nine, and I'll have finished doing all my sums.'

Frank and George began a rousing chorus of *for they are jolly good fellows*, the rest of the company joined in, and Mr and Mrs Curtis blushed and grinned.

'You look tired, Daisy May,' said Amy, who Daisy couldn't help but notice was arm in arm with Ewan as they made their way towards the trolley stop.

'I'm fine,' said Daisy. She glanced at Ewan, who was whispering to Amy now. She wished he wouldn't be like this. After all, they wouldn't be seeing each other for a while, and didn't he realise she would miss him?

Oh, let him sulk, she thought, as Jesse came up on her other side and hugged her round the neck. Let him mutter to Amy if he wants. I don't care anyway.

'Pay day, children,' Frank said happily.

It was half past nine the following morning. The actors were congregating at the stop to get the trolley into the smarter part of town where Mr and Mrs Curtis had their digs.

'I reckon Alfred sounded as if we've done all right,' said

Jesse, grinning.

'So there should be good bonuses all round,' George rubbed his small, plump hands. 'Julia, where's Amy?'

'She's just gone up the road to get her cleaning. She'll be here in a minute,' Julia told him. 'Look, she's coming now. What's the hurry, boys – need to see a man about a dog?'

'We need to catch a train. We're going to have a few days down in Devon, where we can go sketching and have picnics on the beach. What about you ladies?'

'We're here in Birmingham till Sunday,' Julia told him. 'Then I don't know where we'll be going.'

'I need to get my roots retouched, so that's what I'll be doing this afternoon. I think I'll have a manicure as well,' said Amy, looking critically at her nails.

'Maybe I'll go to Rackham's and try on all the expensive modes.' Julia grinned at George. 'Darling, don't look at me like that, I won't pinch anything. I might even buy a frock or two, if they're in the sale or going cheap.'

'Remember you haven't got a job, my dear, so don't go raving mad.' Amy dumped her parcel of dry cleaning on the pavement and lit a cigarette.

'But I'll be making an investment.' Getting out her compact, Julia started touching up her mouth. 'If I get all dolled up to the nines, and then sit in a cocktail bar and flash me pins about, I'll pick up a gentleman who'll soon see me right. Daisy, where's your boyfriend? He's going to miss the bus.'

'He's on his way, I'm sure,' said Daisy, and turned to see Ewan coming round the corner with his case.

When the bus pulled up, Jesse pushed past Ewan, took Daisy's hand and dragged her up the stairs. Sitting down beside her, he laid his arm across the back of the seat and started playing with her hair.

'What are those marks around your wrist?' asked Julia, who was sitting behind them.

'Yes, they look rather nasty, you ought to put some Germolene on them,' said Amy, sniggering.

'Oh, but they're old wounds,' said Daisy, turning round to frown at Amy, who was never very sympathetic at the best of times. 'His father used to tie him up and beat him.'

'He must have been some bastard of a father. They look more like S and M to me,' muttered Amy, grinning. 'Well, Jesse Trent? Did you really have a frightful father who should have been had up before the beak for cruelty to children? Or are you a pervert?'

'Shut up, Amy,' muttered Jesse, as he fumbled for a cigarette.

Across the aisle, Ewan glanced up, caught Daisy's eye, but then he looked away again, and carried on reading from a script.

'Well, darlings, this must be the place.' Amy led them up the neat and tidy garden path, and then she rang the bell.

'Come on,' said Julia. 'I haven't time to hang around all day, looking at the flipping scenery. I've got to find myself another job. Mr Curtis, if you please,' she said, when the front door was opened.

'He's gone, love,' said the middle-aged woman in a floral apron, folding her arms beneath her bosom and scowling at them all.

'We'll see Mrs Curtis, then,' said Amy, stubbing out her cigarette and dropping the butt end on the clean-swept path.

'They've both cleared off. They left before anyone else was up this morning. If you ask me, they've done a runner.'

The woman glared at Amy. 'You pick that fag end up, you mucky trollop. I don't keep a doss house.'

'But how will we get our money?' Frank demanded.

'How will I get mine?' The landlady began to close the door. 'Theatricals,' she muttered. 'I've had it up to here with them. Professional gentlemen, they're all I'm taking now. They smuggle floozies in, they leave the toilets looking quite disgusting, they drop their fag ash everywhere, but they pay their way.'

The door slammed shut.

'The thieving, rotten bastards!' Julia exclaimed, as they all stood on the steps, shocked and disbelieving. The woman was at the window now, glaring at them and willing them to go away. 'I bet you they've been planning this for months.'

'Where does this daughter live?' asked George. 'Does anybody know her married name?'

'Oh, for God's sake, idiot,' said Amy. 'They haven't got a daughter. They weren't even married. Dolly Curtis is a bloke, as you'd all have realised if you'd ever listened to her language. Ladies don't say khazi, that's old army slang.'

'But Mrs Curtis, she can't be a man. She had – '

'Great saggin' whatsitsnames?' Julia shook her head at George. 'I saw her in the buff once, an' a horrid sight it was, the flab all hanging everywhere, but she had a little pecker, too. Ewan, love, you got the money for your fare to Glasgow?'

'No,' said Ewan. 'I was banking on a bonus.'

'You'll just have to get on to the train, and then stay in the lavatory, pretending to be ill,' suggested Amy. 'That's what Julia and I do when we're short of funds. When are they expecting you in Glasgow?'

'I told them I'd be there later today.'

'You'd better get your skates on then, my darling.' Julia led the company down the path. 'Come on, girls and boys. Let's go and see this highland laddie off to bonny Scotland.'

'Ewan,' said Daisy quietly, 'I'll lend you the money for your fare.'

'You keep your money,' muttered Ewan. 'You'll need it if you're going to London with that bastard Trent. I'll bet he has expensive habits.'

'Ewan, please don't be like this!' cried Daisy. 'The Comrades, isn't it? I'll write to you next week.'

'As you wish,' said Ewan, and then he strode off down the road, leaving the others standing in a huddle at the gate.

Amy went running after him. 'Ewan, I can spare a couple of quid,' she told him, panting. 'A fiver, even, if you need it.'

'Amy, you're very kind, but I'll be fine.'

'You could still get her back, you know.'

'I doubt it.' Ewan shook his head. 'She wants to go with Trent.'

'She's such a fool.' Amy sighed. 'Well, maybe one day, eh? When she sees the error of her ways? My darling, when you're in the talkies, send me tickets for your premières?'

'Of course I shall.' Ewan leaned towards her and kissed her on her rouged and powdered cheek. 'Thanks for everything,' he added. He watched her walk back to the others, then went to catch his train.

Julia had gone to hang around in one of the big hotels, hoping to find a salesman who would buy her a few drinks. But Amy had nothing else to do until the afternoon, and so she went with Daisy and Jesse to the railway station.

All three of them stood on the platform, waiting for the

Euston train. 'You watch your step, my girl,' said Amy sternly. 'You keep your eye on him.'

'What do you think I'm going to do?' asked Jesse, slapping at his pockets. 'Damn, I'm out of fags. Amy, love, I don't suppose – '

'No, I flipping couldn't, so you'd better go and buy some,' Amy told him sharply. 'Go on then, shoo! You've only got five minutes.'

As Jesse went hurrying off to find a kiosk, Amy looked hard at Daisy. 'It's not too late,' she said.

'It's not too late for what?'

'Julia and I are going to try to get a summer season. There's always something, end of the pier shows if we're really desperate, pierrettes and blackface, all that sort of thing. Girls are always pulling out because they're getting married or they're up the duff or something, so we'll soon be suited. Come with us, why don't you? We could do a sister act. They always come in threes.'

'I want to go to London.'

'You're besotted, aren't you, Daisy May? Well, when you get sick of Mr Trent, or he gets sick of you, or you get stuck, you write to me, care of my brother in Carlisle. He'll send a letter on.'

Amy tore a page out of a notebook, scribbled something down and stuffed it into Daisy's hand. 'Just don't believe a word he says, all right? I've met his sort before, all mouth and Brylcreem, hard luck stories by the score. All that stuff about his father beating him is rot, believe you me.'

'But he has the marks, so why do you say – '

'Daisy, you've been with us for a season. You're nothing like as ignorant and innocent as when we met you first. But you must stop believing the best of everyone, especially of men.'

'I don't believe the best of everyone,' said Daisy, thinking *if you only knew*.

'No?' said Amy. 'You had Alfred's number from the start? Just remember, sweetheart, make people earn your trust, don't hand it over like a Christmas present, and don't believe the best of Jesse Trent.'

'What's going on then, still discussing me?' said Jesse, coming up behind them and lighting a cigarette.

'Listen, Mr Smartarse, look after this little girl, all right? I've got a couple of brothers. You know what I'm saying?'

'I'll look after Daisy,' promised Jesse. 'I'll defend her with my life.'

'I hope for Daisy's sake it never comes to that, because I'd put my money on you scarpering, not staying around to fight.' Amy put down the parcel of cleaning which she'd lugged round Birmingham all morning and untied the string. 'Here, Daisy May, this is for you,' she said.

'What is it?'

'What does it look like?' Amy shoved the skirt and jacket of her best tweed suit at Daisy's chest. 'Go on, take it! You haven't got any grown-up clothes. You look about eleven in that coat. If a copper notices you getting on the London train together, Mr Smartarse here will be had up for kidnapping a child.'

'But Amy, you can't give this to me.'

'Yes, I can,' said Amy. 'It doesn't fit me any more. I'm getting fat. I can't do up the buttons on the skirt.'

The Euston train came roaring in, throwing out sparks and belching great white clouds of smoke and steam. Amy darted forward, kissed Daisy on the cheek, and then she glared at Jesse. 'Look after Daisy, Mr Smartarse Pervert,' she said threateningly. 'You never know who might be watching you.'

Ewan got off the train at Glasgow Central, hoping nobody was watching him.

He'd spent the journey avoiding guards and ticket inspectors, who had seemed to be everywhere on the train, and now he had to jump the final hurdle. Or get through the barrier, anyway.

Just walk through it, he told himself. Look preoccupied and in a hurry, then hopefully you won't be stopped.

He waited for a surge of passengers, then put his head down and charged through, and made it to the other side.

Where should he go now? Straight to the theatre, he supposed, to see the manager, get a list of lodgings, and ask for an advance against his salary?

That would make him popular, he reflected, get the whole engagement off to a cracking start. Or maybe he would go and have some dinner – he was starving.

As he stood on the station forecourt trying to decide what he should do, a fashionably-dressed but overweight old woman stabbed his ankle with her walking stick and then glared up at him, apparently offended he'd dared be in her way.

God, he thought, as he began to walk towards the buffet, thinking he might go mad and spend a shilling or one and sixpence on a cup of coffee and a sandwich, I've had enough of women.

'Excuse me, could you wait a moment?'

A small, dark girl in an unflattering black overcoat and pale grey Tam o'Shanter that looked like her school beret came hurrying towards him. 'I've come to meet a Mr Ewan

Fraser off the train from Birmingham,' she continued, breathlessly. 'I've asked a dozen people, but I'm thinking we must have missed each other – unless you would happen to be him?'

'Yes, I'm Ewan Fraser,' he replied.

'I'm Sadie Lawrence,' said the girl. 'I'm at the Comrades, but I'm not on stage this evening. I hope you've had a pleasant journey north?'

'I couldn't wait for it to end,' said Ewan. 'Do you have some digs arranged for me? Or do I find my own?'

'They're all arranged,' said Sadie. 'We're meeting Mungo and the others in the Thistle later, and I'm sure you're going to get on famously with them. So now, how would you like – '

'I'd like something to eat.' Ewan picked up his case and started walking.

'I say, wait a minute,' cried the girl, and scurried after him.

Chapter Thirteen

Phoebe stood in front of the theatre, trying to screw her failing courage to the sticking point.

She looked the building up and down. God, it was a horrible, tawdry place, far worse than the Haggerston Palace music hall in the East End of London, where she'd been in variety, and which she'd always thought must be the dump to end all dumps. She'd never have thought a child of hers would sink as low as this.

It was a drizzly afternoon, the sort of day that never got really light, and there was nobody about. But places like this were never open all the time, she thought, they wouldn't have had daily matinees even in the war years when people were desperate for entertainment, when they didn't begrudge a bob or two to take their minds off all the awful things that were happening in France and Flanders.

But even if there wasn't a performance going on, there must be somebody about, she reasoned, painting scenery or checking lights.

She tried the double doors and found them locked. She went round to the side and picked her way along a dirty alley strewn with litter. She found the stage door, which was also locked, but noticed a little ginger ferret of a man, snoozing at a window which opened on a stairwell.

'I can't do nothin' for you, ma'am,' he said, when she eventually roused him. 'They done their last show 'ere on Friday, an' that was the end of their engagements 'ere in Brum. No, I dunno where they've gone. But I tell can you now, my love, you ain't missed anything.'

'You must know where they stayed?' insisted Phoebe. 'They'll 'ave given their landladies their forwardin' addresses, for their post an' stuff.' She squared her shoulders. She hadn't come so far and taken so much trouble to give up now. 'Where are the theatrical digs round 'ere? You got a list?'

The doorman scratched his head. He didn't know what to do. The only folk who asked him for that sort of list were debt collectors, tradesmen chasing actors who had run up bills, then done a bunk.

But this pretty woman in her expensive coat, and what he would have sworn were real silk stockings, couldn't be a debt collector. She was too well-dressed. She wore a proper whizz-bang of a hat, all feathers, lace and velvet, the sort of hat you never saw in Brum, or not in this part of the city, anyway.

Now she was rummaging in her crocodile-skin handbag and getting out her purse, and in her purse he could see rolls of banknotes. 'I think we got a list somewhere,' he said.

'Well then, my good man, I'd be very obliged if I could see it,' Phoebe told him, smiling. She offered him a couple of crackling green pound notes.

Euston was dark and gloomy, suiting Daisy's gloomy mood. She didn't know why she felt so low – wasn't she setting off on an adventure, wasn't she going to be in a revue?

Maybe, but maybe not. There must be a thousand other girls as pretty and as talented, who could sing and dance as well as she could, even better, probably.

She'd walked into the job with Mr and Mrs Curtis, but it had been a fluke, she saw that now. She'd had some small success in little places in the provinces, and this had turned her head, and made her think she could do anything.

Now she was fast realising that London would not, could not be the same as Walsall, Doncaster or Wolverhampton. Jesse's faith and optimism had blinded her with dreams of spurious glory, and she'd got carried away.

While they were on the train, Jesse had talked her into a splitting headache, regaling her with stories of all his past successes, and bragging about the star he meant to be, either on the stage or in the talkies.

'Yes,' he'd continued, dropping cigarette ash on her knees, 'talkies are definitely the coming thing. I think I'd be brilliant in talkies. I'll have to see if I can get a screen test. My profile's perfect, and my teeth are excellent, so close-ups wouldn't be a problem. I could do modern or historical drama, comedy or serious stuff, no question. I could get good parts.'

He'd leaned towards her, dark eyes shining. 'Daisy, I have plans.'

He didn't have any money, though. He'd spent his last two shillings in the buffet car on beer.

Since Daisy didn't smoke and didn't drink, she was quite well off, and even though she hadn't received her last week's wages or her bonus, she had saved five pounds.

But she knew London was expensive, and she wasn't banking on five pounds getting them far. Ewan had refused to take her cash, and on reflection it was just as well.

They climbed down from the train.

'I wonder where the Curtises are now?' said Jesse, as he hailed a porter.

'Somewhere very uncomfortable, I hope.' Daisy told the porter they would carry their own cases, thank you very much. She didn't have sixpences to waste on porters.

'How could they?' she demanded, as they made their way across the concourse. 'I thought they were our friends. We worked so hard for them.'

'Oh, these touring managers, they're all the same,' said Jesse. 'The Curtises won't be the first or last to run off with the cash.'

'You mean it happens often?'

'Yes, of course, and in these dismal days it's going to happen more and more.' Jesse put his arm round Daisy's shoulders. 'Come on, blossom, let's look on the bright side. You're in the capital of the British Empire with a handsome man.'

'I have no job,' said Daisy, 'and I don't have anywhere to stay.'

'We'll soon sort something out, don't worry.' Jesse grinned. 'Let's go and treat ourselves to pie and chips, and then we'll find a mission.'

'A mission?' Daisy frowned at him. 'We had those in India. They were where beggars went to get deloused, to beg some rice or leave their grandmothers to die.'

'Well, we're beggars, aren't we? Actors are traditionally beggars, rogues and vagabonds. Anyway, coming back to missions, there's a place in Edgware Road, and it's run by Church of England nuns. It's just for women, so it shouldn't be too squalid.'

'I'm not going there.'

'Just for tonight, my darling,' wheedled Jesse, 'and tomorrow we'll get things sorted out. But don't tell them at the mission you're an actress, or they'll think you mean you're on the game, and throw you out.'

'What should I tell them, then?'

'You'd need to say you've just come down from Dorset,

that you're looking for domestic work, that you don't have anywhere to stay, and a kind policeman told you to ring their bell.'

'What will you do?'

'Oh, don't you worry about me!' Jesse grinned and winked. 'I'll find a corner somewhere. Listen, they'll chuck you out at eight o'clock tomorrow morning, tell you to go to church or look for work, even though it's Sunday. Whatever you do, don't let them keep your luggage, even if they offer. You'll never get it back.'

'Jesse, I've decided I won't go to a mission.'

'Oh, Daisy darling, please don't be so awkward!' Jesse stopped and took her by the shoulders, gazing deep into her eyes. 'It's only for tonight. I'll meet you at the Lyon's Corner House, Trafalgar Square, at nine or half past nine tomorrow morning.'

'You promise?'

'Yes, I promise.' Jesse let her go. 'I don't like to ask, but could you let me have a bob or two?'

'I suppose so.'

'Thank you, love. I'll pay you back.'

'You'd better,' Daisy told him. 'Let's go and have a meal. I'm starving.'

They found a dingy café near the station, shared a meal of pie and chips, then went to find the mission.

'Actually, I've no' had my supper,' Sadie Lawrence told Ewan as they walked into the buffet.

'What would you like?' asked Ewan as a reflex, then cursed himself for being a courteous, nicely brought up boy. He felt the last few shillings in his pocket melt away.

'A plate of stovies would be grand,' said Sadie.

'You'll have oatcakes, too?'

'Of course.' Sadie took out a little leather purse and gave him a half crown. 'I'll treat you, Mr Fraser,' she said kindly. 'You can treat me back when you get paid.'

'Thank you, that's very nice of you,' said Ewan, pleasantly surprised.

'My pleasure,' Sadie said, and smiled.

'Who is in the company?' asked Ewan, as they waited for their plates of stovies and he thought that maybe Sadie Lawrence was quite attractive, in an impish sort of way.

'Well, it's just the five of us – you and me and Mungo, and a couple of other fellows. I'm the only lassie, owing to the lack of female roles.'

'I'd have thought there would be roles for lassies in experimental drama?'

'You'd be very much mistaken, Mr Fraser.' Sadie Lawrence grimaced. 'Modern drama is full of roles for men. I'm often called upon to play a boy. When we do Shakespeare, female students from the drama school are sometimes drafted in to help us out.'

'Do you do a lot of Shakespeare?'

'Yes, indeed we do,' said Sadie Lawrence. 'Somehow, Mr Fraser, the company has to pay its way, and even make a profit, and this means getting audiences in. The honest burghers out in Partick will come and see *Twelfth Night* or *Julius Caesar*, but they're no' so keen to spend their hard-earned bawbees on a piece from Soviet Russia.'

'You don't have to call me Mr Fraser all the time,' said Ewan, starting on his stovies.

'Very well, then – Ewan.' Sadie Lawrence bit into an oatcake and then she smiled flirtatiously at him. 'I'm sure you're going to fit in with the Comrades.'

'You said I would be staying with – Mungo, is it?' Ewan mopped up his gravy with some oatcake, and realised he was starting to feel better. As Mrs Morrison had always said, a stomach full of stovies was a sovereign cure for any ill. 'Where would that be, in a boarding house?'

'Oh, no,' said Sadie. 'It's much better than a boarding house. You just wait and see.'

Jesse and Daisy turned down Baker Street, then into George Street, and finally came out on Edgware Road.

'This is it,' said Jesse, stopping beside a tall, gaunt, soot-stained building. 'Go on then, ring the bell. I'll see you in the morning.'

He kissed her briefly on the cheek, then strode off down the Edgware Road, leaving Daisy wondering if she'd ever set eyes on him again.

Since she didn't know where she was in London, or where else to go, she felt she had no option but to ring the mission bell.

'What do you think?' asked Sadie, beaming.

'It's amazing.' Ewan stared round the loft space, letting his eyes adjust to the dim light. The empty Glasgow warehouse was almost derelict on the outside, but it was much improved within.

Sadie and the others had taken over the top storey. They had a stove and pots and pans and kindling, half a dozen kitchen chairs and a big kitchen table. Mattresses and bedding were spread across the floor.

'Those are yours,' said Sadie, pointing to a mattress and a pile of army blankets. 'Make yourself at home.'

'What does the owner think about you living here?' asked

Ewan.

'He's on the run from creditors,' said Sadie. 'It was in all the papers. He's not been seen since last November. We moved in here a month ago, and now we have a commune.

'We're Communists,' she added. 'We don't recognise the right of any individual to say, this place is mine. When the revolution comes, everything belonging to the people will be held in common. Listen, Ewan, property is theft, don't you agree?'

Daisy pressed the bell again, rather harder this time. She waited fifteen, twenty minutes until a black-robed, stern-faced nun finally came and opened the front door.

'A policeman sent me here,' said Daisy, wondering what the everlasting punishment for lying to nuns might be. Then she told her story in her best Dorset accent, and to her relief the nun decided to let her in.

'You're in luck,' she said, as she led Daisy up a flight of bare stone stairs, her robes swishing behind her on the treads. 'The casual ward has only one bed left. Otherwise, we'd have had to send you to the Salvation Army hostel, that's in the Marylebone Road, and a little country girl like you would have found the hostel very rough.'

Daisy looked around and wondered how much rougher the Salvation Army place could be.

'This is where you leave your case,' the nun said, pointing to a padlocked cage. 'I'll go and get you a ticket.'

'But I'll need my case,' objected Daisy, clutching it.

'Quite, so you can have it back tomorrow.' The nun looked Daisy up and down. 'You're not in Dorset any more, my dear. This is the big, bad city. It's full of wicked people who would cut your throat for half a crown. If you take your case up to the ward, it will be empty in the morning. Just take out your washing things tonight.'

Daisy did as she was told, sneaking out her purse as well and slipping it in her pocket.

She'd thought she was used to slums and ruins, but this was something else. The mission was a musty, fusty building that had water running down its pea-green painted walls. It smelled of cabbage soup and laundry, and there was an almost overpowering stink of gas.

She thought she could hear reedy, plaintive crying. Or perhaps it was a cat? Did nuns keep pets?

'Be very quiet now,' said the nun, as they climbed and climbed, passing bare stone landings which led to double doors. 'Try not to let your heels click on the stairs, or else you'll wake the babies.'

'Babies?' whispered Daisy.

'The babies and their mothers, poor foolish girls who let men take advantage,' said the nun, severely.

The ward to which the nun took Daisy was high up in the roof. It was unfurnished except for rows and rows of iron beds, on which a strange assortment of women, girls and hunched-up bundles snored or lay like corpses.

Daisy used the cold, echoing washroom, then lay down fully clothed upon the bed. She pulled a hairy blanket over her, trying not to notice that it smelled of sweat.

But although she didn't think she'd sleep, she closed her eyes. When she opened them again, the morning light was streaming through the windows, brightly illuminating all the squalor. She could hear London pigeons courting, chittering and squabbling on the roof.

'Get up,' said a dark-haired, dough-faced girl, who was sitting down on the next bed, and pinning up her hair. 'You'll miss your breakfast, else.'

'They give us breakfast?'

'Yes, of course they do, if you tells 'em you ain't got no money.' The girl grinned slyly. 'Sister Mary Agnes always noses through the stuff they got locked in the cage. So I 'ope you 'ad the sense to stick yer lolly down yer drawers?'

Breakfast turned out to be a bowl of lukewarm, stiff, grey porridge, full of hairy lumps and gluey globules. 'That's the snot the nuns put into it, to mortify our flesh,' observed the dough-faced girl.

But Daisy was very hungry, so she choked the porridge down.

'Good luck, my child,' said the middle-aged sister who reunited Daisy with her case, and who made Daisy think of Mrs Hobson back in Dorset. 'Before you go, tell me, my dear – why did you come to London?'

'To look for live-in work,' said Daisy.

'If you don't find any, what will you do then?'

'I've got the addresses of all the domestic agencies, and so I hope I will,' said Daisy, edging towards the stairs.

'You'll need some bus fares,' said the nun. 'Do you have any money?'

'I've got a little, thank you, sister.' Daisy thought, I won't accept more charity, even if it's offered. I feel enough of a fraud already.

'Then please leave your offering in the box,' the nun said, nodding towards a crucifix on the wall which Daisy hadn't previously noticed. On a shelf beneath the crucifix was a wooden box which had a slit in it.

'Yes, of course. I'm sorry.' Daisy found her purse, and then in her confusion she slipped in half a crown, which she could certainly not afford.

'It's usual to kneel and say a prayer,' went on the nun, pointing towards a threadbare velvet cushion on the floor. 'If you're any sort of Christian, even a Presbyterian or Methodist, you should know to bow before Our Lord.'

'You survived, then,' Jesse said, and grinned.

'Yes, just about.'

Daisy thought the smell of coffee was the scent of heaven. 'What about you, where did you spend the night?'

'Oh, I found a bar, got into conversation with a bloke, and he bought me some drinks. Then, after chucking out time, I walked the streets until the cafés opened in the early hours.' Jesse yawned. 'If I have another cup of coffee, I'll be all right.'

'Thank you for looking after me,' said Daisy, who had almost cried with relief to see him sitting there.

'It's my pleasure.' Jesse smiled a tired smile. 'The mission, was it all right?'

'It was a roof over my head.'

'I've heard it's grim,' said Jesse. 'I'm sorry it couldn't be the Savoy.'

He took the previous evening's paper from his pocket. 'I forgot to say, I hope you didn't tell them you had any money? They'd have tried to get you to make a contribution to their funds. So now we have to find a room to let.'

'Two rooms, Jesse.'

'One room will be cheaper.'

'I can't share a room with you.'

'We'll see,' said Jesse, opening the paper at the pages featuring rooms to let. 'A common lodging house, I think. Somewhere south of the river will be much better value.'

'What about theatrical digs?'

'You're joking.' Jesse laughed, but mirthlessly. 'We can't afford theatrical digs in London.'

They walked all day, looking at dingy lodging houses, dirty tenements and filthy basements.

Finally, they found a place in Clapham, two so-called furnished attic rooms in a crumbling fire trap that smelled of cats and sewage, for which they had to pay a deposit of two pounds to a woman living in the basement.

'So now we're really on our uppers,' said Jesse, who'd kept up his muttering about one room being better, cheaper and more sensible most of the day.

'Let's go and have some supper,' Daisy said, to shut him up – he couldn't talk and eat at the same time. 'I saw a fish and chip shop on the corner.'

As they walked back home again, Jesse put his arm round Daisy's shoulders and hummed some catchy little tunes she didn't recognise. They cheered her up but also made her feel rather melancholy, too.

She was very tired, she was lonely, and she couldn't help but feel how lovely it would be to stay with Jesse Trent tonight.

But that was how so many girls got caught. She didn't want to end up like her missing mother, having a baby in some place for girls who had no sense and let men take advantage, as the nun had put it, and having to hand her child over to a married stranger.

Or, which was even worse, having to hurt herself with knitting needles, and then dispose of blood-soaked parcels.

They let themselves into the gloomy hallway. 'Goodnight,' she said to Jesse, as they reached their attic rooms. 'You must be really tired.'

'I'm not too tired.' Jesse bent to kiss her on the forehead. 'Come in for minute?'

'I don't think I should.'

'Daisy, don't make me beg you.'

'I'm sorry, but I can't.'

'You do look all in.' Jesse sighed and yawned and stretched exaggeratedly. 'So go and get your beauty sleep. You most probably need it, and I sure as hell need mine.'

But Daisy couldn't sleep. She locked her door, then took some paper from her case and wrote to Ewan. As she wrote, she felt how much she missed him, missed knowing he was always there, and always looking out for her, and always on her side.

At first, she wrote a lot of nonsense, about how she and Jesse had found some decent digs, and how they were going to see some agents, how they were sure they'd get themselves fixed up with something soon.

But then, as tears blurred her vision, and the asthmatic clicking of the meter warned her the electricity would soon be running out, and she knew she didn't have a sixpence, she added, *I'm missing you already, and I wish you could be here.*

She wound the golden chain he'd given her round and round her fingers, held it tight, and thought of him. Then she took it off and slipped it down between the lining and the casing of her leather handbag, hiding it from Jesse Trent.

Ewan's Sunday had gone very well.

Mungo Campbell and the other actors said they'd been afraid the manager would engage some feeble English bastard. So they were delighted to find that Ewan was a fellow Scot.

He'd been to Glasgow only once or twice before, just passing through, so being shown around the city by Sadie and the others was a revelation.

Mrs Fraser had always hated Glasgow. She said it was an awful, common place, and full of awful, common people. But Ewan soon decided that he loved it – loved its buzz and huge vitality, loved the wonderful, exuberant Victorian architecture which was so very different from the muted elegance of Edinburgh's pretty Charlotte Square. If Edinburgh was a quiet, decorous maiden lady, Glasgow was a lively girl who liked to have some fun.

Daisy would have loved it too, he thought. But where was Daisy now? He hoped she was all right, that the bastard Trent was looking after her, and she'd do well in London.

Chapter Fourteen

When the electricity ran out, Daisy had gone to bed. But she couldn't sleep. She tossed and turned and fidgeted, unable to get comfortable on the flock-filled mattress which was full of lumps and bumps.

All night long, cockroaches and big black beetles ran across the cracked linoleum, while other, larger creatures rustled and scrabbled beneath the floorboards, and in the roof space high above her head.

She'd grown up in India, so she was used to birds and rats and insects coming uninvited into people's homes, and she didn't mind them. But the antics of their British counterparts still kept her awake.

The actual bed was full of wildlife, too. She woke up from a fitful doze to find that she was being bitten to bits, and in the morning her skin was blotchy, red and itching. I must try not to scratch the bites, she thought, I don't want them to get infected.

When she met Jesse on the landing, it was obvious he hadn't slept. 'I'm going to have a shave,' he said, dipping a chipped enamel mug into the bucket of cold water which someone had brought up and left for them.

They had mentioned washing, and the landlady had told them there would be arrangements. It seemed as if the half full bucket was what she had arranged.

'You could try and do something with your hair,' said Jesse, as turned to go back to his room. 'You should wash your fringe, at any rate. It's looking very greasy.'

'Yes, I know,' said Daisy, and wished he hadn't noticed.

Men weren't supposed to notice things like that, or not to comment, anyway.

They'd spent most of Sunday wandering round, hunting for digs and gazing wistfully at all the West End theatres. While they snacked off food from vendors' stalls, they saw their own names up in lights, and imagined dining at the Ritz or Café Royal.

But now, on Monday morning, after sharing bacon and fried eggs in a somewhat seedy workmen's café, they walked to the West End again, where they bought a copy of *The Stage*.

Then they spent all morning in two adjacent telephone kiosks making calls to agents, getting nowhere. Every part was filled, and every agent's books were closed. Nobody was interested in their great reviews in Stoke-on-Trent, or their notices in Macclesfield. They were just two more provincial players, come to London to join thousands who were also unemployed.

In the afternoon, they traipsed round Soho, where management after management refused point blank to see them. Secretaries shooed them out of offices already full of hopefuls lounging against discoloured walls or sitting on hard chairs.

One or two agents had a list on which they were told they could leave names and details, so they did, but without much hope of being called.

They didn't have a telephone, anyway.

Soon their feet were blistered, and by nightfall they were cold and starving. Daisy still had some money left over, but they knew they should try not to use that, at least not yet. After rummaging in all their pockets, they scraped together one and fivepence. As they made their way back home, they noticed girls of Daisy's age or younger, loitering in shop doorways, grinning desperately at passing men.

By Friday, they'd run out of faith, of optimism, and almost out of Daisy's money. 'We'll have to get non-acting jobs,' said Jesse, as they shared a fourpenny bag of chips, warming their hands by cupping them around the greasy paper.

'But if we get jobs,' objected Daisy, 'what do we do when agents find us something? What about auditions, if we're working?'

'We fit our work around auditions, obviously.'

'What work do you suggest?' Daisy rubbed some flea bites on her arm, desperate to have a good old scratch. 'If there were any jobs, there wouldn't be three million unemployed.'

'We've each got a suitcase, we have a pound or two to buy some stock. We sell things door to door.'

'You mean we go to Woolworths, buy dishcloths, towels and brushes, and try to sell them at a profit?'

'We go to market stalls, love, they'll be cheaper.' Jesse grinned. 'We fill our cases, and we put on a show.'

'Splendid, everyone,' said Dennis Foster. 'I think we've got a show. Mr Fraser, you're doing very well.'

That's a relief, thought Ewan, who wasn't sure about the play itself. It seemed to consist mainly of ranting about the appalling living conditions of the working classes, and prophesying bloody revolution.

But, since he was a natural mimic, reproducing the guttural accent of the Clydeside shipyards didn't present a problem. He just hoped Mungo, Sadie and the other Comrades wouldn't probe too deeply into his own origins, and say he was a fraud.

He didn't want to be a fraud.

'Right, *Antony and Cleopatra* now.' Dennis Foster, the manager and producer at the Comrades, looked at Ewan. 'Mr Fraser,' he went on, 'you can have a crack at Antony.'

Since Antony was an officer in the army, like his father, this was a role which Ewan was proud to play.

Mungo was to be Octavius Caesar, and Sadie played Cleopatra, in a hideous black wig. 'You're very good,' she said to Ewan, after the first rehearsal, whipping off the wig and tossing it back into the property basket.

Mungo had cleared off already. He was probably desperate for a pint. But, still in character – or so it seemed – Sadie was apparently disposed to hang around.

Now she smiled seductively at Ewan. Gazing up at him, she wound her long, thin fingers round and round his tie. 'What about going to the Queen's?' she whispered. 'Just the two of us?'

'I think, my serpent of old Nile, we should go to the Thistle with the rest of them,' said Ewan, as he gazed into her hazel eyes.

'Oh,' said Sadie, and her shoulders slumped.

'But perhaps another time,' he added.

'I'd like that very much,' said Sadie, and straight away she brightened up again.

Then, like Antony, he felt his power.

Jesse certainly put on a show.

Daisy had been reluctant to spend their last few shillings on cotton tea-towels, oven cloths, and mops and brushes made in India. But Jesse finally talked her into it, and she had to admit it – he'd been right.

The initial response from housewives in the smarter suburbs was almost always negative. No thank you, not today.

But Jesse never took no for an answer, and before they'd closed the door on him he had his suitcase open, and his dubious wares out on display.

He was shameless about telling them the cheap cotton tea-towels were finest Belfast linen, that the coarse bristle brushes were made in England and were going to last a lifetime.

The large ones were six shillings each, which he admitted did seem quite expensive. But of course you couldn't put a price on quality.

'You overdo it,' Daisy told him. 'You behave like someone in a fairground, selling patent medicines.'

'Yes, and like a patent medicine salesman, I try to entertain them. I brighten up their day. They get an oven cloth as well.'

'You charge them far too much.'

'If they can't tell cotton from genuine Belfast linen, that's their problem. You sell your stuff too cheaply, anyway.'

'I'm not a fraud, like you.'

'Sweetheart, I'm an actor!' Jesse tossed a gleaming silver florin up into the air and caught it, grinning. 'They pay to see a show.'

A show was what they got. Jesse's pockets were soon full of money, and his case was empty.

'Let's get the rest of your things sold,' he said to Daisy. 'Then we can have steak tonight.'

Daisy's mouth began to water at the very thought of a delicious, blood-red steak.

'Listen, sweetheart, life is a performance,' Jesse said the following morning, as they walked up a road they hadn't targeted before. 'We're not holding anyone at gunpoint. If they buy our stuff, they do it of their own free will.'

'You mesmerise them, Jesse. You're like a weasel with a rabbit, or a mongoose with a snake.'

'It's the only way. All right, you start with number seven. I'll work the other side, and let's see who does best.'

'Genuine Belfast linen,' Daisy assured the bachelor or widower – a man who didn't have a woman, she assumed, judging from the stains all down his tie, and the fact he carried a feather duster – who came to the door of number seven and looked her up and down.

'A shilling each, five shillings for half a dozen,' she added, smiling winsomely. 'If you take a half a dozen, they'll set you up for life.'

A couple of minutes later, the bachelor or widower handed over two half crowns for six cotton tea-towels worth about a shilling.

Daisy thought, I ought to be ashamed.

'Excellent,' said Jesse, when he met her on the corner with an empty suitcase and a handbag full of change.

'I still feel like a highwayman,' said Daisy.

'Do you, sweetheart?' Jesse smiled his charmer's smile, the one the housewives clearly couldn't resist. 'You mustn't. People like you and I, you know – we make this dull old world a better place. That chap you went to first, for instance. How old was he, sixty, sixty-five?'

'At least,' said Daisy.

'So just imagine what his life is like, retired, living in a boring suburb on a private income or his old age pension. The most exciting it ever gets for him is potting up his geraniums or walking in the park. But one morning, there's a beautiful young woman standing on his doorstep, smiling at him, talking to him, happy to spend ten minutes with him. Darling Daisy, you'll have made his day.'

'You're mad,' she told him, laughing.

'You mean I'm fun.'

'Yes, I agree you're fun.'

'I'm also witty, charming, handsome, talented and – '

'Modest?' said Daisy, picking up her suitcase.

'Modesty gets you nowhere.' Jesse grabbed her other hand and danced along the pavement, so Daisy danced as well. People stopped to stare at them, but most of them smiled, too. One old man applauded.

'Damn,' said Jesse, 'another opportunity missed. We should have brought a hat.'

'I think we should go somewhere else tomorrow,' Daisy told him later, as they sat in a little café having lunch and counting up their takings. She saw they'd made a handsome profit. They could afford to pay the rent and eat for a whole week. 'We'll get a bus going out of London, sit on it until we reach some tree-lined avenues, then we'll do our routine.'

'I knew you'd get into character in the end,' said Jesse, and hugged her round the neck. 'We'll make an actress of you yet.'

When Ewan didn't open the box in which he kept the memory of Daisy, he was enjoying life.

A mix of Shakespeare and experimental drama stretched him, interested him and kept him busy. Sadie was always smirking at him, eyeing him flirtatiously and making it very obvious she liked him, and this helped to heal his wounded heart.

Daisy had written six or seven letters now, all sent to the theatre because she didn't have any other address.

At first he'd been so angry and upset about her going off with Trent that he'd torn the first two up unopened. But he read the next few, and finally he decided to reply.

He didn't give much away. He just said that the Comrades were a jolly decent set of chaps – he didn't mention the chapess – and everything was going very well. He was doing Shakespeare, and some challenging experimental drama inspired by Soviet Russia.

Daisy was delighted to get a letter at long last, and read it on the bus.

'I suppose I ought to ask you how he's getting on,' said Jesse, looking out of the grimy window and lighting up a cigarette. A cheap one these days, he'd had to give up the Sobranies when the cash ran out, and hadn't started buying them again.

'He says the other people are very nice, and that they're doing some Shakespeare – which of course was always his intention – and also, let me see, what did he call it, challenging experimental drama inspired by Soviet Russia.'

'He means they spout a lot of left wing drivel at half a dozen people every night, and have no scenery.'

'You don't approve of Communism, then?'

'It's certainly an interesting theory, and as for up the workers, shoot the royal family, nationalise the factories and house the homeless in the mansions of Mayfair – I'd go along with that.'

Jesse yawned and rubbed his eyes. 'But it won't catch on here. Most people like to own things, and anyway the British working classes idolise the monarchy. So nobody is going to shoot our own dear king and queen.'

'I should hope they're not!'

'They won't, don't worry. Okay, let's go and sell some brushes, shall we? If the revolution's coming, we'd better take every chance we get to make the principles of free enterprise work for us.'

'What do you fancy doing tonight?' asked Jesse, several hours and many brushes later. 'Do you want to see a show, a talkie? We could afford the cheapest seats, and probably stretch to ices, too.'

'I say, a treat,' beamed Daisy.

'We deserve it.' Jesse was very pleased with life today, perhaps because a woman in a slinky silken dressing gown had not only bought a dozen tea-towels and a couple of brushes, but had asked him in for coffee, too. He'd come out half an hour later looking rumpled, but insisting they'd only chatted about her daughter's wedding.

Daisy decided not to mention the lipstick on his cheek. 'I'd like to have a proper bath,' she said. 'If I could do anything I liked, it would be to lie in a hot scented bath for hours and hours and hours.'

'Let's do it, then. Let's go to the Clapham public baths and get ourselves cleaned up. I can have a proper shave, and you can wash your hair. Believe me, love, it needs it.'

'Beast,' said Daisy, punching him.

'Ouch, don't hit me, Daisy, I'm a delicate little flower,' he cried, and parried her punches, laughing. 'You're such an aggressive little thing!'

'A dirty thing as well,' growled Daisy, punching him again, but laughing, too.

'So purify yourself. Then, when you're clean,' said Jesse, deflecting Daisy's blows, 'I'll take you to the talkies.'

The outing to the talkies was not a huge success.

The film itself, a musical called *Puttin' on the Ritz* with Harry Richman and Joan Bennett, was absolutely wonderful, and Daisy thought, that's what I want to do, be up there on celluloid. But afterwards Jesse wanted her to go back to his room, and Daisy said she couldn't, and he sulked.

'You're a tease,' he grumbled.

'No I'm not,' she said. 'When we first came to London, you knew it was to look for work. I never led you to expect – '

'You did, you know you did.'

'I like you, yes, of course I do, but I – '

'I'm going out.' Jesse clattered down the stairs and slammed out of the house. Daisy sat down on her bed and seriously considered going home.

But, but, but – she drummed her fingers on the chipped enamel washstand. She thought, I can't go back to Dorset. If I do, I'd have to admit defeat, and Mum will say, I told you so.

She locked her door – she didn't want Jesse coming back drunk and making a big scene, or if he did she would prefer he did so on the landing – got out her writing paper, and then she wrote to Rose.

It was ages since she'd written home, she now reflected guiltily. They'd wonder what had happened. But she hoped Rose and Alex hadn't worried. They probably hadn't been too concerned, she told herself. She often didn't write for several weeks. They'd have assumed that she was still with Mr and Mrs Curtis, wouldn't they?

She told Rose that the company – she didn't say it now consisted of just herself and Jesse – had moved to London. She added she was going to auditions for new shows. Fingers crossed, she thought, she'd get some soon.

Then she wrote to Ewan to say she was delighted he was doing so well. She said she hoped she'd have a chance to visit him some day, and see a Comrades Theatre production.

She listened out for Jesse, heard midnight striking from some distant steeple, but still he didn't come in. She wondered if he might stay out all night, or if he'd walk and keep on walking, if she might never set eyes on him again.

She finally heard him clumping up the stairs at four o'clock, banging into things and swearing softly to himself. She hoped things would be better in the morning.

They were – a bit. When Daisy met him on the landing, he was somewhat surly. But as the day went on he brightened up. He sold a lot of brushes, and said that now they had some cash in hand he thought they'd better start to look for proper work again.

Daisy decided looking so young was probably not helping. So she bought a pair of scissors from the market trader where they got their tea-towels and gave herself a clumsy, hacked-off bob.

'I need to look more modern for auditions,' she told Jesse, when he stared in horror and asked her what the hell she thought she'd done? She'd made herself look like a boy.

'Although it suits you,' he decided, when he had calmed down, and she had let him tidy up the mess she'd made by chopping so haphazardly at the back. 'You've got a very well-shaped head. All right, we need to put an act together. Let's go to Hampstead Heath and practise. We'll take a picnic, shall we, and terrify the swans.'

So they did, and spent all day rehearsing, arranging a ten minute song and dance act which they hoped would entertain any theatrical agent who would condescend to see them.

Jesse was very critical of Daisy. 'You need more singing lessons,' he said. 'You don't breathe properly.'

'How would I pay for singing lessons?'

'What about your parents, wouldn't they help you, if you asked them?'

'They'd be much more likely to send the money for the next train home. They think I'm still with Ewan and the company, being chaperoned by Mrs Curtis. Mum would have a fit if she knew I was on my own here, with the likes of you.'

'What's wrong with the likes of me?' Jesse already had her in his arms, and now he pulled her closer, gazing deep into her eyes.

'You're a man,' said Daisy. 'Men get women into trouble. They love them, then they leave them. Sometimes they don't bother with the loving bit, provided they can get their wicked way.'

'I'm not like that,' said Jesse.

'Of course not, you're a saint.'

'But I love you, mop head.'

'Where did you go last night?'

'I walked into the city, found a place to have a drink or two, and then walked home again.'

'That's all?'

'That's all, I promise you.' Jesse's dark brown eyes looked just like melting chocolate now. 'Daisy, come to bed with me? You can't imagine how it torments me, knowing you're lying there three feet away. I can hear you breathing, and I think how it would feel to run my fingers through your lovely hair, or what's left of it.'

'You know I can't,' said Daisy.

'Why, are you too holy?'

'I don't want a baby.'

'I'll make sure you don't have one.'

'Plenty of women have heard that before, but the world's still full of little mistakes and indiscretions.'

'Oh, Daisy!' Jesse sighed. 'You sound like Amy Nightingale. Since we came to London, you've become so cynical, so worldly-wise.'

'One of us has to be. Anyway, you shouldn't try to corrupt me. I thought you'd been brought up to be religious?'

'I gave up all that guff when I left home.'

Daisy saw the postcard in the window of a shop: female vocalist wanted, mostly shift work, ring this number.

'It'll be in a drinking club or part time brothel,' Jesse told her gloomily. 'They must be really desperate if they're advertising in shop windows. I think I'd better come along. Maybe they'll employ me as a doorman or a barman. I can keep an eye on you.'

But it wasn't a brothel. It was a little dance hall in Tulse Hill. Daisy sang for old age pensioners doing shuffling quicksteps, and for couples dancing in the marathons that were currently all the rage – crooning, half asleep herself, to the exhausted, desperate couples wanting to win a ten pound prize for staying on their swollen feet the longest.

Jesse was getting desperate as well. He couldn't find any acting work at all. He couldn't get auditions. He couldn't even get a dead end job like Daisy's singing shifts. Daisy herself was being a cruel tease.

'It's a waste of money, renting two rooms when we need just one,' he grumbled, as they caught the bus home after she'd sung her heart out in Tulse Hill.

'We can't share a room,' insisted Daisy.

'Why? That old witch in the basement wouldn't care, as long as the rent is paid.' Jesse looked into her eyes, and she saw his own were dark and blazing with desire. 'You'll give in eventually,' he whispered.

Daisy was afraid he might be right, but locked her door at night in any case.

They finally decided to split up, to do the rounds of managements and agents independently, and then to pool resources.

There was nothing doing. Daisy almost gave up hope. But then, to her astonishment, she was called for an audition for the chorus line in a revue, in a little theatre that was almost the West End.

After huffing a bit, and wondering why the agent hadn't called him – he'd left his details with that agent, too – Jesse decided he would tag along.

When they saw the line of hopefuls stretching round the block, they looked at one another in dismay.

'But this is why we came to London, to be in a show,' said Jesse, counting up the people who were ahead of them. He made it a depressing sixty-eight. 'So we can't give up now.'

'Of course we can't,' said Daisy, who had made it an even more depressing seventy-five.

'How do I look?' asked Jesse, brushing tobacco ash off his lapels.

'Lovely,' Daisy told him. 'They'll offer you a contract on the spot. What about me?'

'You're fine.'

She'd hoped she was a little more than fine. She'd made an enormous effort to look positively gorgeous.

She'd washed her hair in Sunlight soap, then brushed

it hard until it was a glossy golden helmet. She'd sponged Amy's old tweed skirt and jacket until she thought they looked as good as new. Well, from a distance, anyway. She'd used the last of a stub end of lipstick which Julia had given her and which she'd been hoarding for occasions such as this. She'd polished up her shoes so that they looked like autumn conkers.

Now she was praying hard.

Jesse smoked and yawned and said that what he really needed wasn't an audition, but a beer.

'You go and get one if you want,' she told him, as he muttered, fidgeted and grumbled. 'I'm staying in the queue.'

'If you get called while I'm not here, you won't have a partner.'

'There must be thirty or forty gentlemen standing in this line. I dare say one of them would dance with me.'

'I think I'd better stay.' Jesse lounged against a billboard advertising current shows. 'If this lot don't have finance, though, we're all wasting our time.'

The doors were opened, and the queue began to shuffle forward.

'You're not on the list,' the girl told Jesse half an hour later, as she ticked off Daisy's name.

'It must be a mistake.' Jesse gave the girl his biggest smile, the one that sold three dozen brushes every day.

'Yeah, they all spin that line,' the girl said, clearly unimpressed. 'I'm sorry, sir – we don't need you this morning, so could you move along?'

'We're a double act,' said Daisy.

'Oh?' The girl regarded them suspiciously. 'You're Daisy Denham, I think you said?'

'Yes, that's right, and Mr Trent's my partner.'

'We always do a double act,' said Jesse.

'Do you?' But Daisy saw the girl was weakening, bathed in the warm glow of Jesse's charm. 'All right,' she said, 'go in.'

'Music?' said the pianist.

'*Puttin' on the Ritz*,' said Jesse.

'Why am I not surprised?' The pianist grinned, and looked them up and down derisively, but then began to play.

Jesse and Daisy did the double act that they'd worked out on Hampstead Heath. They and twenty others were asked to stay behind, and a few hundred disappointed hopefuls shambled out, darting jealous glances as they went.

The producer addressed the people still on the stage. The show was being done on a tight budget, he explained. The cast would have to provide their costumes – top hats, tails and patent leather dancing shoes for men, evening dresses, long kid gloves and silver shoes for women.

'Does this mean anyone needs to leave?' he asked, and looked around enquiringly.

But not one person moved.

Daisy didn't have an evening dress, had never owned an evening dress, couldn't make an evening dress and certainly didn't have the cash to buy one.

But, looking round the other people lined up for the chorus, she knew this was her chance. She wouldn't get another one. The others were all hungry enough to sell their little sisters into prostitution, if it meant being in a London show.

'We'll have to hire,' said Jesse, as they made their way back to their digs.

'We can't hire shoes, hired shoes will give us blisters. We'll need to buy our own.'

'Okay, buy shoes, hire clothes, all right?'

Thanks to living on chips and pies, and selling dozens of oven cloths and brushes, they had just enough to buy some second hand shoes, hire clothes from a theatrical costumier's bargain basement, and feed themselves until they first got paid.

'But why not?' asked Jesse, as they walked home from the pub, where they'd celebrated getting jobs in the revue.

'Jesse, I can't,' said Daisy.

'It's like I've always said, you're just a tease.'

'I am not a tease.'

'What would you call it, then?'

It was awful having Jesse look at her like that, so hurt, so sad, all that reproach and longing in his dark brown eyes. It would be so easy to give in, so easy to admit she wanted him, because of course she did. She'd always wanted Jesse Trent, from the first moment she had seen him standing in Mrs Fisher's hallway.

Ewan had given her warmth, affection, comfort, all the things she knew she ought to value. But Jesse meant excitement, passion, danger – and part of Daisy wanted those, as well.

It was taking all her self control to keep in mind that it would be more than awful if she had a baby, if she had to go crawling home to Dorset in disgrace, with her baby wrapped up in a shawl.

'I love you, Daisy,' Jesse said, his dark eyes soft.

Daisy didn't know who she loved – Ewan or Jesse, either of them, neither of them? When she next wrote to Ewan, telling him about the new revue, as usual she left many things unsaid. But she did finish up by saying, *I often think of you.*

Ewan quickly learned the Comrades took their commune very seriously. The warehouse loft was clean and tidy, and everyone took turns to sweep and cook.

He'd always thought that cooking was something women did, but now he had to learn some basic skills. If he wanted any washing done, he had to do it.

'Why does no one mind us being here?' he asked one morning, as Mungo and he filled buckets at a standpipe, having waited in line with various shifty-looking people who were also camping in the warehouse. 'Why don't the sheriff's men come round with bludgeons? Why don't the police evict us?'

'We don't do any damage, and the building's empty, anyway,' Mungo told him, shrugging. 'We're unpaid night-watchmen. The police are probably happy to have us here. I'm sure they'll tell us if they change their minds.'

As he lugged his buckets up the stairs, Ewan decided that although he was a socialist, and certainly intended to remain one, once in a while he and Sadie ought to have some decadent, bourgeois fun.

There wasn't a matinee that afternoon. The other Comrades had left rehearsal promptly and gone to attend a meeting down on Clydeside. But Ewan took Sadie to a crowded ice cream parlour run by cheerful, garrulous Italians, which was full of music, smoke and noise. They'd have something to eat, he said, and go to the meeting later on.

'What would you like?' he asked, as they sat down on a smart black bench behind a chrome and bakelite table.

'Let me see the menu?' Sadie took it from the smart young waitress and studied it suspiciously, running one long finger down the list. 'Ewan,' she said, 'all this is very expensive for what is basically sugar.'

'Sadie, you're not paying,' said Ewan. 'You bought me stovies, so it's my treat today. What do you fancy?'

'I'd love an ice cream sundae,' Sadie told him wistfully. 'I've not had one of those since I was seven and one of my aunties took me to Dundee.'

'Then you shall have one now.' Ewan smiled at the waitress. 'Thank you, miss – I'd like a sundae, too.'

The sundaes came in great tall glasses, towering concoctions of sweet sauce and fruit and cream. Sadie said she wasn't keen on cherries. So Ewan had to eat them. Then Sadie got some chocolate on her cheek. Ewan wiped it off, and as he did she caught his hand. 'You're a very bad influence,' she whispered, and gazed into his eyes.

'Do you think so?' Ewan leaned towards her and kissed her on the mouth, tasting both ice cream and her own sweetness, and thinking that her lips were firm as berries.

'You're corrupting me.'

'You don't appear to mind being corrupted.' Ewan kissed away a little blob of strawberry sauce. 'In fact, Red Sadie, I would say you like it.'

'Aye, perhaps I do, just now and then.' She kissed a streak of chocolate off his chin.

The sundaes melted in their glasses, but they forced themselves to finish them, spooning up the sauce and cream and feeding one another, making a mess and laughing about it.

As Sadie pointed out, when she finally put her spoon down, some underpaid and underprivileged worker had gone to all the trouble of making them. So leaving them would be a wicked waste and cruel shame.

They never got to the meeting, and Mungo told them

off, saying they'd missed a perfect opportunity to support a workers' worthy cause.

Ewan thought it was just as well Red Mungo hadn't asked them what they'd done that afternoon. He would have had an ideological fit.

After just a few days of rehearsals for the new revue, nobody felt ready, but the management said the show must open. The company financing it, Daniel Hanson Enterprises Limited, apparently insisted. So the bills were printed and the show was advertised. The bookings started trickling in.

'It'll be all right,' said the producer, as he surveyed his ragged chorus line, and smiled encouragingly at his off-key singers. 'I'm sure we'll do the business.'

He ran his finger round his collar, and Daisy saw his face was damp with sweat. 'Mr Daniel Hanson,' he continued grimly, 'is not a gentleman who likes to be let down. So, boys and girls, be sure to do your best.'

To everyone's relief, the first night went quite well. On the whole, the notices were good, and the producer said – in jest, they all supposed and hoped – Mr Hanson wouldn't need to get his men to smash their kneecaps now.

But Jesse wasn't altogether pleased, because one critic on a daily paper singled Daisy out for special mention.

'*As for the pretty blonde soubrette with the enchanting smile, forget-me-not blue eyes and stunning figure, whose short solo in the second half was perfectly delightful – I'm sure Miss Daisy Denham will go far,*' the critic said, but didn't mention the handsome, debonair and hugely talented Mr Jesse Trent.

'Your turn soon,' said Daisy, at the end of one evening performance when Jesse was still rumbling on about it.

Goodness, he was such a baby sometimes.

'I need a drink,' said Jesse, grumpily.

'Let's go and have one, then.'

But Jesse wasn't listening. He'd turned to look at someone who was also in the chorus line, a girl with dyed red hair who looked on the wrong side of thirty-five, but dressed and made up young. 'You all right, Belinda?'

'Tip top, Jesse.' Belinda flashed some fishnet-stockinged leg in his direction and bared her less than perfect teeth. 'What about you?'

'I'm fine. Where are the others going for a drink tonight, do you know?'

'The Old Nag's Head,' replied Belinda, and she tossed her head flirtatiously.

'See you there,' Jesse said, grinning.

'Excuse me?' said Daisy.

'Oh, but you don't drink,' said Jesse.

'What?'

'Just kidding, sweetheart.' Jesse hugged her round the neck. 'We'll let you tag along.'

Phoebe walked down the cobbled side street, thinking about her youth and wondering where the years had gone.

The smell of the dusty little theatre brought the whole thing back – those nights during the war, the men and officers hanging round and looking hopeful after every show, picking up the chorus girls and taking them to pubs and night clubs.

One officer in particular, there'd been. One handsome, fair-haired Royal Dorset with beautiful blue eyes and an enchanting smile, with silver in his pockets and a silver tongue to match.

The stage door was open now, and people were pouring out. A blonde girl and a dark-haired man were coming down the stairs, he was nibbling at her ear, and she was half pushing him away, but laughing, too.

Phoebe had been studying the picture she'd been given by Rose. The girl's sweet face was hot-pressed on her brain. But what if she was wrong?

She stepped into a pool of lamplight. ' 'Scuse me, are you Miss Denham?' she began.

'Yes, I am,' said Daisy smiling, thrilled to have a fan at the stage door, but wondering why the woman didn't seem to have a programme or an album, if she wanted Daisy's autograph?

Phoebe had rehearsed this moment over and over and over in her mind. She had her speech all ready. But now she forgot her lines. 'Hello, Daisy darlin',' she began. 'I'm Phoebe – I'm your mother.'

Chapter Fifteen

'I love you, Ewan, but I'm not in love with you,' said Sadie, who often talked like this, as if she were discussing it with herself. 'Romantic love's a base and bourgeois concept. It's totally discredited. It has no place in twentieth century thinking – wouldn't you agree?'

'Yes, I suppose so, Sadie.' Then Ewan nodded, assuming this was what she wanted him to do. He pushed one hand into his trouser pocket, where a couple of Daisy's recent letters lay creased and crumpled up.

He ought to write to Daisy soon, he thought – he should congratulate her on her big success in the revue. He'd read her notices, and in spite of himself he'd been impressed. He'd been so pleased to hear that she doing so well. He wouldn't mind going to see her, actually, even if it also meant he'd have to see the bastard.

'What are you grinning at now?' demanded Sadie, trying to scowl at him, but when he looked up he saw that she was grinning, too.

'Come here, my little apparatchik.' Ewan pulled her close and then he kissed the top of her dark head.

'Get off, you loon,' she muttered, but she didn't push him away.

The Glasgow Comrades Company was rehearsing for the première of a brand new drama set in Tsarist Russia, in which heroic workers battled against a brutal Tsarist boss.

Ewan played a worker who stabbed and killed the boss because the boss had raped his wife. The worker's subsequent arrest, imprisonment, travesty of a show trial and gruesome execution were acted out on stage, in as much lurid detail as Dennis Foster the producer thought the Lord Chamberlain's office would allow.

Of course, his mother would have hated it, reflected Ewan. All those nasty people being horrid to her boy. All that unnecessary, ill-bred shouting. All that blood, for even Ewan had to admit his death scene did go on a bit.

But when they opened, he got excellent notices in all the left-wing papers, commending his great passion and commitment to the cause of workers' freedom. So he kept his bourgeois reservations to himself.

At least, he thought, nobody here expected him to speak as if came from Surrey. In fact, the producer had wanted all the workers to have strong Glaswegian accents, while the villainous bosses and their lackeys should sound English to a man.

Sadie was a fully paid up member of the Communist Party. She told Ewan that her father had worked for thirty years in various Clydeside shipyards, and it was a disgrace to have a Labour government in power, and so many millions of workers unemployed.

She spoke her lines with fervour and, as Ewan's wife, raged and carried on like anything about the awful things done to her man, and by extension to workers everywhere.

'I'd always thought red hair like yours looked better on a lassie, but on you it's bonny,' she told him, after one performance in which Ewan had died especially noisily and energetically, cursing the capitalists and all their works, to great applause.

'Thank you, Sadie.' Ewan smiled. 'It's very kind of you to say so.'

'I wasn't being kind. I – '

'Fraser, are you going for a beer?' Mungo, another tormented worker, clapped him on the back and grinned at him. 'I'm sure you'll need it, after all that shouting.'

'I'm coming, too,' said Sadie, pulling on her coat. She'd done her hair a little differently this evening, Ewan noticed. She hadn't combed it flat and slicked it down. Instead, she'd tried to make it pretty, and she had succeeded. She was even wearing lipstick.

Bourgeois decadence, he told himself. If it's determined, it can even worm its way into the heart of a nicely brought up socialist girl like our Red Sadie.

They sat with Mungo and the other workers in the Thistle, drinking beer. At chucking out time, Sadie put her hand on Ewan's arm. 'Why don't we go somewhere else tonight?' she whispered softly, looking up at him with big, round eyes.

'Where do you suggest?' he whispered back.

'We could go to my parents' place.'

'But won't your mother mind?' Ewan could imagine what his own would say if he turned up with Sadie on his arm.

'She's away at her sister's in Arbroath.'

'What about your father?'

'He's gone to a meeting, where they'll sit and put the world to rights until the small hours. He won't come home tonight.'

'It sounds to me, Red Sadie, as if I have no choice.'

'I don't believe you do.'

Mungo and the others exchanged embarrassed or suggestive glances, then stole away into the night.

'But how did you find me?' Daisy asked, when the three of them had all got over being astonished, and were sitting in an expensive restaurant in the Strand.

'It wasn't easy, darlin',' admitted Phoebe. 'I 'ad to trawl round all the ruddy digs in Birmin'ham before I found out where you'd stayed. Then, when they told me they thought you'd gone to London – well, I thought, talk about a needle in an 'aystack!

'But then I pulled meself together, come down 'ere, an I 'ired a taxi by the day. I started goin' round the theatres askin' if they'd 'eard of you. I was close to givin' up, I'll tell you!

'Then I saw this notice in the papers, all about your show, said it was good. The bloke had specially mentioned a Miss Denham in the chorus, and me old 'eart did a little flip. So then the doorman at my 'otel up west, he tells me yes, he knows the place. It's maybe a bit rough, he says, but they has try-outs there, an' sometimes stuff transfers to the West End.

'You're a naughty girl, you know. Why did you take so long to tell Rose and Alex where you'd gone? When I last spoke to Rose she said she'd heard from you at last, and I was to give you a good hidin' for not writin' for so long.'

But Daisy wasn't interested in Rose. She had her eyes still fixed on Phoebe's face. She realised this must be the dark-haired woman who had haunted all those dreams.

She had a real mother now, she thought, and it was wonderful. She'd never been so happy. It was as if she had come home.

'Come on, love, drink up,' encouraged Phoebe, making Daisy blink. 'I mean, we're celebratin', ain't we?'

She motioned to the waiter to top up Daisy's glass. She gazed around the restaurant. 'Dear old London, eh?' she sighed. 'God, it seems like only yesterday that I was just a kid, an' startin' out meself. But the last time I was sittin' 'ere – oh, it must've been seventeen or eighteen years ago.'

'You used to come to this place, then?' asked Jesse, looking at the polished woodwork, inlaid marble panelling and gilded chandeliers.

'Yeah, a boyfriend used to bring me regular.' Phoebe lit a cigarette. 'I was on the stage meself, you know, in the varieties.'

She launched into a long resumé of her many triumphs, boasting about the officers she had known, how they had wined and dined her and how marvellous it had been, all the parties, dances, all the fizz …

'Where are you staying, Mrs Rosenheim?' asked Jesse, when Phoebe finally took a break from showing off to drink some more champagne.

'I got a suite in a hotel, in Piccadilly.' Phoebe looked at Daisy. 'What about you, love? You got good digs?'

'Oh, yes, they're fine.' After all the tales of splendour, Daisy didn't want to admit to living in a dump, that there were mousetraps everywhere, and damp ran down the walls. If the revue transfers to the West End, she thought, I'm going to find another place to stay.

As the restaurant started closing, Jesse went into the Strand to try to find a taxi. Phoebe took Daisy's hands, and then looked deep into her eyes. 'You don't mind me comin' to see you, darlin'?' she asked, anxiously. 'Only you ain't said much.'

'I'm still trying to take it in.' Daisy gazed at this stranger who said she was her mother, but who was more exciting, beautiful and glamorous than any mother Daisy had ever known.

'Well, we'll be better acquainted soon,' said Phoebe, smiling happily. 'When I gets you back home to the States, an' takes you all around, I know we're gonna have such fun!'

'You want me to go home with you?'

'Oh, love, of course I do,' cried Phoebe. 'I just can't tell you 'ow I've dreamed about this moment, when I'd be reunited with my darlin' little girl. I don't ever want to let you go.'

'Well, that was exciting,' Jesse said, as he and Daisy sat on the last bus, alone on the top deck as all the lights of London winked at them.

'I've never been so surprised in all my life.' Daisy lay against him, her head upon his shoulder. 'What do you make of Phoebe, Jesse? Do you think she's nice?'

'She's lovely.' Jesse nodded. 'She's very attractive, too. It's obvious where you got your looks.'

'But I don't look anything like her, do I? She's very dark, I'm very fair.'

'You're both very beautiful.' Jesse kissed her sweetly, and then he kissed her passionately. Then he stopped, and Daisy found she wanted to be kissed again.

She'd drunk too much champagne – far less than Jesse, and nothing like as much as Phoebe, but she wasn't used to alcohol, and now she was thinking she shouldn't have drunk any.

She felt light-headed, tired but relaxed, and also – much to her embarrassment – she realised she was hungry for a man.

She looked again at Jesse. He was so attractive, he was generous and kind, he'd looked after her so well since they'd arrived in London, and he said he loved her, and perhaps he even meant it? Why shouldn't she sleep with him?

Jesse stroked her forehead, ran his fingers through her

hair, printed little butterfly kisses all along her jaw line. 'Daisy?' he whispered, softly.

'Yes,' she said. 'But, Jesse, you will be careful?'

'I'll be careful, sweetheart,' promised Jesse. 'I'll look after you.'

When he undressed, and she saw the scars across his back, the marks from all those beatings, she could have cried. Poor man, she thought, he's had a really rotten deal in life. Now he deserves some love.

He took his time, he didn't hurt her, he didn't frighten her, and although she sometimes got the feeling that he was performing, stepping back occasionally to gauge audience reaction, she was glad she'd done it. She was a woman now.

'You were careful, weren't you?' she asked him anxiously, when he had finished.

'Yes, I was careful,' he said, yawning. 'Good night, sweet dreams,' he added, turning on to his side and going to sleep.

Ewan woke up in a single bed under a skylight in a Glasgow tenement, somehow knowing where he was, but not remembering how he'd got there.

Then he became aware of someone else in bed with him, someone soft and warm, and suddenly it all came hurtling back.

He groaned and sat up carefully. He felt so sick, and hoped he wouldn't actually throw up.

On the way back to the tenement, Sadie had bought a bottle of cheap Scotch. He thought he must have drunk the lot, and how he was going to do a matinee this afternoon, he didn't know. There was a glass of water on the night stand. He picked it up and sipped some gratefully.

Sadie woke up now, and twisted round to look at him. 'Good morning, Ewan,' she began, and grinned. 'How are you today?'

'I've been much better.' Ewan blinked and shut his eyes, for the harsh Glasgow dawn was blinding him. 'What did I do last night?'

'You tried to take advantage of me.' Sadie giggled, and walked her fingers up his arm. 'But you'd had far too much to drink. You look more sober now.' She rubbed her foot against his leg. 'Do you want to try to take advantage of me again?'

Ewan could feel the softness of her, smell the musky scent of her, could feel himself responding.

'Yes,' he said, and took her in his arms. 'I'd definitely like to try again.'

Daisy wrote to Rose again, explaining about the revue, and saying she'd been really busy, telling Rose that she was with a company financed by a Mr Daniel Hanson. Mr Hanson was a very important, powerful impresario. Maybe Rose had heard of him?

She sent Rose all her notices – three or four by now – and a programme with her name in it. She also said that she'd met Phoebe, but she didn't go into detail.

Phoebe had been to see the show at every opportunity, always sitting in the front row stalls. But when Daisy met her in a West End café after a matinee, and told her who was backing the revue, Phoebe suddenly went white. She looked as if she was about to faint.

'What's the matter?' Daisy cried, alarmed.

'Mr Daniel Hanson.' Phoebe shuddered convulsively, as if she had a fever. 'I know him of old,' she muttered, 'from when I was in the varieties meself.'

'We hardly ever see him,' added Daisy.

'Yeah, an' you want to keep it that way, love,' said Phoebe, as she groped in her bag for cigarettes.

'Why, isn't he very nice?'

'Mr Daniel Hanson is a bugger, 'scuse my French. I walked out with 'im once, durin' the war years.' Now, with hands that were still shaking, Phoebe lit a cigarette, inhaled. 'When I got caught with you, 'e threatened to make me sorry I'd been born. 'E wasn't your dad, you see – thank God for that – an' 'e didn't want to think another fella had been interferin' with 'is girl.'

'I see,' said Daisy, feeling a bit sick herself.

''E ran vice rings, Dan did, 'e 'ad people's legs broke if they didn't do what he said, or if they upset 'im. The police was in 'is pocket. They still are, I dare say.'

Phoebe shook her head, she grimaced in disgust, but then she smiled. 'Rest day tomorrow, ain't it? I thought we could go up Oxford Street, an' buy you somethin' nice. The boyfriend can come along as well, that's if 'e's got nothin' else to do. I likes to 'ave a bloke to carry all me bags, especially if he's kinda cute like yours! Daisy, 'ave you thought any more about that stuff I said?'

'You mean, go to America with you?'

'Yeah, it's time we got to know each other better, don't you reckon?' Phoebe picked up the silver teapot, poured out more Earl Grey. She snapped her fingers to the waitress for more cakes. 'You're so talented, you could do so well. You could be on Broadway. I can already see your name in lights! My Nathan, he could help you. He's a big shot now. He's got connections.'

'In the theatre?' Daisy asked, thinking that's the first I've heard of it.

'My Nathan's got connections everywhere.' Phoebe spread her hands. 'America's not like Britain, where you has to know your place. Look at me and Nathan – we come to New York City without a penny to our names, but we worked an' worked an' worked, an' now we're doin swell.'

'I'd miss my parents, though.'

'Darlin', you're forgettin' *I'm* your mother.' Phoebe's dark eyes narrowed, but then she smiled graciously. 'Rose and Alex and the kids – yeah, they could visit. We'd be glad to see 'em, show 'em a bit of life.'

'I'll think about it,' Daisy promised, tempted.

'Britain's all washed up,' continued Phoebe. 'It's a mess. Darlin', look around you. It's all dirt and gloom and misery, not like in the States.'

'You don't have unemployment and depression in the States?'

'Oh, sure, we got some problems,' said Phoebe, airily. 'The Crash affected everyone, an' that I can't deny. But things is on the up.'

Phoebe covered Daisy's hand with hers, gave it a gentle squeeze. 'It's the land of opportunity, the good old USA. Listen, I was a kid from the East End. I 'ad no education, but I knew 'ow to graft. So now I wears fur coats, I got a business, I 'as a dozen girls workin' for me. I couldn've done that 'ere. There ain't the will, the energy, the sparkle here in England.

'Daisy, I knows people, lots of people, not little fish like Daniel bloody Hanson. I knows the ones who matter.'

'Phoebe – '

'Mum,' said Phoebe. 'I'd like you to call me Mum, my darlin'. Or maybe Mommy, eh?'

'As I said, I'll have to think about it.'

'Well, don't you take too long, my love.' Phoebe lit another cigarette. 'I'm goin' 'ome next Saturday. I want you to come with me, an' before you says it, yeah, I know – you're very fond of Jesse. But 'e could tag along. I'll even pay 'is fare. Your understudies'll be glad to take your places in the show.'

'But we have contracts.'

'Oh, sweet'eart, tear 'em up,' said Phoebe, grandly. 'Now, about tomorrow, where we gonna meet, at my 'otel? Listen,' she added urgently, 'I got to get you away from Daniel and his henchmen. People like that, they ain't no good to you. I don't think even Dan's long, slippery fingers could reach you in the States.'

The following morning, Jesse said he didn't feel like traipsing round the shops. He thought he'd pulled a tendon in his foot, and it was rather painful. Maybe he should rest it.

'You go, and have real swell time,' he said.

'Well, all right. I'll bring you something nice,' said Daisy, buttoning up her jacket and smoothing the lapels, and blessing Amy for her kindness.

'Something expensive,' Jesse added. 'Gentleman's cologne, perhaps, from some exclusive little shop in Regent Street or Piccadilly. The old girl can afford it.'

'I'll see what I can do.' Daisy kissed him, smiled and waved her fingers. 'You be good,' she said.

'I shall. I'll lie in bed and read the paper.'

'Blimey, Daisy, where do you get your clothes?' demanded Phoebe. She tweaked the collar of Daisy's jacket, testing the quality of the fabric, and finding it wasn't up to her exacting expectations. 'We'd better get you somethin' decent, if you're comin' 'ome with me.'

So Daisy and Phoebe started shopping, and spent a fortune. They didn't have time for lunch, but by three o'clock they were so tired they got a taxi back to Piccadilly, and went to have afternoon tea at Fortnum's where, as Phoebe put it, they might stick their noses in the air, but they did a decent cup of char.

'I been to see you nearly twenty times,' said Phoebe, tucking her arm through Daisy's as they made their way upstairs. 'You gets better an' better every day.'

'Thank you,' Daisy said, wishing that Phoebe wouldn't cling so tightly, but not wanting to hurt her mother's feelings by seeming to shake her off.

'But,' continued Phoebe artlessly, 'I bet Rose an' Alex has been to see you far more times than I 'ave?'

'No, actually, they haven't,' Daisy said. 'It's the farm, you see. They don't have much in the way of help, so they don't have the time to get away.'

'Daisy, if my little girl was on the London stage, an' if I was anythin' like a proper mother ought to be, I'd make the flippin' time to get away!'

At the entrance to the restaurant, Phoebe caught the eye of the head waiter, who came smartly up and led them to a table by a window. He pulled out both their chairs and got them comfortably seated, then handed them their menus with a flourish.

A waitress came up then and fussed around them, making sure they had fresh napkins, finger bowls and cutlery. So many servants, Daisy thought – it was like being in India again.

'But then that's Rose all over,' added Phoebe, pulling off her fine kid gloves. 'She gets obsessed with things, does

Rose. My sister always said so. Rose 'as got a one track mind, Maria used to say. Right now, it's 'er flippin' chickens is occupyin' 'er time, an' she ain't got a moment for anythin' or anybody else – not even for you, my darlin' girl. But never mind, my lovely daughter, your real mommy loves you, an' she wants to see your show.'

Phoebe scanned the menu. 'So, angel, what d'you want today? Some little sandwiches, and some of them French fancies what that fat woman's eatin' over there? They looks tasty, don't they? Them, an' 'alf a dozen little scones, with Devon clotted cream?'

'Mmm, delicious,' Daisy said, slipping off her jacket. She wished Phoebe would shut up for just one minute. Or at any rate, not talk about poor Rose in that nasty, supercilious way.

'That's what we'll 'ave, then.' Phoebe summoned the waiter, gave her order, and sent him on his way. 'You thought any more about goin' to the States with me?' she demanded, as the waitress set out fine bone china and lit the little spirit stove which would warm their scones. 'Just for an 'oliday at first. But if you like it, you could settle down permanent with me, in my apartment.'

'What about Mr Rosenheim?' asked Daisy.

'What about 'im?'

'Well, I'm not his daughter.'

'But you're mine, an' he loves me, an' so he'd make you welcome.' Phoebe smiled. 'He's lovely, is my Nathan. You'd like him, he'd like you.'

'I'm sure I'd like him, Phoebe, but you haven't said very much about him.'

'Mommy,' corrected Phoebe.

'Where did you meet him?' Daisy asked.

'My Nathan?' Phoebe grinned. 'I've known 'im all my life. Nathan was the boy next door, back in the old East End. I was always goin' to marry 'im.'

'But he'd make me welcome?'

'Daisy, sweet'eart, 'e can't wait to meet you, 'e's told me so 'imself. I 'ad a wire yesterday, in fact. So, darlin', what d'you say?'

'Give me another day or two to think,' said Daisy, glad to see the waitress coming over, pushing a little gilded trolley laden with plates of delicate little sandwiches and cakes, and all the other things they'd have for tea.

Phoebe merely fiddled with her sandwiches and scones, but she drank several cups of tea. 'I 'ave to watch me figure,' she explained. 'I ain't gonna dance it off, like you. Go on, 'ave a fancy.'

'I don't eat much sweet stuff, it gives me spots,' Daisy said apologetically. She'd eaten only half a fancy, and for some reason she'd gone off the scones.

'You ain't got any spots, you silly girl. So come on, eat up,' snapped Phoebe. 'I ain't payin' out good money for nothin'.' But then she blushed, and shook her head. 'Sorry, love,' she said. 'I didn't mean to be so sharp. I 'spect you've wondered about me all your life?' she added, picking up the silver sugar tongs.

'No, I didn't find out about you till a year ago,' admitted Daisy. 'Mum – sorry, I mean Rose – told me last summer I was adopted.'

'Oh.' Phoebe looked both embarrassed and annoyed. 'So up until then, you thought you was Rose's and Alex's kid?'

'Well, naturally.'

'They been good to you?'

'Yes, they've been wonderful.' As Daisy said it, she

realised she meant it, and she felt a pang of longing for the people who would always be her mum and dad.

'They tell you about your real dad?' asked Phoebe.

'No, and I didn't ask them,' Daisy said, and shrugged. 'I thought perhaps they didn't know.'

'Oh, they knows all right.' Phoebe crushed a sugar cube with more than casual violence. 'You know the bloke what lives at Easton Hall, near Rose and Alex's place?'

'Yes, Sir Michael Easton. But I don't actually know him. He doesn't have anything to do with us.'

'I wonder why,' said Phoebe savagely. 'Listen, 'ere's the facts. I knew 'im in the war years, when I was on the 'alls, an' he was a regular stage door Johnny. All us girls was very sweet on 'im, on account of 'e was very 'andsome an' generous with 'is cash. So anyway, we 'ad a little fling, and you was the result.'

'I don't believe you!' Daisy stared in horror. 'How could you have met Sir Michael Easton, and if I'm his daughter, why doesn't he want me? Why don't I live with him?'

'Calm down, Daisy, darlin, keep your voice down.' Phoebe touched her daughter's hand, but Daisy jerked it back, as if her mother's were red hot. 'In the war years, people got about a bit. Rose was a nurse in London, as I 'spect you know, an' she was friendly with my sister.

'Mike was sweet on Rose, an' he come up to London once to see 'er. Me and my boyfriend walked into this restaurant, and there she was with 'im. She was in 'er nurse's uniform, an' he was an officer. God, 'e looked so gorgeous! We was introduced – '

'So it all went on from there.' Daisy glared at Phoebe, blue eyes glittering. 'Sir Michael wanted to marry Mum, you know.'

'Yeah, I did know that. But Rose, she didn't want to marry 'im, she told me so.' Phoebe looked at Daisy. 'Darlin', she's very 'appy with 'er Alex, she told me that 'erself.'

'You spoiled it all for Mum!' cried Daisy, glaring. 'You deliberately wrecked her life!'

'No, Daisy, you don't understand, I – '

'It's all your fault, the mess they're in at home, the fact we haven't got any money – '

'Daisy, just 'ang on just a minute,' interrupted Phoebe. 'God, I shouldn't have told you so abrupt – '

'No, I'm glad you told me!' Daisy stood up, blue eyes blazing. 'I should have been told all sorts of things, years and years ago! You've all lied to me!'

Daisy pushed her chair away, snatched up her old tweed jacket. 'You abandoned me!' she cried, as the entire restaurant turned to stare. 'If Rose and Alex hadn't adopted me, I'd have ended up in some disgusting East End orphanage, along with all the other nameless bastards. All the time I was growing up, you never had any contact with me, never wanted to know about me, never even sent a birthday card.

'But then, all of a sudden, you walk back into my life, buy me lots of expensive junk, ask me to call you Mommy and want me to go home with you. Well, forget it, Phoebe, it's not going to happen. I'm going now. I never want to set eyes on you again.'

'Darlin', don't forget your bags!' cried Phoebe, as Daisy strode off across the deep pile carpet.

But Daisy kept on walking. When she was in the street again she thought, I must stop making scenes in restaurants and walking out on people, it's becoming quite a habit.

Chapter Sixteen

Ewan was definitely corrupting Sadie, taking her to places where there were chromium tables and red leathercloth banquettes, and where he bought American toasted sandwiches – not stovies, bridies, white pudding fritters or other wholesome Scottish fare.

He also took her to the talkies where she watched the musicals with arms folded and pursed lips, but when he glanced at her he could see she was enjoying herself, that her foot was tapping, and she was having wicked, bourgeois fun.

'It's not that I object to people dancing,' she said wistfully, as they came out into the evening twilight. 'But dancing isn't relevant to the struggle.'

'You're allowed a few hours off,' said Ewan. 'The struggle will somehow carry on without you, if you take a little break.'

'Maybe,' admitted Sadie, as she ran her fingers through her newly Marcelled waves. She'd had it done to find out what it felt like, having hot iron rods dragged through her hair. She needed to understand why otherwise intelligent women put themselves through stuff like this – or so she said. She seemed put out when Ewan said it suited her, that she looked very pretty.

If she didn't watch it, Ewan thought, one day Red Sadie was going to wake up and find she was – unlike Red Mungo, the dauntless champion of the workers – middle class.

Living in a commune, sharing everything and looking out for one another, that was grand. Ewan wasn't disputing it.

But, like the other Comrades, he was getting somewhat tired of living in the warehouse. Mungo had been moaning about climbing all those stairs when he was drunk. Other, more disreputable, people had been moving in and occupying the lower floors.

The police were prowling round the place more often, and Ewan said perhaps the four men in the company should think of trying to find another place, a boarding house or something? Sadie, of course, could go back to her parents' house.

Their notices were fine, he added, they were earning reasonable money, so if they didn't want to find a boarding house, why not rent a tenement apartment?

'Perhaps,' said Mungo, flexing his red worker's hands and cracking his worker's knuckles. 'If it's cheap, and if the landlord isn't a bloated capitalist oppressor of the proletariat, we might consider it.'

'I'm moving in as well,' said Sadie, who was clearly anxious not to be left out. 'We'll still be a commune, and still committed to the struggle.'

'You're a guid wee wifie,' Mungo said, approvingly.

Daisy arrived back at her digs in Clapham hot and tired. She'd walked home all the way, and the day was far too warm for Amy's smart tweed suit.

She was still furious with Phoebe, but she was more furious with herself for being such a fool, for being taken in so easily, being so very willing to be seduced by Phoebe's gaudy, tawdry charm.

As she climbed the stairs up to her room, she began to feel a little calmer. If Jesse's foot was not too sore, they could walk down to the Lamb and Flag, then she could tell him what had happened, and he would sympathise.

Or, if he was still resting it, they could stay at home, and she could make some supper on the gas ring on the landing. She'd go and get some ham or something from the corner shop – they'd put it on the slate – and then she and Jesse could have ham and fried potatoes in his room.

She tapped on Jesse's door. She heard a muffled giggle, and Jesse saying, sssh, and then, hang on a minute! But Daisy was in no mood to mess about. Opening the door, she marched straight in.

Jesse was lying face down on the bed, his wrists tied to the head rail. Belinda from the chorus line was lying next to him, wearing a black silk petticoat and smoking, a birch switch in her hand. Jesse's back was hatched with streaks of blood.

Daisy stared in horror.

Whatever were they doing?

Why was Jesse letting Belinda hurt him?

What was going on?

But then it all clicked into place. The whole room stank of sex and alcohol. It smelled so rank and foxy that she gagged. The bile rose in her throat.

The ground caved in beneath her feet a second time that day. She felt so stupid, so ashamed, so totally ridiculous that she could have cried.

She turned and fled. She ran back down the stairs and out of the front door, gasping for what passed in London for fresh air.

She was packing in her room when Jesse came to talk to her, wearing just a velvet dressing gown he'd stolen from some costume hamper, smelling like a brewery, his black hair ruffled up like raven's feathers.

'It wasn't what it looked like,' he began, his voice soft and caressing. 'Darling, you mustn't go. You mustn't leave me. I – '

'Don't talk to me,' snapped Daisy.

'Sweetheart, you must understand that sometimes I have needs.' Jesse sat down on Daisy's bed and tried to take her hand.

She slapped him off.

'You're so young, so inexperienced,' he continued, gamely ploughing on. 'You're still on the nursery slopes of sex. So I couldn't have asked you to do that – at least, not yet. But whatsername's an instrument, that's all. She doesn't mean a thing to me.'

'Oh?' Daisy clicked the locks shut. 'But while you were with whatsername, I didn't mean a thing.'

'Daisy, you mean everything to me!'

'I should have listened to Amy,' muttered Daisy, more to herself than Jesse. 'Amy and Julia, they both had your number from the start. God, I was so horrible to Ewan – '

'Oh, that's right, drag your precious Ewan into it,' sneered Jesse. 'That's what you women always do. The man you love upsets you, so you start carrying on about some hopeless deadbeat who used to drive you mad.'

'Don't you dare slander Ewan!' Daisy cried. 'One day, he'll be a star, you wait and see!'

'I'll hold my breath,' yawned Jesse, raking a languid hand through his becomingly tousled hair.

'My God, you're such a poser, such a fraud, such a performer!' Daisy glared at him. 'Listen, Jesse Trent. I don't care what you do, what needs you have. I might be inexperienced, but I'm old enough to realise that people must like different things in bed. I'm leaving you because you lied to me. All that rubbish about your father, all the sympathy you milked from me, it was all fabrication, wasn't it?'

'Perhaps I did embroider just a little. But – '

'What does your father really do?'

'He's a carpet salesman.'

'Do you come from Yorkshire?'

'Not exactly – my parents live in Dunstable. Dad wanted me to be a bank clerk, civil servant, something boring and respectable. But I wanted to be an actor. So I left.'

'Do you ever see your family?'

'No, I borrowed a little money the last time I was there.' Jesse shrugged. 'It would be rather awkward to go back.'

'You mean you stole their savings. You really are a rogue and vagabond.'

Daisy picked her case up, but Jesse grabbed her wrist. 'Darling, you can't walk out on me, into the big, bad city. Where do you think you're going to go? Oh, did Phoebe ask you – '

'Yes she did and no I'm not,' snapped Daisy. 'I'm going back to Dorset.'

'You mean you're going home?'

'Yes, Mr Double Dealer, I'm going back to Charton with my tail between my legs. I'm going crawling back to Mum and Dad.' Daisy shook him off and stared him out, her blue eyes flashing dangerously. 'You want to make something of it, do you?'

'Just hang on a minute. What about Mr Hanson – have you thought of him? He gave us our first break in London, and everybody says it's very dangerous to cross him. What about his show?'

'Damn the show,' said Daisy. 'Damn Mr Hanson, damn his show, and damn you, too.' She put her case down, rummaged in her handbag, and found the bottle of cologne she'd bought with her own money, not with Phoebe's. 'Jesse?'

'Yes?'

'This is for you, so make the most of it.' Daisy dropped the heavy crystal bottle on his foot, picked up her case and ran downstairs, leaving Jesse cursing on the landing.

The train took hours, but the walk from Charton station to the bailiff's cottage was less than half a mile. So she was nearly home, and she was glad.

But she wasn't yet ready to face her parents, because even after sitting on the train for all those hours, and thinking until she had a pounding headache, Daisy was still all churned up inside.

Why hadn't Rose replied to all the recent letters she had sent from London? She usually replied to Daisy's letters by return of post.

Oh God, thought Daisy, maybe Rose was going to say Alex and I have done our duty, fed you, clothed you, sheltered you. But you're not our child. You've found your natural mother now, so off you go, and don't come here again.

It would serve her right, she thought. She'd been such an ungrateful little cow. She didn't deserve to be their daughter any more.

Phoebe had apparently assumed that Daisy would abandon Rose and Alex, and swan off to America for good. Daisy had to admit she had been tempted by a vision of her name in lights on Broadway, and had for a few seconds believed that Phoebe's husband was some kind of big shot who'd be able to arrange it.

As for Jesse – she couldn't imagine why she'd ever thought he was attractive, ever thought she was in love with him. As she walked up the path to the bailiff's cottage, the smell of bridges burned down to their foundations filled the soft, night air.

She hadn't realised it was quite so late. The Dorset sky was a bluish-reddish-orange-purple, promising a perfect day tomorrow, and the moon was still a pale ghost, but it must be well past ten o'clock. The cottage lights were out, and she supposed they must all be in bed. Of course, she thought, they had to get up early for the milking.

She hadn't got a key, so she knocked softly on the door, and a few minutes later Rose came down and opened it.

'Mum?' said Daisy fearfully, seeing at once from Rose's face that something must be wrong.

'Oh, Daisy, darling! I'm so relieved you've come!' Rose threw her arms round Daisy neck and hugged her tightly, and Daisy could feel tears on her cheek, although she knew she wasn't crying. 'But how did you know to come today?'

'What do you mean?'

'You didn't get my wire?'

'No.' Daisy's heart was hammering. 'Tell me, what's the matter – is it you, or Dad, the boys?'

But Rose was sobbing now and couldn't speak. Daisy took her back inside, sat her at the kitchen table, put the kettle on and made some tea.

'Mum?' said Daisy softly, as she set out cups and saucers and found a bowl of sugar.

'It's Alex.' Rose managed to choke it out at last. 'I don't know what's wrong with him. He's not been well for a few days – that's why I sent the wire – but yesterday morning he collapsed. Now he's in hospital in Dorchester. They've done a lot of tests, but they don't know what's wrong.'

'But he's not dying?' demanded Daisy, urgently. 'Mum, it's not that serious? He's not going to die?'

'I hope not, but – '

Rose shrugged and looked so helpless and so little that Daisy could have wept. 'What about the boys?' she asked.

'Oh, the twins are fine.' Rose smiled through her tears. 'They've been such bricks! I'm sorry if I frightened you,' she added. 'It was the shock of seeing you, standing on the doorstep at this time of night. It was as if I'd summoned you, and you had come home. But we should go to bed. I'll have to be up at five tomorrow morning. Come on, I'll make your bed up.'

'I'll do that,' said Daisy. 'You go back to bed and go to sleep.'

'If you're not too tired, I'd like to have your company for a few minutes more.' Rose brushed her hand across her eyes. 'I can't sleep, anyway.'

So Daisy made more tea, and talked to Rose a little longer, and then she went to bed. But she didn't sleep – too much had happened for her to sleep. All night she heard Rose pacing up and down, the scrape of matches as Rose lit cigarettes, the clatter as she put the kettle on, again, again.

When she got up, bleary-eyed and sluggish at five the following morning, she found that Robert and Stephen were as glad to see her as Rose had been last night.

They've changed, thought Daisy, as she watched them hurry across the yard. The brats are growing up.

They were still two scruffy-looking kids, but they were doing all the milking, looking after their mother and the farm, and taking the responsibility that Daisy knew she should have taken. She shouldn't have gone gallivanting off, and showing her legs to anyone with a bob or two to spare.

'What do you think is wrong with Dad?' she asked. 'Mum, you can tell me, you know, even if you don't want to tell the twins. You don't have to treat me like a child. I don't have to be protected.'

'He's been working much too hard,' said Rose.

'That's all?'

'I hope so, Daisy. I can't afford to lose him. I'd be nothing without him.'

Rose and Daisy stood at the kitchen table, mixing mash for Rose's chickens, while the twins were seeing to the cows before they went to school. 'Your father might look hale and hearty, but he's not strong, you know,' continued Rose. 'He was badly wounded in the war, then he got shot in India, and he's never quite got over that.'

She poured the mash into two buckets. 'After the India business, they said they couldn't keep him in the army. He wasn't fit enough. He never complains to me, but it's often obvious he's in pain.'

'When will you go to visit him?' asked Daisy.

'This afternoon,' said Rose. 'I'll catch the bus to Dorchester.'

'I'll come as well.'

'Good, he'll want to see you.' Rose glanced up at Daisy. 'Darling, I'm rattling on about myself, but how are you, and what have you been doing with Phoebe?'

'Oh, it's like I told you in my letters, we met for lunch a couple of times. We had some little chats,' said Daisy, blushing at the memory of the scene she'd made in Fortnum's.

'But you did get on?'

'Well, we didn't *not* get on.' Daisy picked her bucket up,

and shrugged. 'But we didn't have very much in common. I probably won't be seeing her again.'

Rose and Daisy got the bus to Dorchester that afternoon. As she walked into the public ward, Daisy saw at once that Alex must be very ill. He was thin and haggard, and his skin looked yellow. There were long, grey streaks in his black hair, which she was sure had not been there the last time she'd been home.

But he was obviously delighted to see Daisy. He wanted to know about her show in London, he said how thrilled he'd been to see her brilliant notices from all around the country, said how proud he was to have a daughter who was such a star.

'I'll stay in Charton until you're on your feet again,' she promised, when – all too soon – the sister rang the bell and started shooing visitors out, as if they were so many wayward hens.

'I'll soon be better, there's nothing seriously wrong with me,' said Alex, as she bent to kiss him. 'It's such a tonic to see you, love,' he added. 'You can't think how we've missed you.'

'I've missed you too, Dad,' Daisy told him. 'Listen, you hurry and get well again.'

'I'm just shirking.' Alex grinned at Rose. 'Your mother panicked. She called the doctor, and had them cart me off to this place – eh, my darling?'

'We'll see you tomorrow,' Rose said softly, and she even managed a brave smile. But Daisy saw the fear in her eyes, and suddenly understood how it would feel to lose someone you loved.

The doctors took more of Alex's blood, shone lights into his eyes, did lots of other tests, and finally agreed that there was nothing wrong with him. Or nothing they could fix, at any rate. He didn't have tuberculosis, diabetes, jaundice, or anything like that.

But he was obviously exhausted, they told Rose. He needed lots of rest, and she must see he got it. He was discharged from hospital into his wife's and daughter's care, told to eat a lot of meat and fish and eggs, drink a daily pint or two of stout, and build up his strength again.

'So that's what you must do,' said Daisy, watching him as he ate his dinner, feeling she was looking at someone she could help, could heal, could by sheer force of will make well and strong again.

She would pull her family through, she thought. She wouldn't go traipsing off again. She knew that here in Charton was where she wanted and where she ought to be.

Daisy's Wellingtons stood in the porch next to her father's, hers all caked with mud and muck, while his stayed clean and dry. She worked so hard she fell into bed exhausted at nine o'clock each evening, and then got up at five the following morning for another gruelling day.

She also watched the calendar, fingers twisted and hoping for the best, aware it would serve her right if she'd been caught, if she was fated to join the wretched club of idiot women who believed the lies men always told.

She thought of still-warm parcels shoved in dustbins. No, she couldn't do that, she didn't know how, and it would be wicked, anyway. She thought of all the gossip there'd be in the village when it started showing. She could imagine Rose's disappointment when she had to accept that Daisy was her mother's daughter in every single way.

'Listen, God,' she said, 'my mum and dad have got enough to cope with, so they don't need this, as well.'

'Why didn't you tell me about Sir Michael?' she asked Rose, as they trudged home from Charton, loaded down with shopping, one beautiful June day.

Daisy couldn't really understand why they didn't have their groceries delivered, like everybody else. But Rose wouldn't have it because, she said, if you sent in an order, the tradesmen sent you anything. She wasn't paying out good money for flour with weevils in it, sugar that was damp, or rusty tins of pilchards that had been in Mr Gorton's shop since Adam was a boy. She preferred to choose, get her stuff fresh. She wouldn't have an account or buy on credit. She said she preferred to pay her way.

'Mum?' persisted Daisy.

'What would have been the point?' Rose put one of her oilcloth shopping bags down for a moment, and flexed her aching fingers. 'He's never admitted he's your father. Darling, I'm not being unkind to Phoebe, don't think that – but we have no proof. It's just her word against his, and he denies it.'

'Perhaps I ought to meet him.'

'Well, of course that's up to you,' said Rose.

'What's he like?' persisted Daisy. 'I mean, perhaps he wasn't very nice when he was young. But people change.'

'I haven't seen Mike to speak to for fifteen years or more,' said Rose, picking up her shopping bag again. 'So really, darling, I honestly couldn't say what sort of person he is now.'

Chapter Seventeen

As she walked down the gangplank, scanning the crowds for one beloved face, Phoebe reflected sadly that she hadn't intended it to be like this at all. The wires and letters she had sent from England must have given everyone she knew in New York City quite the wrong impression.

She hadn't had the time or the emotional energy to send the last instalment of the story. So perhaps there'd be a feast prepared. They might have killed a fatted calf, or at any rate bought up the contents of the local delicatessen. They'd be ready to welcome Phoebe and her long lost daughter to the Lower East Side.

It was going to be awful.

She wiped away a tear or two, and scanned the crowds again.

But then, as she was almost beginning to think he hadn't come, and her cup of bitterness was full to overflowing, she saw Nathan stumbling through the throng, pushing through the hawkers, brass band players, general gawpers and all the other people who'd turned up to greet the ocean-going liner. Then she was in his arms, and she was sobbing with happiness, despair and half a dozen other mixed emotions.

'You on your own?' she asked him, when they'd kissed and she had hugged him back, and had a look at him, when she was satisfied that he'd been eating properly in her absence, and was well.

'Yes, my dear,' said Nathan. 'I thought it would be better than having a great gaggle of people standing on the quay, all jostling and pushing and staring at this girl. The boys all sizing Daisy up, the women deciding whom she ought to marry, and all that sort of thing.'

Phoebe silently thanked God for tender mercies.

'But Vinnie and her cousins have been in with brooms and dusters,' went on Nathan. 'The whole apartment is immaculate. Daisy's bedroom's ready. There's a new dressing table and a new quilt on the bed. The room's been painted pale cream with touches of sunshine yellow, like you told me. Vinnie's made the whole place look a treat.'

Getting out a clean, white handkerchief, Nathan wiped Phoebe's tears away and smiled encouragingly. 'So, this daughter of yours, where is she, then?'

'She – she ain't coming, Nathan.' Phoebe began to cry again. 'It all went wrong. My Daisy, she don't want to be my daughter, cos she 'ates me.'

'Oh, Phoebe!' Nathan pulled her close to him, let her bury her face against his shoulder while she sobbed. 'Oh, my darling, after all you said! I thought it was all going so well. Phoebe, I'm so sorry.'

'Yeah, well, it can't be 'elped,' choked Phoebe.

'Come on, love,' said Nathan, and started pushing through the crowd. 'Let's get you home again.'

They went home in a cab, Phoebe's head on Nathan's comfortingly familiar shoulder, his arm around her waist.

'It wasn't such a great success, then?' Nathan asked her sympathetically, when they were on their own in their apartment.

'Yeah, you could say that.' Phoebe sat on the sofa, kicked off her high-heeled shoes and put her feet up. She closed her eyes and started massaging her aching forehead.

But Nathan soon took over, soothing away her headache, just as he always managed to soothe away a little of any

232

pain that racked her heart.

'At first, I thought it was all goin' so well,' said Phoebe, wretchedly. 'Rose was 'appy enough for me to see my little girl, an' when we finally met up, Daisy was sweet to me. But when I told her all about when she'd been born – I thought I was doin' right to be honest, Nathan, but it seems I should've kept me trap shut – Daisy got all upset, an' said I'd ruined Rose's life.'

'Poor Phoebe.' Nathan's gentle fingers stroked her temples, and she lay back against him, wondering what she'd ever do without him. 'About you, though, my dear – any news?'

'No,' said Phoebe. 'I'm not going to 'ave another kid. I feel it in me bones.' She sighed and shook her sleek, dark head. 'Nathan, I was a fool to think she'd like me, an' want me to be 'er mother. It's not who actually 'ad you, it's who brings you up that really counts. I should have known that, shouldn't I? Bein' brought up by a foster mother meself.'

'So why don't *we* adopt?' Nathan stopped his massaging, and gently turned his wife around to face him. 'These days, things are very bad in Europe, and they're going to get worse. Children as young as eight are coming here from Poland and from Russia all alone. The agencies and charities can't cope with all the orphans in New York. Phoebe, maybe we could do some good.'

'I'll think about it,' Phoebe said.

'I'm so glad you're back.'

'So am I, my darlin', so am I.' Phoebe managed a little smile. 'I shouldn't be so flippin' greedy, should I? It's not every girl that's got a husband who's as good as you, her own little business, an' a lovely home.'

'What's Daisy like?' asked Nathan.

'She's lively, smart, she's got a gob on her, an' she's very pretty,' Phoebe said. 'I've got a photo somewhere in my luggage, I'll show you when I find it. But anyway, she's got a lovely figure, she's a blonde, she's got them sort of sparkling blue eyes. In colourin', she's the dead spit of 'er dad. But she don't even know 'im, an' I don't think she'd want to know 'im, either.

'Course, she thinks of Alex as 'er father, an' Rose is always gonna be 'er mum. So, although I'll always be the woman who gave birth to 'er, Daisy's never gonna be my child.'

Daisy had decided she didn't really want to meet Sir Michael. She wasn't disposed to like him, not after what he'd done. She had the world's best father, anyway.

She gave a cow a shove and edged it through the doorway into the milking parlour. Robert had the churns all ready, sterilised and shining. The twins had found a wind-up gramophone in the ruins of Melbury House, and now Stephen put a record on.

'What's all this in aid of, eh?' asked Daisy, as old-fashioned pre-war music filled the parlour with its decorous strains.

'The cows like music,' Stephen said.

'They know we have to milk them, but they don't really like it, that's why they kick and fidget,' added Robert.

'But they calm down if you play them music, and they give more milk,' continued Stephen.

'Yes, they do,' said Robert, and he grinned at Daisy's frown. 'Dad didn't believe us when we told him first. But now he says there must be something in it. Ruby's and Clover's yields have nearly doubled since they discovered ragtime.'

'They're not pets, you know,' said Daisy, sternly. 'You shouldn't get so fond of them. Sooner or later they'll be off to market, or to the slaughterhouse.'

'Yes, and that's another thing,' said Robert. 'We think that when they're for the chop, we should have a man come over here to do the job, not send them somewhere else to die, it isn't fair on them. Dad says he'll think about it.'

'Daze, have you seen the rabbit farm since you came back from London?' Stephen asked.

'No, I haven't had time.'

'It's going great guns now, you'll be impressed.'

After they'd finished milking, the twins took Daisy to visit their own enterprise. She saw that it was more than rabbits now. Guinea pigs and piebald mice and fancy rats lived in the stable block, in cages which the twins had made.

'Still selling livestock to your friends at school?' she asked, amused.

'Yes, and to the boys at lots of other schools as well,' said Robert, proudly.

'Rats are very popular,' said Stephen, 'particularly the white ones with pink eyes. They're the most intelligent, you know.'

'So I understand,' said Daisy, and she thought of Ewan, who had also had a white rat as a pet.

What was Ewan doing, she wondered, was he still in Glasgow? Did he ever think of her, and – if he did – was his opinion of her even lower than hers was of herself?

Ewan was wondering if he believed in witchcraft. If Daisy hadn't bewitched him, why was he still in love? Why did he think of her, day in, day out – almost all the time?

It was ridiculous, he thought, still to be hankering after Daisy Denham when he had another woman now. A clever, pretty woman who was strong and independent, and who was clearly much attached to him.

Sadie was right, of course. Romantic love was an illusion, something poets wrote about, but real people never felt, said Sadie, unless they were retarded or weren't committed to the struggle.

So was he retarded? Or was he not committed to the struggle?

'You're such a dreamer, Ewan, aren't you?' Sadie asked him, when they were lying on a patch of grubby city grass one morning, in a public park. 'Of course, it's no' a crime to be dreamer. But when the revolution comes, action will be what it's all about.'

'Then we had better have some action, hadn't we? Or at least away and do our matinee,' said Ewan. 'Come on, get up. We mustn't keep our audience waiting.'

He put the box in which he kept the images of Daisy in the deepest dungeon of his mind. As he and Sadie walked back to the theatre hand in hand, he realised Daisy had forgotten about him, anyway.

She hadn't answered any recent letters. She hadn't even sent a postcard. She was too busy having fun with Trent.

Daisy worked very hard, so hard that she had little time to think, remember or regret.

But, deep in her heart, she knew that she was playing at being a farmer. It wasn't the life she needed. That life was on the stage, when she could be herself, but lots of other people, too. She realised she was someone for whom just one reality would never be enough. She almost understood why Jesse needed to reinvent himself so often, to pretend to be so many people, to tell so many lies.

'You mustn't work too hard, my dear,' said Rose, when

Daisy came in from the milking parlour one evening in July and promptly started making mash for the hens.

'But there's so much to do, and anyway I like being busy,' Daisy said, wondering if gin and exercise – jumping off kitchen tables, wasn't it, and riding hard to hounds – might do the trick. Then she felt very wicked for wanting to destroy a little life. If indeed there was a little life.

When she finally went to bed, she didn't want to dream. But she found she often dreamed of Ewan, of the smile that lit his face whenever he had looked at her, and which she'd meanly thought was stupid at the time.

But she was the stupid one. She understood that now. She'd been so cruel to Ewan, had belittled his affection, gone chasing after Jesse and followed him to London, and look where that had got her – up the duff, as Julia and Amy would have put it. She was getting fatter every day.

What was she going to do?

When should she tell Rose?

What would Alex say?

Alex was getting better. He wasn't fit enough for any physical work, not yet. But he was walking round the farm and criticising, which was very good. When he'd been so ill, he hadn't cared what anybody did, if the cows had not been milked, or if the hens stopped laying.

Mr Hobson and one of his sons came to do the heavy work that the twins and Daisy couldn't manage, bossing her and the boys around, but in a genial, tolerant kind of way.

But the revived, revitalised Alex was a martinet. He dressed them down when something wasn't perfect, and told them off for cutting any corners, until Rose reminded him he wasn't in the army any more. Daisy watched them with affection, thinking how good it was to have the master of the house fit again.

Daisy wondered if she'd ever have the courage to own up. She knew Alex wouldn't turn her out, he wouldn't lecture her, or anything like that. But he'd be so upset on her behalf, and then he would be angry. She feared for Jesse's life.

Daisy and Rose took turns to get the bus to Dorchester, to buy the things they couldn't get in Charton. Daisy enjoyed the ride, which was a rare chance to put her feet up and relax. In Dorchester, she could look round the shops, and buy *The Stage*.

It was her turn to go to town this week.

She did her shopping, gazed in dress shop windows at clothes she couldn't afford to buy, then bought some flowers for Rose, some toffee everybody liked, and a copy of *The Stage*.

There was a long article on experimental drama. It all sounded very heavy, intellectual stuff. Surely there couldn't be an audience for that sort of thing? Surely people went to see a show expecting to be entertained, not bored or mystified?

Ewan had gone to Glasgow to act in plays like that. But lying on the stage and howling, or spending an hour staring at the audience and having them stare back – that didn't sound like the Ewan she had known and, too late, had loved.

As the bus pulled into Charton, Daisy put away the magazine. But as she shoved it in her shopping bag, on the back page she spotted a short item that made her pull it out again. A new rep in Leeds was due to welcome Ewan Fraser, Sadie Lawrence and Mungo Campbell, all from the Comrades Theatre Company, Glasgow, for the autumn season.

Leeds, said Daisy to herself, and started thinking hard. If I went to Leeds, perhaps I could sort something out. I don't know what, but surely there wouldn't be any harm in writing to the manager in Leeds. If this is a brand new company, they might still be casting. Or they might need an ASM, at any rate.

When she got home, she wrote a letter.

Ewan was feeling somewhat disappointed, but resigned.

They'd been doing so well, but then the backers had pulled out. The houses had been small, admittedly. But the reviews had all been excellent – he now had several folders full of complimentary cuttings – the audiences had been receptive, and he'd learned a lot.

'I still don't think we should be going to Leeds,' said Mungo, looking morose and chewing crossly at his finger nails.

'We have to eat,' said Sadie, who was sitting between them on a wall outside the darkened theatre, chewing at a bridie – she'd bought a shilling bag of them – and drinking from a bottle of beer that they were passing round in a brown paper bag, in case a policeman happened to pass by.

'But is it better to eat than sell our souls?' demanded Mungo, glowering.

'Oh, don't go getting ideological with me today.' Sadie glared back at him. 'It's no' the place or time. Do you want a bridie, or do you not?'

'I'll eat Mungo's,' offered Ewan, reaching for the bag.

'You damn well won't,' said Mungo, grabbing it. 'As long as you two understand – we take this job to earn some money, to get ourselves set up, and then we try to find some serious, honest work again.'

'I think we should be glad that Sandy Taylor happened to see us when he was in Glasgow, and thought we would be useful,' Ewan told him, wiping flakes of pastry off his chin. 'I'm going, anyway.'

'Fraser, I'm no' convinced you'll be an asset in the coming struggle,' muttered Mungo, 'and don't drink all the beer.'

'Mum, I've got an audition,' Daisy said, a fortnight later.

'Really?' Rose was peeling vegetables at the kitchen sink. 'I thought you'd got that theatre business right out of your system. I hoped you'd be staying here in Charton, until we find a man to marry you.'

'Mum!' cried Daisy, horrified.

Rose turned round and smiled. 'I was joking, dear. Your dad and I were saying the other night, it's time you were getting itchy feet again.'

'Oh,' said Daisy, relieved but annoyed to be so very easily understood. 'But you wouldn't mind if I did a short season now and then?'

'It's what you want to do, and people should be allowed to chase their dreams.' Rose sat down at the kitchen table. 'Alex is much better now, and we did quite well this summer, mainly thanks to you. We can just about afford to hire a part time cowman, and maybe share him with another farmer. The twins are doing more and more now, bless their little hearts. You go for your audition, and good luck.'

A few days later, Daisy sat on the train to Leeds, wondering if this new adventure was a big mistake. Well, she thought, it wouldn't show for a while, and if she actually got a job, at least she'd earn some money, and she could send something home.

She'd also get a chance to make it up to Ewan, to say

she was sorry for being such a bitch. She was so looking forward to seeing him again. The thought of it buoyed her up and made her smile, even though she was in such a mess.

When she had the baby, maybe Ewan – but no, she mustn't race ahead.

She ate her ham and pickle sandwiches and grimaced at her reflection in the window. In a few hours, she'd be in Leeds, where she'd be eating humble pie.

Chapter Eighteen

When she arrived in Leeds, she took her case to the left luggage office and paid the clerk one of her precious shillings to leave it there. It didn't do to turn up at auditions looking too optimistic. Anyway, her suitcase weighed a ton, and she didn't think she ought to be lugging heavy loads through city streets in her condition.

If they didn't want her, she decided, she wouldn't hang around. She wouldn't let on that she knew Ewan, or ask where she could find him, or anything like that. She'd simply get the next train home, sitting up all night if necessary. She couldn't afford a sleeper.

She wondered how many other people the manager was seeing, if she had any chance, or if she was just chasing wild geese, or wild Ewans.

Mr Taylor had arranged to meet her in a Victorian pub in Leeds town centre. She'd never gone into a pub alone before and, as she walked across the room, she was aware of being sized up in a way that wasn't entirely pleasant. Surely it didn't show, not yet? After enquiring at the bar, she was relieved to find the manager was already there.

He turned out to be a youngish man – mid-thirties, she'd have guessed. One of the newer breed of actor, manager and producer, he wasn't an Alfred Curtis lookalike, straight from a Charles Dickens novel. Mr A S Taylor had an open, shrewd and honest face, wore ordinary clothes – no monocles or spats for him – and knew a barber. There was nothing of the theatre about Mr A S Taylor, at least not on display.

'Why did you leave your last job?' he began, as the white-aproned waiter placed the manager's pint of best and Daisy's half of lemonade on the table, and as Mr Taylor scanned her letter. 'Let me see – you were with Daniel Hanson's company, weren't you?'

'Yes, that's right, in London.'

'But you just walked out?' The manager glanced up and shook his head. 'I've never heard of anyone walking out on him before, or living to talk about it, anyway!'

'We had a serious illness in the family, and they needed me at home.'

'The show must still go on, you know,' the manager said, impressively. 'This family illness – everything's resolved now, I presume, and you're fit yourself?'

'Yes, absolutely,' Daisy assured him, crossing her fingers underneath the table, willing him to take her on and pay her decent money, so she could send some home.

'Well, that's good to hear,' he said, 'because I'd work you hard. As well as playing your own parts, you'd be understudying, walking on, shifting properties, painting scenery, doing anything and everything. The members of this company all muck in, and I've no time for prima donnas, male or female – do you understand?'

'I understand.'

Mr Taylor had Daisy's cuttings spread across the table, and she thought, at least I've had reviews, and that must count for something. Even if most of them are for that awful *Blighted Blossoms*, and only three for the revue.

'*The Telegraph* picked you out for special mention,' the manager continued. 'But we're not doing any musical comedy, you know.'

'I want to do straight acting now,' said Daisy. 'I've prepared some pieces for you, if you'd like to hear them?'

'You mean you'd do them here, in the pub?'

'Yes, if you wish.'

'Maybe not, but your enthusiasm is certainly commendable.' The manager grinned sarcastically, considering her, appraising her and screwing up his face. 'Very well, Miss Denham,' he said, at last. 'I'll take you on. But you'll have to sign a binding contract. You won't walk out on me.'

'Of course I won't,' said Daisy.

'You'd better not. I'll set the dogs on you. We're already running this company on a flipping shoestring.' But then the manager smiled more graciously. 'Okay, first read-through at ten tomorrow morning, in the upstairs room here, that all right? I'll let you have a list of digs.'

'Mr Taylor, may I ask you something?'

'Yes, of course.'

'I saw in *The Stage* that you'd engaged some people from the Comrades, Glasgow.' As she thought of Ewan, Daisy felt her face begin to glow. 'Did their company fold?'

'Their audiences were falling off, and the management had to cut its losses.' Mr Taylor shrugged. 'It's not surprising, really. They were doing gloomy, left wing drama for half empty houses.'

'How did you find out about them?'

'I happened to see them when I visited my sister up in Glasgow, and I thought – great power, great commitment, but terrible material. There are some very fine young players among them, very enthusiastic, not afraid to take some risks, and clearly keen to learn. So I was glad to snap them up.'

The manager shook his head. 'Good Communists these chaps might be, all burning with the fire of revolution. But empty bellies have no ears, and starvation's not an appealing prospect in whatever cause. So three of them were happy to take my filthy capitalist shilling. Miss Denham, do you happen to have a pen?'

Daisy walked back to the railway station, got her case, then spent another threepence on her bus fare to the theatrical boarding house that Mr Taylor said was sure to have a vacancy.

When she saw her room, she realised why. It made the place in Clapham look like a palace. She wondered just how ruinous a house would have to get before it actually started falling down.

As well as all the usual insect life, the place was home to dozens of rats and mice, and two lazy, clearly ineffectual ginger cats who were never brushed, had forgotten how to groom themselves, and whose fur got into everything and lay in orange clumps on every surface.

But it was cheap, the landlady was friendly, and the food at supper turned out to be plentiful, if stolid: lots of mashed potato with greyish, lumpy sausages full of gristle, then prunes and tapioca, all washed down with dark brown builders' brew.

So, she decided, 14 Milton Mansions would have to do for now. She sent Rose a postcard to say she had arrived, and would be staying for a while.

Anxious to make a good impression, she was first to arrive the following morning. 'Just go on up, my love,' the barman said, when she rang the bell and said she was with Mr Taylor's show.

As she climbed the creaking stairs to the rehearsal room, her heart was hammering and her palms were damp. What would Ewan say, what would he do, was this a big mistake? She'd been so keen to see him that she hadn't thought it through. What if he just nodded, if he scowled, or if he cut her dead and turned away?

But it was too late to run. She'd signed the contract with its penalty clauses, so she couldn't afford to leave. She had to see at least this season through. Maybe nobody would notice if she got a little fatter day by day?

The dusty, yeasty scent of the rehearsal room above the dingy pub brought a flood of memories rushing back. She found herself inhaling deeply, savouring the smell, and letting herself think back to those rehearsals with Mr and Mrs Curtis, who had been so kind to her and taught her such a lot, and with whom she'd had her first professional chance, even though they'd paid her almost nothing, even though they'd turned out to be crooks.

She stared out of the dirty window at the busy street below, remembering Amy striking attitudes, stroking and patting her spun-sugar hair as if it were a favourite pet, and Julia with her everlasting lipstick.

She thought of Frank and George in their silk shirts and pretty ties, their make-up carried in boxes that had once contained Havanas, so they wouldn't look like deviants, and get attacked by thugs. She thought of Jesse, dark and dangerous as a panther, prowling round the stage, of Ewan in a panic because he couldn't find his violin …

Then the door behind her opened, Daisy turned, and suddenly he was there.

He'd grown a little taller, and he moved more gracefully as he came into the room. But he was still the same old Ewan Fraser, copper-haired, green-eyed, well-made and handsome. Now those green eyes positively glowed, with what she hoped was pleasure to see her standing there.

'H-hello, Ewan,' she began, looking at him somewhat nervously.

'Daisy?' Ewan stared a moment longer, blinking as if he couldn't believe the evidence of his eyes. But then he smiled, a warm and welcoming, thrilled-to-see-you smile, and she knew it was going to be all right. 'I didn't recognise you for a moment,' he continued, beaming. 'It's because you've had your hair cut. It's wonderful to see you!'

'It's lovely to see you!' cried Daisy, who was now feeling almost faint with happiness and gratitude, whose arms were open wide, in her mind already in his embrace.

'Ewan, there you are at last.' A small, dark girl who had a pretty pixie face came bursting in, ran up to Ewan and hugged him round the waist. 'Where did you go?'

'I had to buy some gaspers.'

'Oh, I see.' Standing up on tiptoe, she kissed him on the cheek, leaving Daisy in no doubt that these two must be lovers.

Then she turned to Daisy, curiosity in her hazel eyes. 'You must be the new girl, come from Dorset, I believe? I just saw Sandy in the paper shop. He told me he engaged you yesterday.'

Daisy was struggling to choke back her shock and disappointment. 'Yes, that's right, I'm Daisy Denham,' she eventually managed to reply.

'I'm Sadie Lawrence.' Sadie's grip round Ewan's waist grew tighter and, as Daisy watched, the knife of jealousy in her heart began to twist in earnest.

'You were in a musical, weren't you?' Sadie continued, in a tone suggesting that being in a musical wasn't far removed in general iniquity from kicking helpless kittens.

'I was in revue, but I've done serious drama. I – '

'Oh, yes indeed, I'm sure you have, you'll be an all-round entertainer.' Sadie pursed her lips. 'Ewan, we have ten minutes before the read-through, and there's something we need to have a little talk about. In private,' she added, tugging at Ewan's arm and dragging him towards the fire escape.

Ewan shrugged at Daisy, smiled again, but then went off with Sadie.

Two more members of the company came up the stairs, followed by two more, all chattering and laughing, then a heavy, sullen-looking man in worker's corduroys and a collarless cotton shirt.

Sandy Taylor came in last, brought them all to order, then introduced the newcomer, giving a brief resumé of Daisy's career so far.

Daisy couldn't help but notice Daniel Hanson's name provoked a shudder in a couple of the players. Phoebe had muttered darkly about him, too. Perhaps she'd had a lucky escape from him?

Then scripts were handed round, and soon the read-through was well under way.

'Miss Denham, are you all right?' asked Sandy, when they broke for lunch.

'Yes, I'm fine,' lied Daisy. 'Why do you ask?'

'You're looking very pale.'

'I'm always pale,' said Daisy, smiling hard.

Daisy felt rather sick and ill all day. She started wondering if this was the famous morning sickness. If it was, could you have morning sickness all through the afternoon?

She had awful stomach cramp as well, the kind of griping, twisting agony that made her want to retch. Maybe she was in for months of this? But then, that evening, when she went to bed, she found she wasn't pregnant, after all.

Instead of feeling the relief she knew she should have done, however, Daisy felt bereaved, and lonely, sick at heart. A baby would have loved her, would have been someone to love.

She realised now how much she needed loving, and somebody to love. Since she'd known she would be seeing Ewan, she'd fantasised about them starting over where they had left off. Maybe, she had thought, even though the baby wouldn't actually be his child, they could be a little family ...

But it seemed that Ewan hadn't wasted any time in moping and in being broken-hearted, as she had arrogantly feared. She needn't have felt guilty about going off to London, after all.

She cried herself to sleep that night.

Ewan still couldn't believe it. When he'd walked into that dusty room above the pub, he thought he'd seen a vision. It was only the arrival of the others that convinced him he wasn't actually dreaming.

She was just as pretty, but she didn't look the same. She was taller, her face had lost all of its childish roundness, and she looked grown up, world-weary, sad. He wondered what had happened in London, if she'd ever tell him, if he needed to go and murder Trent.

'Ewan, what are you thinking about?' asked Sadie, as she was getting ready for bed that evening. They'd booked themselves into a boarding house as man and wife, Sadie kicking up a bit because she didn't want to pretend she was married, but eventually understanding that, if she wanted to sleep with Ewan on a regular basis while they were in Leeds, this was the way it had to be.

'I was going over my lines,' he said, and walked towards the window.

'That new girl, she's quite pretty.'

'Yes.' Ewan didn't know if he should confess, but also knew that if he must, this was the time to do it. 'She was in the company I was with before I came to Glasgow, actually.'

'You didn't know she was coming here?'

'No, it was a big surprise. I thought she was in London.' Ewan frowned and tried to think straight, to replay the scene yet one more time. When he'd seen Daisy standing there, had he also seen a glint of gold around her neck? Did she still wear his chain?

Probably not, he thought. She'd most likely sold it, pawned it, lost it long ago.

When he saw her again the following morning, he looked very carefully, and – definitely no chain.

After a week's rehearsals, they had three plays up and running, and two more almost ready. In a company where everyone was young, lines were committed to memory very quickly, and professional arrogance was in relatively short supply. Everyone needed this to work, and knew it.

Sadie made it obvious to everyone she wasn't keen on Daisy, and certainly didn't want to be her friend. As time went on, Sadie's animosity scorched Daisy like hot blasts from a volcano. Daisy hoped and prayed she'd never need to ask the other girl for a loan of make-up, pins or stockings.

She was relieved to find that Sadie also wanted to make this tour a big success. She didn't upstage Daisy, she didn't try to make her fluff her lines. She didn't let her very obvious personal dislike affect the plays. But, off stage, Daisy was constantly aware of the burning hatred in Sadie's hazel eyes.

They got into the theatre. The scenery – such as it was – had all been put in place. The lighting man was sober. The first play would be opening to the public that same night.

'Mungo's very good,' said Daisy, as she and Ewan stood in the wings while Sadie and Mungo Campbell, the other actor from the Glasgow Comrades who had taken Sandy's shilling, ran through a scene together.

'Maybe he doesn't have to kiss her quite so hard,' said Ewan, who was watching Mungo closely.

'Yes, he does – he's desperately in love with her, they're planning to elope.' Daisy glanced at Ewan. 'But only in the play, of course. Off stage, it's obvious she's in love with you.'

Ewan merely shrugged.

When the actors took a break, Sadie came rushing over to Ewan, shoving Daisy to one side so she could sit with him. She grinned at him flirtatiously and rubbed herself against him, like a cat – a cat who knew she'd got the cream, and meant to lick it up.

Daisy saw she'd lost him, and her heart was sore.

Chapter Nineteen

Who was he trying to fool?

Ewan knew his eyes were following Daisy everywhere, that Sadie saw him watching, and was jealous.

He couldn't decide what he should do, anything or nothing. He didn't want to hurt poor Sadie, who he knew depended on him, loved him, needed him.

He didn't want to be the sort of man who played cruel games and trampled over other people's feelings wearing hobnail boots. A man like Trent.

Daisy hadn't given him any encouragement, anyway.

Although there were days when Daisy wished that she was anywhere but Leeds, when Ewan and Sadie seemed to be a living, breathing, mortifying example of the perfect loving couple, she knew she had to stick it out.

She and Ewan were thrown together all the time. In two of the plays, they had been cast as lovers, and Daisy had to remind herself that when he looked at her with joy or longing in his eyes, he was a player, he was acting.

But it was so difficult to see him, touch him, kiss him, flirt with him, and know it was a sham, that whatever he might have felt a year ago, these days he felt nothing for her at all.

Every passionate kiss was in reality chaste and cold. Sometimes, he didn't even kiss at all, just brushed her mouth with his, and he was always more than ready to pull away.

On rest days, the whole company invariably went out as one, for Sandy believed in fostering a good community spirit, and in everybody being friends.

Then Sadie hurt her foot, and couldn't join an expedition the company had planned to Ilkley Moor.

'But you all go,' said Sandy, who added that he wasn't really a walker anyway, and he'd stay with Sadie. 'It's a lovely morning, it's a shame to waste a rest day, and you need fresh air and exercise. You've hired your boots and sticks, and you won't get your money back.'

'Yes, off you go,' said Sadie, and looked at Daisy meaningfully, as if she were saying, don't think you're going to have any fun with Ewan, because he's mine.

Daisy thought, you mustn't worry, Ewan isn't interested in me, and we'll have four or five other people with us, anyway.

'You're looking puffed,' said Ewan, as Daisy struggled up a slope.

They were a couple of hours into their ramble, having left Sandy and Sadie drinking in the saloon bar of the little countryside hotel where they had all got off the bus.

'I'll be all right,' said Daisy. But she had turned her ankle earlier on, and now she couldn't keep up with Mungo Campbell and the others. She sat down in the shelter of a rock, pulled off her boot and rubbed the joint, which looked pink and swollen. 'Maybe I'll sit here a bit and read, and you can pick me up when you come back.'

'So come on, Fraser,' Mungo said. 'Away, and leave the lassie with her book.'

'She could make a fire for us, perhaps,' said one of the other men.

'Aye, get the kettle on, she could, for when we come back down the hill.' Rummaging in his battered army issue khaki backpack, Mungo produced a workman's billy-can, a twist of tea leaves, a copy of the *Daily Worker* and a lemonade bottle full of water.

'I'll stay with Daisy, if she doesn't mind.' Ewan sat down too, and yawned. 'I'd quite like a nap.'

'You're having too much sex, man,' Mungo told him, scornfully. 'Wee Sadie's worn you out. Very well then, keep the lassie company. But if you make a brew-up, mind you don't use all the water.'

As Mungo and the others strode off, Daisy looked at Ewan. 'You didn't have to stay,' she said, and felt her cheeks grow scarlet.

'I know I didn't. But you've hurt your ankle, you look tired, and it didn't seem very kind to leave you.' Ewan glanced at Daisy's swollen ankle. 'You need a cold compress. Otherwise, you'll never get your boot back on, and then what will you do?'

'Mungo said we mustn't waste the water,' murmured Daisy, looking at her foot.

'Oh, bugger Mungo.' Ewan got out his handkerchief and poured cold water over it, and then he wrapped it tightly round Daisy's damaged ankle. She tingled at his touch on her bare skin, and hoped he wouldn't look up and see her face.

'In ten minutes or so, when it feels numb, you must put your boot back on,' he said. 'Lace it up as tight as you can bear it, and then you'll be all right.'

'Thank you,' Daisy said politely, picking up her book. 'I'll be fine now, Ewan,' she added, primly. 'You can go to sleep.'

But Ewan lounged there, looking at her, pulling at a clump of purple heather. 'Daisy,' he began, 'I hope it's not too difficult for you, having to act with me?'

'Of course it isn't difficult,' Daisy told him, her eyes fixed on her book. 'It's very nice to see you, and have a chance to act with you again.'

'It's lovely to see you.' Then, Daisy happened to glance up, and Ewan smiled, and her heart did cartwheels. 'When I walked into that room above the Wakefield Arms, and saw you standing there, it was like Christmas and my birthday all rolled into one.'

'Ewan, don't,' cried Daisy.

'Ewan, don't what?' said Ewan.

'Be so nice to me.' Daisy forced herself to look at him, to meet his gaze. 'I was really horrible to you. I belittled and embarrassed you. I flirted with that awful man. Then I went off with him, although I knew you'd be upset. I'm sorry, Ewan. I'm delighted that you're happy again with Sadie.'

'Thank you.' Ewan tugged more heather, twisting it round and round his fingers. 'Daisy?'

'Yes?'

'You and Trent – it didn't work out?' Now Ewan was staring fixedly at a rocky outcrop on a distant hill.

'There was really nothing to work out. When we went to London, we were trying to find engagements, that was all.'

'But you liked him, didn't you?'

'I don't want to talk about it.'

'He seduced you.' Ewan kept his gaze fixed on the hill. 'He talked you into bed, then left you. Didn't he, the bastard?'

'It's more or less what happened, except that I left him.' Daisy shrugged. 'I was stupid. I thought I was in love, but I was chasing rainbows.'

'But you're over him?'

'I'm definitely over him.'

'I won't pretend I liked him, but I'm sorry things went wrong for you.' Ewan turned back to face her and looked into her eyes. 'Listen,' he said, 'I know we've had some rather awkward moments, you and I. But whatever happens, I'll always be your friend.'

'I – thank you, Ewan.' He was so near, they were alone, and she was so tempted to pull him close, to kiss him, then tell him she was sorrier than he could ever know, was heartbroken because she knew she'd lost him.

'Why don't you have your nap now?' she suggested.

'Why don't you have one, too?' He lay back on the heather. 'Come on, you're tired,' he added, stretching out one arm so she could lie beside him, so she could rest her head upon his shoulder. He smiled at her, his green eyes chips of emerald in the sunshine. 'It won't mean anything.'

I know, thought Daisy, sadly, and that's why I can't do it. 'I'm going to read my book,' she said. 'You go to sleep.'

So Ewan crossed his arms upon his chest and shut his eyes. Daisy sat and stared down at her book, but didn't read a word.

When Mungo and the others came back, Daisy had a fire going, and the water boiling.

'I see you've worn young Fraser out,' said Mungo. 'I dunno what all you women see in him.'

'You've a dirty mind,' said Ewan, opening one eye. 'We've just been sitting here and talking.'

'A likely story, man.' Mungo grinned and cracked his raw, red knuckles, eyeing Daisy wolfishly. 'Where's my *Daily Worker*?'

'I burned it,' Daisy told him. 'It made excellent kindling, actually.'

'A hindrance to the struggle – that's what you are, woman,' muttered Mungo, and then slumped down beside them, scowling furiously.

The season was turning out to be a very mild success, covering its expenses, paying the actors' and producer's salaries, and making just the tiniest of profits week by week. But this was as much as Sandy Taylor had dared hope, he told the company, in these increasingly wretched days of unemployment, heartache and despair.

'We live in mean and grubby times,' he said, and Daisy knew exactly what he meant, for life was grey and thwarted – or hers was, anyway.

Anxious to avoid the happy couple, she took to spending much of her free time in the local spit and sawdust pubs with Sandy and Mungo Campbell. Sitting in the bar and getting kippered by all the foetid smoke from workmen's pipes, she and Mungo listened to Sandy's stories about the older, married women he had loved and lost.

'You're like the Prince of Wales,' said Daisy, trying to sound more sympathetic than she really felt, for privately she was a bit disgusted by young men who fancied tough old hens.

'Yes, but if I were the Prince of Wales, I'd only have to tap the husband on the shoulder, and he'd move aside, not square up to me,' said Sandy, scowling down into his pint of best.

'Away, man – you're a pervert, you want tae fuck your mother,' Mungo told him, scornfully. 'The lassie should be younger than the laddie every time. It's a law of nature. Me, I'd never dip a fat old sheep, if I could get a lamb.'

'Campbell, you're never going to dip the lamb you've got your eye on,' retorted Sandy. 'We've all noticed the way you look at Sadie. If I were Fraser, I would stick one on you.'

'Fraser wouldnae even try it,' Mungo growled belligerently. 'He knows I'd lay him out.' He flexed his worker's hands, and cracked his knuckles one by one. 'But the de'il only knows what a lass like Sadie sees in him. I'd have thought she'd want a real man. A working man.'

Unlike Ewan and Sadie, who seemed to have put their left-wing sympathies in storage while they were in Leeds, Mungo still spoke the language and wore the uniform – the collarless shirt and corduroys, the flannel neck cloth and big heavy boots – of the ordinary working man. He played his parts in all the rather anodyne, lower middle class dramas they were putting on in Leeds, somewhat sarcastically.

But Daisy couldn't blame him when her own heart wasn't in it. As she trotted through her various roles of dutiful daughter, innocent ingenue and kindly sister, night after boring night, getting polite applause and equally polite, respectful notices in the local press, she wondered why she was doing this at all.

That silly melodrama *Blighted Blossoms* had had a lot more bite. The revue had been a lot more fun. Besides, they really needed her at home. Rose's letters had that tone of bright and brittle optimism which Daisy knew meant things were going badly.

We miss you, love, she said. *I'm glad to know you're happy, and that things are working out in Leeds. We'd love to come and see you, as you know. But right now it's impossible for your father or me to get away. I'm sure you understand.*

The chickens are doing well. I have an arrangement with the local egg man now. He comes to collect the baskets every Saturday and Wednesday, and I'm earning enough to pay most of the vet's bills, as well as the boys' school fees.

The twins both send their love, and say they'd like some picture postcards, if you can spare the time to send them some.

Sadie and Ewan carried on being deliriously in love. She positively glowed with happiness, and every smile she gave her lover scraped another graze on Daisy's heart.

Ewan wasn't physically bigger than when she'd met him in the rehearsal room above the pub. But in the past few months he'd sort of grown. He wasn't an awkward boy, he was a man. More to the point, he had the relaxed and easy confidence of a happy man.

He didn't yell at the audience any more. Instead, he played to them, took them into his confidence, and they loved him just like Sadie did. Each night, he got the most applause, and Mungo Campbell's scowls grew even grimmer.

Daisy tried to be brisk and friendly when she spoke to Ewan, but it was very hard. She watched in silent misery as he touched Sadie's shoulder, as he kissed her on the cheek, and lavished upon her all the light caresses that happy lovers do.

She'd been such a fool. She'd thrown a good man's love away.

The day the season finished and the company got out, a letter came from Rose.

The twins are in trouble yet again, she wrote. *But it's serious this time. They were caught on Michael Easton's land, the police became involved, and the boys were charged with trespass and malicious damage.*

As you can imagine, Alex isn't very pleased. Of course, the twins are guilty, and so there's no defence. Alex knows we can't afford the sort of fine the magistrate, who's very thick with Mike, will almost certainly hand down. But if we don't pay, the twins could end up being birched, or sent away. I don't quite know what we shall do.

Daisy sighed. Poor Rose and Alex, good as gold themselves, they'd somehow managed to raise a trio of juvenile delinquents.

She checked her bank book. In the past few months, she'd saved a mere three pounds, which almost certainly wouldn't be enough to pay a fine. She also had to settle up with her landlady, then get herself back home.

Sandy Taylor had got a company together for a spring and summer season in places like Southend and Eastbourne, taking some of the people who were in Leeds along with him.

But Ewan, Sadie and Mungo were going back to Scotland, to try to interest managements in drama studio versions of some of Shakespeare's plays – *Romeo and Juliet*, *Macbeth* and *Hamlet* – which Ewan had adapted for three players, so they would be very cheap to do. He'd been writing letters all that week.

'Good luck to them,' said Sandy Taylor. 'Fraser will have his work cut out, though – Scots don't always go for men in togas, or in tights.'

'I think they're going to do the plays in modern dress,' said Daisy.

'I don't like Shakespeare done in modern dress,' said Sandy Taylor. 'But our Mr Campbell will make a good Mercutio, the sarcastic, touchy bastard. Fraser will be in his element as Romeo. I can imagine Sadie hanging off a balcony, or more likely ladder, carrying on as Juliet.'

Daisy's heart contracted at the thought of Sadie playing Ewan's Juliet.

'What about you, Daisy Denham, won't you reconsider coming with us to the seaside?' went on Sandy, for Daisy had told him she would not be going to Southend because they needed her at home. 'You can't keep chopping and changing, love, being an actress one year, and mucking out pigs down on the farm the next. As you already know, it's hard to get anywhere in this damned profession. It's much harder still if you don't take it seriously.'

'I do take it seriously,' said Daisy, imagining Rose's worried face and wishing she was at home.

'But do you have that kernel of ambition everybody needs, even when they have a wealth of talent?' persisted Sandy Taylor. 'Do you have the necessary hunger? When you're on stage, you're fine. I've no complaints. You have the makings of an actress, and maybe you could even be a great one, who can tell? But do you want it? Do you have the hunger?'

'Sandy, I'm a two-bit entertainer, not Dame Ellen Terry. I play juveniles and people's sisters in provincial plays.'

'But you could be a star, you know. You have that special quality, you can hold an audience in your hand.'

'Do you think so, Sandy?' Daisy asked him doubtfully, feeling she was being torn in two.

'Yes, I do,' said Sandy. 'One day, I'll be seeing you at Drury Lane – that's if you haven't married some fat farmer and buried yourself in Dorset for all time.'

She got the next train home. But as she sat in the third class compartment, trying to read the paper and take some interest in what was happening in the real world, she wished she was going to Southend with Sandy Taylor and his company. She'd most probably have fitted in.

'She wouldn't have fitted in,' insisted Sadie, as Ewan and she and Mungo got on the train to Glasgow. 'I agree we could have done with someone else, but Daisy's not the one.'

'She's a lightweight,' added Mungo Campbell. 'She's fine

for comedy and melodrama, but she couldn't do the serious stuff. She has a frivolous mind.'

'You're only saying that because she burned your *Daily Worker*,' Ewan told him.

'You're only sticking up for her because she has nice legs and big blue eyes.' Sadie made a face at Ewan. 'I think you might have had a little crush on Daisy Denham.'

A little crush does not begin to cover it, thought Ewan, looking back at Sadie, who annoyed him more and more with every passing day.

Charton looked the very same as when she'd seen it last. Golden in the sunshine, as it must have looked for a hundred, two, three, four, five hundred years, or more.

Rose was not at home. Alex was probably in the kitchen garden with Mr Hobson and his son, or out in the fields with the cows. So Daisy left her suitcase in the cottage porch, and then she went to find the twins.

'Honestly,' she cried, when she found her brothers in the stables, giving their menagerie their supper, 'I can't turn my back for fifteen minutes without you wretched children getting into trouble. What were you doing, you little clots?'

'Letting innocent animals out of traps,' retorted Stephen, cradling a rabbit which he was stroking tenderly. 'Surely you don't think that was wrong? Daze, we released three foxes, a young badger!'

'But you got caught, you idiots!' Daisy glared at them. 'As if Mum and Dad don't have enough to worry about!'

'Oh, look who's talking now!' Robert glared back at Daisy. 'Not so very long ago, you were running off to Scotland with that ginger chap from Easton Hall. Then you went off to London without telling anybody where you'd gone.'

'You hardly wrote to them at all when you were up in Leeds,' continued Stephen. 'If Mum and Dad have more grey hairs than when you saw them last, it's you as well as us who put them there.'

Daisy let that pass. 'What have you done with all the injured foxes and other things you found?' she asked. 'I hope you didn't let them go and limp into the undergrowth, to die a really slow and painful death?'

'Of course not, stupid,' Robert said. 'We put them all in baskets, and then we brought them home. They're here in the stables.'

'Oh, and I just bet that thrills the rabbits.'

'They're in a different part of the stables, idiot – in our infirmary.' Stephen looked at Daisy as if she were a fool. 'We can't afford a vet, of course, but we got some books out of the library to find out how to treat them.'

'We made them muzzles so they couldn't bite us. We cleaned up all their wounds,' continued Robert, 'made splints for all their broken bones, and collars out of cardboard so they couldn't chew their dressings off.'

'So now they're all doing really well, that's except for one poor stoat, who died.'

'The baby badger with the broken leg is getting better, he can walk again.'

'We're going to release him on our land.'

'Dad says we may.'

'What about the foxes – feeding them on Mum's best chicken, are you?' Daisy asked the boys sarcastically.

'No, of course not, they're having to make do with scraps and worms.'

'Easton is a bloody sadist, Daze. Everybody in the village hates him,' muttered Robert, grimly. 'Don't look at me like that, I know it's swearing.'

'They say he was a coward in the war,' continued Stephen. 'Our father was a hero, and he got the DSO. It was in the *Dorset Echo*. Mrs Gorton at the village shop has kept the cutting, and she showed it to us once. But Sir Michael Sadist didn't get anything.'

'Daze, there's no need for all those iron traps in all the woods,' insisted Robert. 'Sir Michael Sadist just likes hurting things.'

'The kinds of traps his keeper uses are illegal these days,' Stephen said. 'We went and looked it up. We're going to tell the magistrate about it when we go to court, and then Sir Michael will be fined.'

'You wish,' said Daisy.

'But Daze, he breaks the law.'

'Listen, you little idiots,' cried Daisy, 'don't you understand? In this part of Dorset, Michael Easton is the law!'

She looked from one twin to another, suddenly furious with Michael Easton, who had too much power for his own good. 'Right,' she said, 'I'm going to see him.'

'Who?'

'Sir Michael Easton.' Daisy put her hat straight, squared her shoulders. 'I should have done it long ago. I'm going to see him now.'

'But, Daze, you can't!' cried Robert. 'Dad says we must keep off Easton's land.'

'He didn't say that to me.'

Still in her best high heels, her last pair of silk stockings and the smart tweed travelling costume Amy had given her as a parting gift, Daisy set off along the gated road, which was the quickest way to Easton Hall – far quicker than the cliff path, even though going this way meant she was trespassing on Easton land.

By the time she panted up the drive which led to Easton Hall, she was sweating heavily from exertion, as well as hot with rage.

Chapter Twenty

After she had rung the bell, after the family butler had looked
her up and down with cool disdain, after she'd eventually
been invited to state her name and business, Daisy was kept
waiting on the steps of Easton Hall for almost half an hour.

The maid who finally admitted her didn't condescend to
speak. She didn't offer to take her jacket, and didn't offer
her any refreshment, even a glass of water, which Daisy
desperately needed, but for which she was too proud to ask.

The Easton family was clearly very rich. They must
have had good brokers, she decided, ruefully. The place
was furnished in the latest style, and the mingled scents of
beeswax, Spanish leather and artificial jasmine filled the air.

There were hothouse flowers in huge arrangements on
almost all flat surfaces, massed explosions of purple, red and
gold, even though the grounds of Easton Hall were full of
daffodils and tulips, and all the lovely, gentle colours of an
English spring.

Daisy was led along a beautifully decorated hallway, hung
with family portraits and carpeted with the softest, silkiest,
cream-white Berber rugs. Then she was shown into a fussy
drawing room, full of expensive, nasty modern china, which
she at once decided must be Lady Easton's taste.

There, she cooled her heels and fanned her face, telling
herself she must stay calm, and that there was nothing to
be gained from telling Sir Michael Easton what she really
thought of him.

She hadn't meant her very first meeting with the man who
was supposed to be her natural father to be quite like this. In

fact, as she had huffed and puffed her way along the gated road to Easton Hall, she had quite forgotten that Sir Michael was allegedly her father. She'd come to Easton Hall for just one reason, to make him drop the charge against the twins.

Then someone came into the room, and Daisy found she was face to face with Michael Easton. Or so she supposed, since she had asked to speak to him. This man was smartly barbered, neatly shaven, and immaculately suited in the height of fashion, so he couldn't have been a servant, anyway.

She looked again and saw that on one hand he wore a leather glove. She remembered Ewan saying something about a missing hand – that he had been injured in the war...

'You're Miss Denham?' he said coldly, as he saw her looking at the glove.

'Yes, and you must be Sir Michael?'

'What do you want from me, Miss Denham?'

He was quite good looking. She thought that straight away, even though she was disposed to hate him. She also saw they looked like one another, for they had the same blue eyes, the same corn-coloured hair, the same straight noses, same long lashes, same slightly darker, arching brows.

But their mouths were different – his lips were thin and mean, while hers were full and generous, like Phoebe's. While his was long and angular, she had Phoebe's heart-shaped face.

'I won't pretend this visit is a pleasure,' he added, when Daisy didn't speak. 'But you might as well sit down.'

So Daisy sat.

'What do you want?' Sir Michael asked again.

'My father has had a summons,' Daisy said. 'I'd like you to revoke it, to let the matter drop.'

'Why should I do that?' Sir Michael's thin lips twisted.

'Those brats were trespassing, committing wilful damage on my land. They should be taught a lesson.'

'Yes, but by their father, not by you,' said Daisy, telling herself that she must keep her temper.

'Denham never taught anyone a single thing worth knowing. It's clear he can't control his wretched children. So someone else will have to do it for him,' said Sir Michael. 'I'm afraid the summons stands.'

'But my father hasn't any money, and he can't afford to pay a fine,' objected Daisy.

'Then of course the children will be birched, or sent to a reformatory where they will be taught respect for other people's property.'

'But they're only kids!' Daisy stood up and faced him, met his calm, superior blue stare. 'Sir Michael, we admit it, they were walking in your woods. They found some animals caught in traps, and set them free. If they damaged any of your traps, I'm sure my father would be more than happy to replace them, or to pay for them to be repaired.'

'I thought you said that Denham had no money?'

'Oh, very well, I'll pay myself, if you'll withdraw the charges.'

'Miss Denham, you don't seem to understand. Your brothers are delinquents. They deserve a flogging, and I intend to see they get one.'

Daisy couldn't believe what she was hearing. Already half ashamed of herself for offering to pay to have the cruel traps repaired, she glared at him. 'Then what they say about you in the village must be right,' she muttered, as she turned to go.

'What do they say, Miss Denham?' asked Sir Michael, so calmly and sarcastically that Daisy was incensed.

'That you're a sadist and a coward,' she replied, as she made her way towards the door.

She didn't reach it. 'No one speaks to me like that,' Sir Michael told her coldly in a voice of steel and ice, as he placed himself between his visitor and the door.

'Well, I just did,' said Daisy.

'Miss Denham, listen to me carefully.' Sir Michael's fine blue eyes flashed angry fire. 'I have some standing in this county. I expect my inferiors to treat me with respect. I see your adoptive parents brought you up to be a hoyden, so perhaps it's not your fault, but you won't leave this room till you apologise.'

'Then I'll have to stay.' Daisy sat down again, folded her arms across her chest and glowered up at him.

'Miss Denham, please don't be so obstinate.' Michael Easton sighed. 'I don't know what else you might have heard about me, but – '

'Believe me, I've heard plenty!' Daisy held up one hand and started ticking off a list. 'Seducer, liar, criminal, arsonist – '

'Arsonist?' A vein throbbed dangerously in Michael Easton's temple. 'Be careful,' he said softly. 'What you say is slander. You could end up in a court of law yourself.'

'So you didn't pay somebody to set our house on fire?'

'Of course I didn't.' Michael Easton laughed. 'Whoever told you that? I – '

'Why do you hate my parents?' interrupted Daisy.

'I don't hate them.'

'Yes, you do.' Daisy met his stare. 'You wanted to marry Mum, she wouldn't have you, and you've never forgiven her for it, have you?'

'You don't know what you're talking about,' Sir Michael said abruptly, but in a slightly less abrasive tone than he had used before. 'You're just an adolescent, with an adolescent's foolish notions, and you wish – '

'I wish you'd leave my family alone! Just let us all get on with trying to make a sort of living.' Daisy held his gaze, her own beseeching. 'Please, can't you forget about this summons? So, a couple of children go walking in your woods. They get upset when they find animals in traps. But how does that hurt you?'

'Your family, Miss Denham?' Sir Michael shook his head. 'I know what the village gossips say and, looking at you today, I can see there is a kind of accidental likeness.'

Daisy didn't want to think about it. 'Whatever our relationship,' she said, 'supposed or proven, Alex Denham will always be my father.' She looked back at him steadily, into clear blue eyes just like her own. 'Please, Sir Michael, drop this court case. Let my father deal with my brothers?'

'I'm so sorry, Daisy.' Sir Michael spread his hands. 'I have my property as well as my reputation as a sadist to defend, and so the answer's no.'

But now he seemed prepared to let her leave, and so she walked out with her head held high.

'What did he say?' asked Stephen, when Daisy finally got back to the stables, hotter, dustier and so tired that she was almost walking in her sleep.

'The summons stands. You're right, he is a sadist, and he's going to see you cop it.' Daisy grimaced. 'Well, I'll get another job, then I can pay your fine.'

'You will, Daze?' Robert grinned. 'You're such a brick! We thought we'd go to Borstal.'

'If Sir Michael's friends with the presiding magistrate,' said Daisy, yawning hugely, 'you still might. I'm going back to the cottage now – are you two horrors coming?'

'No, not yet, we have to put the animals to bed.' Stephen smiled ruefully at Daisy, and ran his grubby fingers through his untidy mop of jet-black hair. 'Thank you, Daze,' he said.

'Oh, don't mention it.' Daisy rubbed her eyes. 'We'll work something out, but now I'm going home to have a sleep. I'm tired, and it looks like rain.'

It wasn't working out, and Ewan was getting tired of Sadie and Mungo always going on at him.

This Shakespeare studio business, it had been his brilliant plan, they grumbled, and they'd both gone along with it, merely to humour him.

But they weren't getting anywhere with Scottish managements, idiots to a man who only wanted farces, comedies, or a Sir Harry Lauder kind of light variety – patriotic, sentimental sing-songs led by men in kilts.

'So that's what we should offer them?' said Ewan. 'Mungo, what's your tartan, the Red Campbell? Do you have a sporran and twisted walking stick all of your own?'

This brought the wrath of God down on his head. 'We should be doing modern drama,' Sadie cried. 'Our mission is to educate the workers, not pander to the lowest sort of taste!'

Yes, they'd done that season down in Leeds. They'd sold their souls to Satan for a while, and saved a bit of money, muttered Mungo. So now they should be spending it putting together a season of their own, doing theatre for the masses, in hospitals, in factories, in barracks – and in prisons, possibly.

Ewan could just imagine prison governors letting the likes of Sadie stand in front of hardened convicts, spouting left wing propaganda, as the men looked up her skirt.

'We'll need more funds, so why can't you get some money from your mother?' demanded Sadie, who had dragged information about his family out of Ewan, and now assumed he was a closet millionaire.

She refused to accept that Agnes Fraser had no money, or none to spare at any rate, and that if she had, she wouldn't have used it to advance her son's theatrical career.

Sadie couldn't or wouldn't understand that everything the Frasers owned was all tied up in land, that these days rents no more than covered costs, that there were numerous covenants and entails which meant they couldn't sell this land and raise a bit of money, even if they wished.

'You're just a feudal remnant, Fraser,' muttered Mungo, balefully.

'You call yourself a socialist, but really you're a traitor to the workers, aren't you?' added Sadie, crossly.

Ewan couldn't be bothered to reply.

Sadie's favourite hobby horse was all the senseless slaughter of the workers in the war, in which her father had been badly wounded, and most of his friends had died.

'My father was in the war as well,' said Ewan. 'He was wounded too. But after they had patched him up, he went back to the trenches.'

'Aye, but he was an officer,' grinned Mungo, rubbing his worker's hands upon his worker's greasy corduroys. 'Everybody knows they had it soft.'

'No, they didn't,' insisted Ewan. 'Officers got killed as well as men.'

'It was a dirty capitalist war, and if all the workers had had their proper say, and understood what they were really being asked to do, they wouldnae have fought in it at all,' retorted Mungo, smugly.

Ewan yawned. Mungo's constant flaunting of his working class credentials was sometimes very tiresome. Not everyone could be a stoker's son. Or was it a boiler-maker's nephew? Ewan couldn't remember, actually. Maybe it was both.

He left them ranting and went off to the pub.

One evening, as he was writing to yet another theatre management, Sadie said she had to tell him something very important.

'What's that, then?' he asked, putting down his pen and wondering what she'd cooked up in the public library where she sat and read the left wing press, and mentally ticking off the gruesome possibilities.

A short run of a play, which was in reality a tedious ideological diatribe, probably to be staged in some drill hall? The workers wouldn't come. They all preferred the music hall or pub.

Rabble-rousing posing as street theatre in Glasgow city centre? They'd get themselves arrested.

A series of public lectures, featuring some dull, dogmatic drama on the side? They'd bore their audience into a stupor, or get pelted with rotten eggs and turnips.

He met her sharp-eyed stare. 'Come on, then, tell me, don't keep me in suspense. What absurd new scheme have you and Campbell thought up now?'

'I'm pregnant,' Sadie said.

He looked at her and thought how much he didn't want to spend his life with this outspoken, bossy harridan. But now he'd have to.

'When would you like us to get married?' he asked Sadie, determined to bite the bullet and do the proper thing.

'Marriage is an outdated bourgeois concept,' she replied.

'Anyway, why do you think it's yours? It could just as easily be Mungo's.'

'You mean you've slept with Mungo?'

'Yes, obviously,' said Sadie.

'But I thought you and I – '

'You thought I was your private property?' Sadie shook her head. 'You really need re-educating, don't you?'

'I need my head examined, certainly.'

Daisy thought, I must be mad, walking across the water meadows in these stupid shoes. When she finally limped into the kitchen of the bailiff's cottage, she was wet through, too.

The clouds had gathered as she hobbled up from the stables, the rain had started falling, and now the sky was purple, like a bruise. There were ominous rumbles in the air. It seemed more than likely they were in for one of those terrific spring or summer storms that sometimes hit the Dorset coast, toppling trees and causing landslides.

Rose had come back from the village, where she had been visiting Mrs Hobson, who'd apparently been anxious that her dear Mrs Denham should meet her eighteenth grandchild.

But now Rose was delighted to see Daisy, and the prodigal daughter was petted and made much of, was made to take off her wet things and put on clean pyjamas, to sit with her blistered feet in a bowl of cool, soapy water, and drink a cup of cocoa. 'You got back in the nick of time,' smiled Rose. 'But were you on the four o'clock? You must have come the long way from the station?'

Daisy realised Rose could not have noticed that her case was in the porch. 'Well, you're always telling me I mustn't trespass on the Eastons' land,' she told her mother. The twins had just come in, and she shook her head at them and frowned, willing them to keep quiet about her recent expedition.

The storm raged on all night, the lightning crackled and the thunder rolled, keeping them all awake. The rain came down in torrents, and the gale force wind howled round the cottage, threatening to bring the chimneys down and take the roof off, too.

Finally they gave up trying to sleep, and all assembled in the kitchen, sitting round a paraffin lamp, sipping milky drinks and waiting blearily for the dawn.

'I never thought I'd hear noise like this again,' said Alex, shuddering as a peal of thunder deafened them, and the cottage quaked.

'You mean it's like the guns, Dad?' Stephen asked, bright-eyed with interest.

'It's like the time we blew the Messines Ridge, in 1917.'

'Gosh, Dad, were you there?' demanded Robert.

'Yes, and so were half a million other unlucky blighters. Most of them got killed,' said Alex, scowling at his son.

The storm abated towards morning, growling off to the east and leaving clean, clear, blue-washed skies. Robert and Stephen went out after breakfast, saying they needed to check up on the pets before they went to school.

But as Daisy filled the usual buckets for the chickens, she saw them set off down the path which led to the shingle beach. They probably hoped to find all sorts of treasures had been washed up there, fossils newly exposed by falling rocks, and possibly a whale.

They came dashing back ten minutes later in a state of great excitement. 'Dad!' cried Robert, running into the kitchen, his dirty, muddy Wellingtons dropping great gouts of orange mud across the clean, flagged floor.

'Whatever's the matter?' Rose demanded, frowning.

'At least take off your boots, you little grubs,' said Daisy.

'Where's my dad?' gasped Stephen.

'He's in the milking parlour, where you should be, helping him.' Rose looked at her sons suspiciously. 'Why, what have you done?'

'Nothing, Mum!' cried Robert, looking hurt. 'But there's been a cliff fall.'

'Tons and tons of rock and half our road,' continued Stephen. 'It's come down on to the beach.'

'This fall – I hope it's not on our land?' Rose enquired.

'Why's that?' asked Robert.

'The road from Charton is a public highway until it's on our land. Then it becomes a private road, and we're liable for its repair.'

'It's on our land,' said Stephen.

'Oh, my God,' said Rose. 'Daisy, will you go and find your father? Please don't tell him it's bad news. I want him sitting down when he hears this.'

Chapter Twenty-One

As Daisy got up to go out, Alex walked back into the cottage kitchen.

He looked relieved. 'The cows are fine,' he said, as he poured himself a cup of tea, sugared it and sat down. 'I was afraid they might have panicked.' Then he noticed their long faces. 'What's the matter with you lot? Lost a pound and found a shilling?'

'It's the road from Melbury into Charton,' whispered Rose.

'The cliff has come away, and some of our road has fallen on the beach,' continued Stephen.

'So we're marooned,' said Robert. 'We can't get into Charton now, or to the railway station, not unless we go through Easton Woods.'

'Or along the gated road that's on Sir Michael's land.'

'But you've told us not to go that way.'

'So we can't go to school,' concluded Stephen.

'You two can walk across our fields,' said Rose. 'You often go that way in any case, especially in summer. But if we need to drive …'

'How will you take the cows to market now, Dad?' Daisy asked him anxiously. 'How will you go to Charton, and how will we get all the stuff we need?'

'I don't know,' said Alex, looking as if he'd just been rabbit-punched. 'Where exactly has the cliff come down?'

Robert and Stephen told him.

'So it's on our land,' said Rose, 'and we'll have to pay for the repairs.'

'I don't see how we're going to do repairs. We don't own the fields alongside that stretch of our road. They all belong to Easton.' Alex raked his fingers through his hair. 'I don't know if he'd let me buy a piece of land so we could make a loop around the fall.'

'I'm sure he wouldn't,' Rose said bitterly. 'Or, if he did agree to sell, the price would be extortionate.'

'It's very narrow there.' Alex shook his head. 'I'll have to go and have a look, and see if we could get round it. But it doesn't sound too promising. As the twins have pointed out, the only other road's on Easton's land. So I suppose – '

'Oh, Alex, we'll be ruined!'

'No, we won't, said Alex. 'I'll just have to go and grovel to Easton, ask him to let me use his road until I can afford to have a new one built across our land to link up with the one going into Charton.'

'But that won't be for years!' cried Rose. 'It'll cost hundreds, to build a proper road!'

'So I'll be doing very heavy-duty grovelling.' Alex looked severely at the twins. 'It's a pity you two have upset him. Daisy, you haven't done anything to annoy him, so maybe you could come with me to see him?'

Daisy felt the blood rush to her face. 'Actually, Dad,' she said, 'I saw him yesterday.'

'Daisy, you said what?' demanded Rose, when Daisy had explained where she had been, what she had done and what she'd said.

'You actually accused the brute of burning down our house?' asked Alex, who had gone white.

'I'm really sorry, Dad.' Daisy felt two inches tall, and it didn't help that the twins were sitting staring at her, open-mouthed and goggling, half impressed and half dismayed.

'What shall we do?' asked Rose.

'Let me think,' said Alex.

'I'm glad you didn't marry him, Mum,' said Daisy.

'So am I,' said Rose. 'But that won't get us out of this mess, will it?'

'Mum, I was only trying to help,' cried Daisy.

'Well, don't try any more,' said Alex, curtly.

'You children, what's got into you?' sighed Rose. 'Well, I suppose it's no use sitting here. I ought to go and feed the hens, though how we're going to get the wretched eggs to market now ...'

'I'll go and feed the hens,' said Daisy, wishing she'd never gone to Easton Hall, hating the very name of Michael Easton, but cursing herself as well, and trying to think what she could do to make amends.

Rose told the twins they needn't go to school, the day would be half over by the time they'd walked the long way round, across a common and through miles of woods. So they went and did their daily chores around the farm, helped Alex with the cows, then went to seek some comfort from their pets.

At ten o'clock a courier came, bringing an official-looking letter for which Alex had to sign.

'I suppose I was expecting this,' he said, and handed it to Rose.

Daisy looked over Rose's shoulder, frowning as she read. Sir Michael's lawyer Mr Reade of Reade and Makepeace wrote that Mr and Mrs Denham and their children should be aware the Easton estate was private property. Any trespassing on land or thoroughfares would therefore be answered with the full force of the law.

'Do you think we ought to go and see him?' Rose asked Alex, doubtfully.

'If we so much as set foot on his land, he'll have us up in court.' Alex shook his head. 'Even if I phone him, he'll probably refuse to speak to me. He means to ruin us, and he knows there's nothing we can do.'

'But there must be something, Dad,' said Daisy. 'What if we go and – '

'Daisy, don't do anything,' interrupted Alex, testily. 'Listen, I'm not saying it's your fault. I realise you were trying to help the twins. But you don't know the half of what that man is capable, or how much he hates me.'

Daisy did some things for Rose, collected all the eggs, then put them in the big, square wicker baskets lined with straw, even though she knew the egg man wouldn't be able to come round in his van to pick them up.

But, she decided, they could get at least some eggs to market. After lunch, she and the twins could carry one basket several miles across the fields to Charton, then they could meet the egg man in the village. Also, they could bring back a sack of feed.

That however, wasn't going to be a permanent solution.

She went to see the twins. She found them happily occupied in their infirmary, making pets of all the animals which they'd sprung from Michael Easton's traps, and which had indirectly caused this mess. She sat with a lop-eared rabbit on her lap, trying in vain to think of something she could do to help. But she couldn't think of anything that wouldn't make matters even worse.

Rose was being so decent about it all, and Alex had gone so quiet and pale that Daisy felt really wicked. It would be so much easier if they'd raged and shouted, if they'd told her what a fool she'd been. That the wind and tempest were to blame as much as she was didn't make it any better.

At the end of a sleepless night, during which she'd heard her father pacing up and down out in the yard, and her mother begging him to come back in and rest, she suddenly had a brain-wave.

She knew she had the number somewhere. One day, when Phoebe had been showing off about her hat shop, she had produced a business card. Daisy was almost certain it must still be in her handbag.

'Mum, may I use the telephone?' she asked, after they'd done their morning chores and after the twins had gone, moaning and groaning about the rank injustice of it all, to make their way across the fields to school. 'I need to ring New York.'

'Do you?' Rose looked doubtful. 'You know, it's very expensive to make transatlantic calls. I suppose you want to talk to Phoebe?'

'Yes, I do – and Mum, don't worry, I'll pay for the call.'

'Oh, that's all right, my love. A few more debts won't matter.' Rose raked her hair back from her brow and then smiled bravely. 'Go on, go ahead.'

It took an hour to get the call through. The operator rang just as Alex walked into the kitchen for his morning coffee.

'Who's that?' demanded Phoebe, sounding groggy.

'It's Daisy. Phoebe, don't hang up on me!' Daisy saw Rose and Alex exchanging curious glances, but she ploughed on gamely. 'I wanted to apologise. I was very nasty to you the last time we met. I'm sorry I ran away that afternoon.'

'Oh, that's all right, my darlin'.' Phoebe coughed, and cleared her throat. 'I reckon I shocked you, yeah? I should've been more tactful. But do you know it's five o'clock in the morning over 'ere?'

'Oh, God, I was forgetting.'

'I'll forgive you, sweet'eart,' Phoebe said. 'So, is that it? We're friends again, an' now can I go back to bed?'

'No, not just yet, there's something else.' Daisy crossed her fingers. 'Phoebe, would you sign an affidavit – '

'Sign an affy what?'

'An affidavit, it's a declaration under oath, to say you had relations with Sir Michael Easton round about the time I was conceived and, that to the best of your knowledge, he's my natural father?'

There was total silence on the line.

Daisy crossed her fingers, praying hard.

'Well, I suppose so,' Phoebe replied, at last. She sounded quite surprised, but not reluctant. 'After all this time, though – Daisy, you're settled with Rose and Alex, ain't you? They been very good to you, you told me so yourself. Surely you ain't thinkin' of tryin' to get yourself another dad?'

'No, but – Phoebe, this call is costing us a fortune, can I assume you'll sign an affidavit if need be?'

'Yeah, sure, I'll sign it. I'll get my Nathan on the job, an' he'll sort something out.' Then Phoebe chuckled. 'You left all them bags behind, you know.'

'Yes, I know. I'm sorry.'

'I brought them back with me. We got some lovely stuff in Selfridges, an' in them posh shops in Piccadilly. Look, I'll post 'em on to you, okay?'

'Okay' said Daisy. 'Phoebe, thanks for everything.'

'You're welcome.' Phoebe cleared her throat again. 'Daisy, darlin', write to me some time?'

'I'll do that,' promised Daisy. 'I'll send you lots of

photographs, as well. Phoebe, you must come over here again. Come and stay in Dorset, and bring your husband, too.'

'Well, what was all that about?' asked Rose, as Daisy hung the receiver in its cradle.

'You'll see, Mum, soon enough.' Daisy buttoned up her cardigan, brushed a few wisps of straw off her skirt. 'I'm going to see Sir Michael again – and Mum, you're coming with me.'

'Oh, I don't know if that's wise,' said Rose.

'Phoebe's going to help us, Mum,' said Daisy. 'So come on, we need to get things moving. Dad, persuade her, will you?'

'Well, I suppose it can't do any harm. Or any more harm, anyway.' Alex suddenly looked more hopeful. 'Daisy's right,' he said. 'We can't appeal to Easton's better nature, he doesn't have one. This is the only way.'

'But I don't understand!' cried Rose.

'Daisy, explain it to your mother as you go along.' Alex plonked Rose's hat upon her head, then kissed her on the cheek. 'Good luck, girls,' he said.

'I'm sorry, Mrs Denham, but Sir Michael's orders are to say he's not at home to you,' began the elderly servant who'd opened the front door at Easton Hall.

'Oh, don't be so silly, Hannah Ward!' Rose looked the woman up and down. 'You've been here – how long, is it? Fifty years? You were in the kitchens once. You used to help the cook. You gave me macaroons and shortbread biscuits, when I was a child.'

'Mrs Denham, please don't make things hard for me!' The servant flushed a deep shade of brick red. 'Sir Michael was quite adamant that you and any members of your family were not to be admitted. Anyway, he's gone to see his steward.'

'When did he leave?'

'Two or three minutes ago, that's all, but – '

'Did he go on foot?'

'Yes, I believe he did.'

'Then we shall catch him up. Come along, Daisy, we'll go through the shrubbery, that's the quickest way.' Rose clutched her hat and hurried off, closely followed by Daisy.

They caught up with their quarry as he crossed the orchard. They ran up to him, gasping, out of breath.

'Michael, wait!' cried Rose.

'Rose?' As he turned to face them, Michael's blue eyes narrowed. 'Rose Courtenay?'

'Rose Denham, as I believe you know.' Rose met his gaze and smiled. 'It must be fifteen years or more since we – '

'At least.' But then, recovering from his shock, Sir Michael grinned sarcastically. 'I know it's polite, on these occasions, to tell a woman she hasn't changed a bit. But time has not been very kind to you.' Then he turned to Daisy. 'I wasn't expecting to see you again. I can't think why you've – '

'We've had a letter from your lawyer,' interrupted Rose. 'I'm sure you know we've had a cliff fall on our land. We've lost part of the road that goes to Charton. So I've come to ask you to let us use your road, until we can get something sorted out.'

'Why should I?' Michael asked.

'You're our neighbour, and neighbours help each other, or they should,' said Rose. 'Michael, Alex and I have never tried to injure you, and so – '

'You have a short memory, Rose,' said Michael. 'I have

nothing more to say to you.'

He turned to go back to the house. But Daisy stepped in front of him, so if Michael wanted to escape, he'd have to dodge past her then run away. 'Why are you being like this?' she cried. 'Just because Mum wouldn't marry you?'

'I don't have to talk to you,' snapped Michael.

'But I'm your daughter!'

'You are not my daughter.'

'Of course I am!' Daisy met Michael's cold, blue glare. 'Just look at me! Look at my hair, my eyes, my nose. It's obvious I'm yours.'

'Rose, take your brat away.'

'I know what happened now.' Daisy glared back at Michael. 'Mum didn't tell me, Phoebe did, and she's willing to sign an affidavit to say you are my father.'

'Who would believe a chorus girl?' sneered Michael.

'Everyone would love to believe a chorus girl,' snapped Daisy. 'Especially if the man who seduced her is a baronet.'

'So who exactly are you going to tell?'

Daisy thought, if I should mess this up, my family will be ruined. 'If you don't allow us to use your road,' she said to Michael Easton, 'I'll go to all the papers. I'll tell *The News of the World*, *The Daily Mirror*, and *The Times*. I'll give them such a story, and they can have photographs, as well.

'Sir Michael, just imagine it. *One of the largest landowners in Dorset's sordid secret. Love child and her mother left to starve.* You'll look cruel, vindictive and ridiculous.' Then something Ewan had mentioned long ago flashed back into her mind. 'You want to be Lord Lieutenant of the county – '

'Who told you that?' demanded Michael.

'Never mind who told me,' Daisy said. 'But if you don't let my parents use your road, by the time I've finished with you, you'll be a laughing stock. As for your chances of being a magistrate, or Lord Lieutenant – they won't even let you shake a collecting tin on flag days.'

'What about you?' growled Michael. 'After all that, you'd lose whatever threadbare reputation *you* might have.'

'Oh, don't be stupid, I have no reputation,' Daisy said. 'I'm a bastard, aren't I? I'm an actress, too. Actresses will go with anyone for half a crown. What did you pay my mother?'

'Get off my property.'

'I'll tell Daniel Hanson that you fucked his girlfriend, and I was the result!' Daisy blushed, astonished at herself for using such a filthy word, but gratified by the look of utter horror on Michael Easton's face. 'He's a London gangster, did you know? He runs all sorts of vice rings, the police are in his pocket, he breaks people's legs, and he'd break yours.'

Michael Easton turned to glower at Rose. 'You put her up to this,' he spat.

'All Rose has done is love me, look after me and treat me as her own.' Daisy glowered back at Michael. 'I'll take you to court. I'll claim a share of your estate. Phoebe and I will drag your name through so much muck and mud – '

'You'd get that whore back from whatever gutter you found her in?'

'Yes, I would. Phoebe isn't scared of you. She and I'd put on a damned good show for all your neighbours, and the press. It would be goodbye Buckingham Palace garden parties, Royal Ascot – '

'Oh, Daisy, careful,' cautioned Rose.

But Daisy took no notice. 'If you don't let us use your road,' she cried, in desperation, 'I'll marry Ewan Fraser!'

Chapter Twenty-Two

Ewan couldn't believe how light and happy he felt now, how relieved he was to be free of Sadie and mad Mungo. He need never see either of them again.

He gave up trying to interest managements in his adaptations, and wrote to every theatre in the land, offering to do anything and everything – shift scenery, make properties, write short dramatic pieces, farces, full length plays as well as act.

He thought of Daisy constantly, and wondered about writing. But then he thought – I must have something firm to offer, something which will tempt her, make her want to act again, even if she doesn't particularly want to act with me.

He hadn't wanted to marry Sadie, they'd have driven each other round the bend, he knew that now. But, given half a chance, he'd marry Daisy.

Michael stared, then suddenly looked so close to losing all his self control that Daisy was glad he didn't have a gun. 'I'm the head of this family!' he cried, 'and I'll forbid it!'

'We can wait until we're twenty-one!' Daisy shouted back defiantly, determined to outface him. 'I mean it. I'm not making idle threats. I shall do everything I said!'

'All your children should be in asylums.' Michael scowled at Rose. But then, all of a sudden, the fight went out of him. 'I'll speak to my solicitor,' he muttered. 'Now, the pair of you, get off my land. Or I shall call the police and have you both arrested.'

'What about the boys?' persisted Daisy. 'I assume you'll

drop the charges against them?'

'I've already said I'll speak to my solicitor,' hissed Michael, and he turned and stalked back to the house.

'We did it, Mum!' gasped Daisy, as she and Rose ran down the gated road, not even stopping to catch their breath until they were safely back on their own land. 'He'll see the sense of it, I'm sure. He won't risk all that scandal just to stop the egg man coming.'

'You did very well, my love, I'm very proud of you.' Rose clutched at her side, trying in vain to rub the stitch away. 'But that Mr Hanson – do you really know him?'

'I was in his London show. I told you, Mum. But I walked out on him.' Daisy grimaced. 'So I hope he'll never track me down, especially if he's as mean as everybody says.'

'Oh, don't worry, love, I'm sure your dad could deal with him. Alex would never let anyone hurt you. But are you going to marry Ewan?'

'No, don't worry, Mum.' Daisy looked down at her finger nails. 'Actually, I'd love to marry Ewan,' she confessed. 'But he doesn't want me. He's in love with someone else.'

'Oh, darling, I'm so sorry!'

'It doesn't matter.' Daisy shrugged. 'There'll be other men and other opportunities for me.'

'Talking of opportunities, what will you do now, dear?' Rose enquired. 'I mean about your acting. The new season's coming, companies will be casting – '

'I think I should stay here in Dorset,' Daisy said. 'I can see Dad still isn't very well. But he goes out in all the wind and rain, and he's still trying to do everything himself.'

'I do help him, sweetheart,' Rose said gently.

'Yes, Mum, I know you do, and you look like death

warmed up yourself. You need some decent help. A couple of farm labourers full time, a proper cowman. A woman to come in every day, collect the eggs, and see to all the hens.'

'We can't afford it, Daisy, you know that.' Rose shrugged. 'Since the war, this country has collapsed. No farmers have it easy these days, and hundreds have sold up. So, compared with some, we're doing well.'

'Why didn't you marry Sir Michael?'

'I fell in love with Alex.'

'But, Mum, you could have been so rich! You could have been the lady of the manor, you could have had expensive clothes, and holidays abroad, and everything. Maybe you could have made him kinder, too. Lady Easton must be bad for him.'

'You're thinking how nice it might have been to grow up in great luxury, with your natural father and with me – is that what you're saying?'

'No, Mum, no!' Daisy was horrified. 'My dad's my father, and nobody could have a better one.'

'I know.' Rose smiled and shook her head, remembering. 'When Michael was denying you were his, and Phoebe was so anxious to put it all behind her and run off to America, Alex suggested he and I adopt you.'

'Otherwise, I'd have grown up in an orphanage, I suppose?'

'Yes, I dare say.' Now Rose met Daisy's gaze. 'I've never regretted anything, you know. I couldn't love you better if you'd been my natural child. I couldn't have been happier than I've always been with Alex.'

'I'm so glad you married Dad,' said Daisy.

'I am, too.' Rose sat down on a stile. 'But nothing is ever black and white, you know.'

'Why, what do you mean?'

'You say perhaps I could have made Michael kinder, but I hurt him, too.' Rose looked down at her hands. 'If Lady Easton is a bitch, it's partly down to me.'

'How do you make that out?'

'Daisy, come here, sit down.' Rose gazed across the headland. 'Chloe – Lady Easton, as she's been for years – was married to Alex once.'

'What?' Daisy frowned.

'But it was a case of having to get married. She was pregnant.'

'What happened to the baby?'

'It was stillborn.' Rose turned to look at Daisy. 'I'm not proud of this, you understand. So anyway, after that poor baby died, Chloe and Alex grew apart. He was in the army, and she was here in Dorset. He was trying hard to stay alive, and that took all his energy. She believed he didn't love her, and eventually I don't suppose he did.'

'Then you met Dad?'

'Alex and I had known each other as children. We were out of touch, but we met again during the war, when I was a nurse and he was wounded, and – things happened.'

'So you broke up their marriage?'

'Yes, I suppose I did,' admitted Rose. 'Then, after the war, Chloe met Michael, and I guess the two of them …'

'They both hate you and Dad for being so happy, for having children, for having all the things they don't or can't. So maybe they don't love each other? What they have in common is that they hate you?' Daisy shrugged. 'It's getting late. We'd better go and help Dad get the cows in. Mr Hobson isn't here today.'

Daisy became the chicken woman, cowman, general help. As Rose had said, it was bad for farmers everywhere, but somehow they survived. So she felt she was doing the right thing, practically for the first time in her life.

One day, as she was looking for some change, she emptied out her handbag on her bed, collecting up the sixpences and threepences and farthings that had got themselves stuck in the creases in the lining.

Two and sevenpence, she thought, it's not a fortune, but it will buy some flour, some sugar …

Then, as she felt around the lining, hoping to find another silver sixpence, her fingers chanced on something else. She realised it was Ewan's golden chain, which she had hidden inside the bag.

She fished it out and held it up. She watched it glinting in the sunshine, remembering when he'd put it round her neck, and she had promised she'd never take it off. I'm good at breaking promises, she thought. I do it all the time.

So should she send it back to him? She didn't know where he was right now. But she could post it to his mother in Glen Grant. Then she wondered if he'd want to have it, or if he wouldn't want to be reminded of the past. These days, she and Ewan were nothing more than friends, and Sadie was the woman he loved now.

She'd think about it, she decided. In the meantime, she fastened it round her neck.

In her spare time, which didn't amount to much, Daisy sang at weddings, in local concert parties organised by Miss Sefton, and sometimes she went dancing at the village hall. The word had soon got round about how Daisy Denham had stood up to the local bully, and she found everybody in

Charton wanted to be her friend.

She took out a subscription to *The Stage* and now and then was tempted to go to an audition. But she was afraid of what might happen if she went away again.

'I'm fine,' insisted Alex, whenever she told him he was looking tired, that she'd see to the cows or dig up some potatoes for the kitchen. 'I don't want a lot of women fussing round me, wrapping me up in cotton wool.'

But Daisy read the papers, and she'd noticed from the obituaries that servicemen who had survived the war also had a habit of dying fairly young. There were a lot of widows in Dorset, and plenty of other women who had helpless invalids for husbands. If anything should happen to Alex, she could not leave Rose to cope alone. She'd have to wait until the twins were older – very much older – to start her life again.

At Miss Sefton's invitation, she started giving dancing classes in the village hall, and sang in the *Messiah* in Dorchester. Rose cut out the notices which praised Miss Denham's pure soprano voice, and stuck them in her scrap book. '*The Dorset Echo*'s music critic is in love with you,' she said.

'I don't think so, Mum,' said Daisy. 'Where's the post today?'

'Here,' said Rose. 'There's only one for you.'

Daisy took the envelope and opened a letter from a girl who had been with the company in Leeds. As she read, she felt her heart sink like a stone in water, spooling down and down. So that was it – the end of hopes, of dreams, of everything.

'What's the matter, love?' asked Rose.

'Oh, nothing, Mum.'

'You look upset.'

'I'm fine.' Daisy didn't speak, but screwed the letter up, pushed it into the red heart of the fire and watched it burn to ashes.

'You miss the theatre, don't you?' Rose asked Daisy, as they fed the chickens one bright sunny morning, while Mrs Hobson looked for eggs.

'No,' said Daisy.

'Darling, I think you do.'

'I don't.' Daisy threw the last handful of corn to a little scrum of clucking hens. 'Anyway, you never wanted me to be an actress. So why are you always going on about it now?'

'I didn't want you to be away from home, so young and inexperienced,' said Rose. 'It's very hard to let your children go. But now you're older, if it's what you really want – '

'It's not – not any more,' lied Daisy.

'You'll make some lucky farmer a fine wife,' said Mrs Hobson, bestowing the highest praise.

'I don't want to be anybody's wife.'

'Oh, go on with you,' said Mrs Hobson. 'You'd have such lovely babies. It would be criminal if you stayed a spinster. There are a dozen men in Charton who'd be glad to have you.'

'A lot of them are tenants of Michael Easton, and he hates me.'

'Well, there's nobody round here likes him. If you went looking for a man Sir Michael Easton liked, and who liked him back, you'd have your work cut out. Mrs Denham, talking of the Eastons, have you heard what they're saying in the village?'

'No,' said Rose. 'I haven't been to the village for a week. I don't take any notice of the local gossip, anyway.'

'You can tell me,' said Daisy.

'Hannah Ward, she happened to be – '

'Listening at the door again?' said Rose.

'She happened to hear Sir Michael and Lady Easton having words. Lady Easton, she was going on at him like a fishwife, Hannah reckoned, telling him he'd overreached himself, what had he been thinking, they'd have to sell the water meadows and all the woodland now, and if Mr Denham got wind of anything, he'd be so pleased!'

'Go on,' said Daisy.

'Then Sir Michael told her to shut up. Then she said she hated him. She couldn't think why she'd ever married him. He said if she didn't want to be married any more, she knew what she could do.'

'What did she say then?' asked Daisy.

'She slammed out of the room and knocked poor Hannah flying. Hannah was bringing in a tray with morning coffee on it, and all the china got smashed to smithereens, and Lady Easton said she wasn't needed any more. She could go to the workhouse, or whatever they call it these days.'

'Oh, poor Hannah!' Rose looked at Mrs Hobson. 'If Lady Easton meant it, if they turn her out, we'll have to see what we can do.'

'Mrs Denham, dear,' said Mrs Hobson, 'Hannah Ward has never been your friend, and you're too soft for your own good.'

As the weeks went on, it seemed things went from bad to worse at Easton Hall. Some rooms were being shut up, the servants told the people in the village. Sir Michael was looking worried, and Lady Easton lost her temper every day.

'I was looking through *The Stage* last night,' said Rose, one autumn afternoon.

'I must cancel my subscription. That would save a bit of cash.' Daisy put her feet up on the fender of the kitchen stove. 'It's a waste of money. I hardly ever read it.'

'Have you read this one yet?' asked Rose, shunting it across the kitchen table.

'No, but keep it for a day or two, I might get round to it.' Daisy yawned and stretched. 'Or light the stove with it, if you prefer.'

'Daisy,' Rose said earnestly, 'if you want to do a season anywhere, we could easily manage. The twins are getting older and bigger, they do lots of jobs around the place.'

'You still need me, Mum. I don't want to be anywhere else. This is where I belong.'

'You belong here anyway, wherever you go, whatever you want to do.' Rose looked at Daisy, her grey eyes dark and serious. 'Sweetheart, don't bury yourself alive in Dorset if being a farmer's wife is not for you.'

'I need to get the cows in.'

'Actually, talking about the cows – Alex has been advertising for a cowman in the local press. We've a Mr Tasker coming round at eight tomorrow morning. If this man suits, Alex will take him on full time. You and the twins won't need to work so hard.'

'Mum, you've got to get the road repaired or even build a new one. You can't afford a cowman.'

'Actually, I think – I hope – we can,' said Rose. 'Alex had a letter from his broker recently. It seems that some investments in America are making a decent profit nowadays.'

'Oh?' said Daisy.

'Yes, Alex seems quite hopeful.'

'So you'll have some money?'

'I think so, yes – and although when we've rebuilt the road we won't be rich, we should be better off.'

'Oh, Mum, I'd like you to be rich!'

'I had enough of being rich when I was younger. Nowadays, if I have enough, I'm happy – and it looks as if we're going to have enough at last.'

'What about the house, will you rebuild it?'

'Maybe we won't have *quite* enough for that,' said Rose, 'But I've got used to living here, we've made the cottage very cosy, and does a family of five need a house with twenty bedrooms, anyway?'

'You still need me here,' said Daisy, pushing her feet into her Wellingtons. 'You and Dad aren't getting any younger, and you shouldn't have to work so hard. I think I should stay.'

'What are you running away from, Daisy?'

'I'm not running away from anything.'

Ewan opened the letter postmarked Dorset and read it quickly, frowning. He was surprised she'd written. If he'd had to make a list of people most unlikely ever to write to him, she would have definitely been on it.

He wondered what to do. Plymouth wasn't far from Charton, or not as far as Glasgow, anyway.

Give it a couple of days, he thought, as his head said keep away, and his heart said go.

So should he listen to his heart?

Daisy was walking home along the cliff path when she saw someone coming from the opposite direction.

A tourist, she supposed. But he wasn't doing any harm, so

she didn't need to tell him this was private land. As the man drew nearer, she realised she knew him.

'Hello, Daisy,' Ewan said.

'Hello, Ewan.' Daisy's heart began to hammer hard against her rib cage. She felt her colour rise. 'What are you doing here – visiting your relations?'

'No, I'm banned from Easton Hall for life. Your mother said that if I walked this way, I'd very likely meet you.'

'You've been to see my mother?'

'Yes,' said Ewan. 'She said you've been upsetting Cousin Mike.'

'Then that makes two of us.' Daisy looked at Ewan, and hoped she didn't look or sound as flustered as she felt. She thought, I'd better get this over. 'One of the people from the company in Leeds wrote and told me Sadie was going to have a baby,' she said quickly, looking at her feet. 'So, Ewan, are you married?'

'What would you say if I said yes?'

'I'd say congratulations, I wish you every happiness, and what would you like first, a boy or girl?'

'Sadie's had the baby, and last week she married Mungo.'

'What?' Daisy's head jerked up, and she stared at Ewan in astonishment.

'Yes, I was quite surprised.' Ewan shook his head. 'At first, of course, she wouldn't even think about it. She didn't need a husband, she kept saying. The baby would be hers and hers alone. She'd take it with her everywhere. It could sleep in its basket while she was on stage, and in the intervals she'd play with it. She could earn her living, and she could support them both.'

'Oh,' said Daisy, and wondered what was coming next.

'But when it was born, the poor wee thing had Mungo's

nose and Mungo's eyes and Mungo's widow's peak, and he was so excited that he more or less wheeled her in a barrow to the registrar's office in Dundee, and made her sign her spinsterhood away.'

Daisy thought, now I've heard everything. 'Where do they live now?' she managed to choke out, 'with Sadie's parents?'

'No, they're with Mungo's people, in the very best part of Dundee. Although our comrade Mungo led us to believe he was a worker and a worker's son, it seems he comes from solid bourgeois stock. Mr Campbell is an orthopaedic surgeon with a thriving private practice. Mungo is going to be an architect. He was only playing at being an actor and a Communist, after all.'

'But Sadie – is she happy?'

'I believe so.'

'Poor Ewan, you don't have much luck with women.'

'Oh, I don't know,' said Ewan. 'I think I've had some lucky escapes, don't you?'

'I don't know how to answer that.'

'Then maybe don't say anything.' Ewan leaned towards her, head tilted to one side. 'What's that around your neck?'

'You know,' said Daisy. 'Do you want it back?'

'Well, that depends,' said Ewan, and he grinned. 'It seems we're going to be married. So it would be common property, in any case. Your mother explained about your meeting with Sir Michael.'

'I was just bluffing.' Daisy reddened. 'You don't need to worry. Did she also tell you he and I – well, we're related?'

'Yes, she did, but I only have to look at you to know what he's apparently been denying all your life.'

'So we're family.'

'Yes, but the connection's very distant. My father was a

second cousin of Sir Michael's mother, if you can work that out.'

'Where are you working now?' asked Daisy.

'In Plymouth, I'm in *Pygmalion*, playing Freddy. But then we're doing Shakespeare for a month, and I'll be Romeo.'

'I see – and playing him as if he comes from Surrey?'

'We haven't yet cast Juliet.' Ewan touched the golden chain, and then he wound it round his index finger. He pulled Daisy close to him, so she was looking up into his eyes. 'Mrs Denham says you're longing to go back to the theatre.'

'I never told her anything of the sort,' said Daisy, as she met his gaze.

'But mothers know these things,' said Ewan, softly. 'Or some mothers do, at any rate. She showed me your album.'

'She shouldn't have done that!' Daisy thought, is nothing private in this family?

'Maybe not, but I'm so glad she did. It gave me courage.' Ewan smiled. 'You've been pasting in my cuttings, too.'

'So what if I have?'

'I think it means that you still care for me.'

'Does it?'

'Do you?'

'I – '

'Daisy, don't torment me, is it yes or no?'

'Yes,' said Daisy, knowing she must own up. It wasn't fair to tease him. 'I must admit I do.'

'Then we understand each other, don't we?' Ewan let the chain fall and bent to kiss her on the lips.

'Your little brothers are growing up,' he added, several minutes later. 'Plymouth isn't so far from Charton. If there was something wrong at home, it's just a couple hours away by train. Daisy, will you come and read for Juliet?'

Daisy looked at him, at this lovely, handsome man who was asking her to read for Juliet, and knew she'd be insane to tell him no.

But did she have that hunger, that kernel of ambition? She suddenly realised, yes – of course she did, she'd always had it, though she hadn't had the confidence to admit it to herself. Now, Ewan had cracked open that obstinate hard shell.

'Daisy?' he repeated, and his gaze was on her face, and his green eyes were shining.

'Yes,' she said. 'Of course I will. I'd love to read for Juliet.'

'That's wonderful,' said Ewan, and his smile made her heart start singing. 'We'd better get in some practice right away,' he added, kissing her again.

'You kept it,' he said, minutes or hours later – Daisy didn't know and didn't care.

'Did you think I'd lose it?'

'I wouldn't have blamed you if you'd sold it. You must have had some difficult times in London.'

'Ewan, I would never have sold your chain. It means too much to me.' Daisy didn't want to let him go. 'Will you come back to the cottage and have some supper? Mum won't mind, she always cooks too much.'

'Actually,' said Ewan as he took her hand, 'I might as well confess. Mrs Denham saw my name in a review, in the *West Country Herald*. She wrote to say that when I had a rest day, I'd be very welcome to come over here for supper. So she's already invited me.'

About the Author

Margaret James was born and brought up in Hereford.
She studied English at London University, and has written
many short stories, articles and serials for magazines.
She is the author of fourteen published novels.

Margaret is a long-standing contributor to *Writing
Magazine* for which she writes the Fiction Focus column
and an author interview for each issue. She's also a creative
writing tutor for the London School of Journalism.

An active member of the Romantic Novelists' Association,
she contributed to the 50th anniversary anthology
Loves Me, Loves Me Not. Margaret's short story is
The Service of My Lady.

For more information on Margaret visit:
www.margaretjames.com
www.twitter.com/majanovelist

More Choc Lit

From Margaret James

First novel in the trilogy

If life is cheap, how much is love worth?

It's 1914 and young Rose Courtenay has a decision to make. Please her wealthy parents by marrying the man of their choice – or play her part in the war effort?

The chance to escape proves irresistible and Rose becomes a nurse. Working in France, she meets Lieutenant Alex Denham, a dark figure from her past. He's the last man in the world she'd get involved with – especially now he's married.

But in wartime nothing is as it seems. Alex's marriage is a sham and Rose is the only woman he's ever wanted. As he recovers from his wounds, he sets out to win her trust. His gift of a silver locket is a far cry from the luxuries she's left behind.

What value will she put on his love?

ISBN: 978-1-906931-28-5

Why not try something else from the Choc Lit selection?

**New home, new friends, new love.
Can starting over be that simple?**

Tess Riddell reckons her beloved Freelander is more
reliable than any man – especially her ex-fiancé, Olly Gray.
She's moving on from her old life and into the perfect
cottage in the country.

Miles Rattenbury's passions? Old cars and new women!
Romance? He's into fun rather than commitment. When
Tess crashes the Freelander into his breakdown truck, they
find that they're nearly neighbours – yet worlds apart.
Despite her overprotective parents and a suddenly attentive
Olly, she discovers the joys of village life and even forms
an unlikely friendship with Miles. Then, just as their
relationship develops into something deeper, an old flame
comes looking for him....

Is their love strong enough to overcome the past? Or will
it take more than either of them is prepared to give?

ISBN: 978-1-906931-22-3

Revenge and love: it's a thin line ...

The writing's on the wall for Cleo and Gav. The bedroom
wall, to be precise. And it says 'This marriage is over.'

Wounded and furious, Cleo embarks on a night out with the
girls, which turns into a glorious one-night stand with ...

Justin, centrefold material and irrepressibly irresponsible.
He loves a little wildness in a woman – and he's in the right
place at the right time to enjoy Cleo's.

But it's Cleo who has to pick up the pieces – of a marriage
based on a lie and the lasting repercussions of that night.
Torn between laid-back Justin and control freak Gav, she's a
free spirit that life is trying to tie down. But the rewards are
worth it!

ISBN: 978-1-906931-24-7

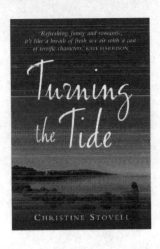

All's fair in love and war?
Depends on who's making the rules.

Harry Watling has spent the past five years keeping
her father's boat yard afloat, despite its dying clientele.
Now all she wants to do is enjoy the peace and quiet of
her sleepy backwater.

So when property developer Matthew Corrigan wants
to turn the boat yard into an upmarket housing complex for
his exotic new restaurant, it's like declaring war.

And the odds seem to be stacked in Matthew's favour.
He's got the colourful locals on board, his hard-to-please
girlfriend is warming to the idea and he has the means to
force Harry's hand. Meanwhile, Harry has to fight not just
his plans but also her feelings for the man himself.

Then a family secret from the past creates heartbreak
for Harry, and neither of them is prepared for
what happens next ....

ISBN: 978-1-906931-25-4

A modern retelling of Jane Austen's *Emma*.

Mark Knightley – handsome, clever, rich – is used to women falling at his feet. Except Emma Woodhouse, who's like part of the family – and the furniture. When their relationship changes dramatically, is it an ending or a new beginning?

Emma's grown into a stunningly attractive young woman, full of ideas for modernising her family business.
Then Mark gets involved and the sparks begin to fly. It's just like the old days, except that now he's seeing her through totally new eyes.

While Mark struggles to keep his feelings in check, Emma remains immune to the Knightley charm. She's never forgotten that embarrassing moment when he discovered her teenage crush on him. He's still pouring scorn on all her projects, especially her beautifully orchestrated campaign to find Mr Right for her ditzy PA. And finally, when the mysterious Flynn Churchill – the man of her dreams – turns up, how could she have eyes for anyone else?

The Importance of Being Emma was shortlisted for the 2009 Melissa Nathan Award for Comedy Romance.

ISBN: 978-1-906931-20-9

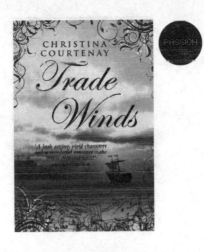

Marriage of convenience – or a love for life?

It's 1732 in Gothenburg, Sweden, and strong-willed
Jess van Sandt knows only too well that it's a man's world.
She believes she's being swindled out of her inheritance by
her stepfather – and she's determined to stop it.

When help appears in the unlikely form of handsome
Scotsman Killian Kinross, himself disinherited by his
grandfather, Jess finds herself both intrigued and infuriated
by him. In an attempt to recover her fortune, she proposes
a marriage of convenience. Then Killian is offered the
chance of a lifetime with the Swedish East India Company's
Expedition and he's determined that nothing will stand in
his way, not even his new bride.

He sets sail on a daring voyage to the Far East, believing
he's put his feelings and past behind him. But the journey
doesn't quite work out as he expects ....

ISBN: 978-1-906931-23-0

Money, love and family. Which matters most?

When Diane Jenner's husband is hurt in a helicopter crash,
she discovers a secret that changes her life. And it's all about
money, the kind of money the Jenners have never had.

James North has money, and he knows it doesn't buy
happiness. He's been a rock for his wayward wife
and troubled daughter – but that doesn't stop him
wanting Diane.

James and Diane have something in common: they always
put family first. Which means that what happens in the back
of James's Mercedes is a really, really bad idea.

Or is it?

ISBN: 978-1-906931-26-1

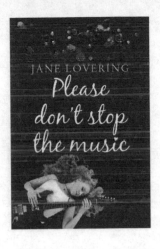

How much can you hide?

Jemima Hutton is determined to build a successful new life
and keep her past a dark secret. Trouble is, her jewellery
business looks set to fail – until enigmatic Ben Davies offers
to stock her handmade belt buckles in his guitar shop and
things start looking up, on all fronts.

But Ben has secrets too. When Jemima finds out he used
to be the front man of hugely successful Indie rock band
Willow Down, she wants to know more. Why did he desert
the band on their US tour? Why is he now a semi-recluse?

And the curiosity is mutual – which means that her own
secret is no longer safe ...

ISBN: 978-1-906931-27-8

**Abducted by a Samurai warlord in 17th-century Japan –
what happens when fear turns to love?**

England, 1611, and young Hannah Marston envies her
brother's adventurous life. But when she stows away
on his merchant ship, her powers of endurance are
stretched to their limit. Then they reach Japan and all
her suffering seems worthwhile – until she is abducted by
Taro Kumashiro's warriors.

In the far north of the country, warlord Kumashiro is
waiting to see the girl who he has been warned about by a
seer. When at last they meet, it's a clash of cultures and wills,
but they're also fighting an instant attraction to each other.

With her brother desperate to find her and the jealous
Lady Reiko equally desperate to kill her, Hannah faces the
greatest adventure of her life. And Kumashiro has to choose
between love and honour …

ISBN: 978-1-906931-29-2

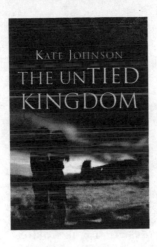

**The portal to an alternate world was the start of all
her troubles – or was it?**

When Eve Carpenter lands with a splash in the Thames,
it's not the London or England she's used to. No one has a
telephone or knows what a computer is. England's a third
world country and Princess Di is still alive. But worst of all,
everyone thinks Eve's a spy.

Including Major Harker who has his own problems. His
sworn enemy is looking for a promotion. The general wants
him to undertake some ridiculous mission to capture a
computer, which Harker vaguely envisions running wild
somewhere in Yorkshire. Turns out the best person to help
him is Eve.

She claims to be a popstar. Harker doesn't know what a
popstar is, although he suspects it's a fancy foreign word for
'spy'. Eve knows all about computers, and electricity. Eve is
dangerous. There's every possibility she's mad.

And Harker is falling in love with her.

ISBN: 978-1-906931-68-1

Introducing the Choc Lit Club

Join us at the Choc Lit Club where we're creating a
delicious selection of women's fiction.
Where heroes are like chocolate – irresistible!

Join our authors in Author's Corner, read author interviews
and see our featured books.

We'd also love to hear how you enjoyed *The Golden
Chain*. Just visit www.choc-lit.com and give your feedback.
Describe Ewan in terms of chocolate and you could win a
Choc Lit novel in our Flavour of the Month competition!

Follow us on twitter: www.twitter.com/ChocLituk